A
KILLING
WINTER

TOM CALLAGHAN

Quercus

First published in Great Britain in 2015 by Quercus Editions Ltd
This edition published in 2018 by

Quercus Editions Ltd
Carmelite House
50 Victoria Embankment
London EC4Y 0DZ

An Hachette UK company

A CIP catalogue record for this book is available
from the British Library

PB ISBN 978 1 78747 249 5
EBOOK ISBN 978 1 78429 018 4

10 9 8 7 6 5 4 3 2 1

Typeset by Jouve (UK), Milton Keynes

Printed and bound in Great Britain by Clays Ltd, St Ives plc

A
KILLING
WINTER

Born in the north of England, Tom Callaghan was educated at the University of York and Vassar College, USA. An inveterate traveller, he divides his time between London, Prague, Dubai and Bishkek.

Also by Tom Callaghan

A Spring Betrayal
A Summer Revenge

For Sara

Dying: nothing new there these days,
But living, that's no newer.

Sergei Esenin

Chapter 1

Fresh blood is especially vivid against snow. Even on a moonless, starless night like tonight, when it spills thick and dark, like oil leaking from the rusting sump of an abandoned Moskvitch. But oil doesn't steam. Oil doesn't spatter red against white, until it trails back to a body half hidden under silver birches. And oil doesn't dribble from the lips of a wound already turning stiff and blue with cold.

The threat of dawn snow hangs in the sky like ash. A few stray flakes already shroud the woman's upturned face, a scattering of lace like a bride's veil across her forehead. Unless a drunk stumbling home from a bar stops for an urgent piss and spots her, a few hours will transform her into yet another snow drift, unnoticed, skirted around, anonymous until the spring thaw. Only when a single boot-clad foot or a mottled hand sign-posts itself out of grimy snow will people wonder why no one heard anything . . .

'*Privyet*, Inspector Borubaev, how are you?'

'Cold, what do you think?'

I waved away the proffered pack, noting the swathe of butts at the uniform's feet, the stink of cheap tobacco rancid on the raw night air. Typical uniform, high-peaked green cap and no brains inside. I watched as he lit a fresh Classic from the stub of his last one, debated tearing him a new arsehole for contaminating the crime scene. But this is Kyrgyzstan. The forensic lab of the Sverdlovsky District Police is a cupboard with an assortment of cracked test tubes, some pre-independence medical textbooks and a box of out-of-date litmus paper. We're still waiting for the electron microscope.

I'd put it off long enough. Time to justify the fistful of *som* they pay me each month. A battered ambulance would turn up sooner or later, to ferry the body down to the morgue. No hurry; it would be a damn sight warmer there than outside.

We were up on Ibraimova Street, just down from the Blonder Pub, on the unlit birch-lined path above the carriageway, where the *moorzilki*, the cheapest railway-station whores, hang out in the summer, by the footbridge. Dumpy, surly women, big-bellied and chain-smoking, swigging cans of Baltika beer, dressed to depress in shapeless T-shirts and tracksuit bottoms, easy down for instant access, easy up for a quick escape. No business ladies here now, though, not at twenty below and more snow coming.

Not a good place to die, if there is such a thing.

I told the uniform to keep behind me and followed the droplets and smears of blood towards the body. They reminded me of the black cherry juice you get on ice-cream cones in Panfilov Park, rich and appetising. I turned up my collar against the wind, but nothing keeps a Kyrgyz winter out. My feet felt like they belonged to someone else, but I consoled myself that at least the body wouldn't stink. Not until Usupov sliced her up on the table. Or rather, sliced her up some more.

'It's a homicide, Inspector, right? It's murder?'

The uniform seemed almost eager; maybe this is what he joined up for, not for pocketing on-the-spot traffic fines to pay for his breakfast. Whether he would want breakfast after this was another matter.

'Could be a nasty shaving cut. Maybe running with scissors.'

'You think?'

He nodded, impressed at the wisdom of the big-city detective. Typical southern peasant, what we call a *myrki*, who should never have been let out of his village, a danger to himself.

A couple of steps further and the cherry juice started to join up into bigger puddles and splashes until it became a frozen river that welled up out of a small white hillock. The body.

'Keep back,' I said, unnecessarily. He'd already seen

the body and, by the smell, left last night's mutton stew at the scene of the crime.

'This your spew?'

Better not to assume. Maybe we've got a weak-stomached murderer on our hands. Maybe he'd wiped his mouth using a piece of paper with his phone number scribbled on it. Maybe the lab could get a blood group. Maybe.

'*Da*. I'm sorry.'

'Your first? Don't worry, we all do, our first time. You'll get used to it.'

But you don't.

I pushed back the memory of the old man, his one-room apartment turned into a slaughterhouse, gutted by his nephew in a vodka-fuelled row over God knows what, and focused on the present, on the ice-blue eyes glazed over with snow, staring up at the final mystery.

Ignoring the cold, I peeled off my gloves, and brushed away the snow covering her cheeks and nose. Gently, the way I used to brush Chinara's hair away from her sleeping face, towards the end, once the morphine took away the worst of the pain. Tenderness is the least we owe the dead; we give them so little beforehand.

Not a girl, a woman, maybe late twenties, thirty at a pinch. Dyed blonde hair, professional, not a home job, a thin line of black roots showing. Slavic high cheekbones, good teeth, no gold. A long coat, wool, well cut, a cashmere scarf around her shoulders. No handbag, but that didn't surprise me. Kyrgyzstan's a poor country; no one's going to look a gift horse in the mouth. And it wasn't as if she'd need her mobile where she'd gone, right? So not a *moorzilka*, then. If she was a business lady, she was a long way from the 191 Bar in the Hyatt Regency when she died.

There were no marks on her face, no look of terror or surprise, just that frozen stare gazing up at the sky. Snow spilt away to the ground as I pulled back the wings of her coat.

A white, high-necked blouse, ripped open. A delicate lace bra, sliced apart at the front, revealing small breasts, nipples shrunken and indigo with cold. Still no wound, but that only made it worse. It was like undressing a shop-window dummy, except you can't mistake the feel of flesh, even when it's dead.

Slim waist, leather belt with a metal designer buckle. And the skirt, pulled up to her thighs. Dark-grey material, from what little I could see of the original colour. But otherwise a swamp of crusted crimson turning to black. White pants, shredded and coiled around one leg. And finally, the wound.

I looked down and wondered what lies and treasons lured her here, before I tugged my gloves back on and stood up. My knees cracked in the cold like ice splintering on a distant lake. My world is a hopeless, brutal place, a land peopled only by regrets and lost love. I fumbled for my cigarettes, waved away the offer of a light, sucked down the cancer.

'Tell the blood waggon I'll see them down the morgue. Oh, and don't forget to mention we're dealing with a double homicide.'

The uniform looked, if possible, even more puzzled. The fur earflaps on his hat gave him the appearance of a cartoon rabbit. He looked around, even peered behind the slender birches.

'There's only one body, Inspector.'

I exhaled, watching the smoke and my breath plume out together into the night, life and death weaving together. The first flakes of the threatened dawn snow kissed my face. I wanted a vodka. Badly.

'You haven't looked inside her womb.'

Chapter 2

It was late afternoon when one of the uniforms at the end of his shift dropped me round the corner from the morgue. It's always seemed disrespectful to park next to an ambulance unloading the evening's bag of bones and guts. And it gave me time to collect my thoughts, and get some cold clean air into my lungs before inhaling the sour stink of a newly opened stomach.

The Sverdlovsky District Morgue is a unprepossessing, shabby building, with the ever popular stained-concrete look; suitable accommodation for the dead in a country where it's difficult for even the living to find a home. Only a small weather-beaten sign reveals its purpose; it's not a place many people visit, and those who do usually enter feet first.

I've spent too many evenings there, under the light bulbs that flicker whenever there's a drop in power, every sound bouncing off the tiled walls, trying not to think of the heavy scents of a butcher's shop.

As the *ment* drove away, the flare of his tail lights spilling over snow reminded me how blood spurted from the throat of the sheep we sacrificed for Chinara's *toi*, the commemoration we hold for someone forty days after their death. The imam muttered a few prayers, the sheep shat itself in the yard and, five minutes later, found itself hacked up into chunks.

I'm a city boy, Bishkek born and bred: I think killing an animal is a hell of a way to commemorate the dead, but that's the way it's always been done in the villages.

I put thoughts of butcher's knives to one side, and pushed through the swing doors. The business end of the morgue is actually underground, down a flight of broken-tiled steps. There's a long emerald-green stain against one wall, where last winter's snows broke in, probably looking for warmth. Every other light fitting lacks a bulb, but there's still enough light to reflect off the metal doors at the corridor's end.

I kicked the worst of the snow off my boots, grateful that there was no *babushka* to scold me for making a mess on her floor, and took my last deep breath.

'Inspector,' Kenesh Usupov muttered, not looking up from the shapeless mass on the steel table in front of him, strip lights glinting off his rimless glasses, 'I suppose you've come about the woman? Five minutes, I'm afraid, I'm just finishing off this *krokodil*.'

I winced, noticing the smell of iodine in the air, overwhelming the usual odours of blood, raw meat and shit. I've seen some horrible things, from babies

8

whose parents broke every bone in their body to grannies raped and kicked to death for their two hundred *som* pension. But a *krokodil* is a vision from hell.

Krokodil is the latest drug craze from Mother Russia, cheaper and much stronger than heroin. You make it yourself at home, using over-the-counter medicines like codeine, mixed and cooked up with iodine, red phosphorus from the striking edge of matchboxes, a dash of gasoline, and whatever else you can lay your hands on. Poison, simple as that.

Krokodil gets its name from the way your skin turns green and scaly where you inject, as infection and gangrene set in. Your flesh starts to die and rot almost at once, peeling away and leaving deep, unhealing sores that gnaw through tissue and muscle down to the bone.

I've seen addicts with no flesh on their arms, the ulna and radius bones exposed and grey-white, women with holes in their legs you could put your fist in, men whose cheeks have split apart as their gums turn to a bloody mash. The reek of iodine saturates clothes, skin, hair, even the walls of the shitty apartments and shooting galleries where the addicts cook up non-stop for days on end. Swim with the *krokodil* and you've probably got six months to live, if you can call it that.

With Kyrgyzstan being so close to Afghanistan and a ready supply of cheap heroin, *krokodil* hasn't eaten us the way it's devoured addicts from Moscow to Vladivostok, but it's only a matter of time.

'A bad one?' I asked, taking care not to look.

'As opposed to?'

'You know what I mean. Bad.'

'Not really. Heart attack took this one. Hardly any necrosis at all. Except for his fingers. They're all gone, just raw stumps with the bones jutting out. Oh, and his penis. Couldn't take a piss, even if he'd had any fingers left to hold his cock. Of course, couldn't work a syringe either in that state, someone else must have spiked him, got the dose wrong.'

'Or right, maybe. One less vein to feed, all the more for me.'

'It's possible, Inspector. But impossible to tell.'

The iodine made me gag, knowing I was sucking rotting tissue into my lungs, but I'd never hear the end of it from my colleagues if I started wearing a mask at autopsies.

'I could come back. When you're ready. For the woman.'

'Don't worry, Inspector, this one's going nowhere, his career's reached a dead end.'

That makes two of us, I thought, as Usupov threw a threadbare cotton sheet over the remains in front of him. I tried not to notice how the material immediately started to soak up some horrible fluid, and followed

10

Bishkek's Chief Forensic Pathologist to the autopsy table at the far end of the room.

'Your girlfriend. Too good-looking for you, way out of your league. Or she was,' Usupov announced, pulling open one of those oversized filing cabinets where he keeps the new and not so newly dead. The metal runners screeched like a razor scraping rust, and a gust of cold air wafted out. As always, the thought flashed through my head that the corpse wasn't really dead, and had just breathed out.

There are nights when I can't sleep, when my eyes feel blistered and cracked from the things I've witnessed, when the dead parade past me like fashion models on a macabre catwalk. I pressed my tongue against the roof of my mouth, to counter the worst of any smell, and intruded once more upon the girl's death.

One of Usupov's assistants had stripped her bare, to pass on her clothes to forensics or, more likely, to sell in the bazaar. Since we declared independence from the Soviet Union in 1991, we've endured the corruption and greed of various governments who've filled their pockets. Everyone looks out for themselves, making a few *som* where they can. And if that means selling the clothes of the dead, well, we're a poor country.

The girl's face was uncovered, ice-white, peaceful.

The purple bruises of lividity – the smearing under the skin where any blood left in a body slowly settles, dragged down by gravity – were already beginning to show around her hips and back. I could see the wear and tear of daily life on her body; an appendix scar slipping down towards her groin, old nicks and cuts on her hands, a childhood graze stencilling one knee.

Naked, she looked younger, more vulnerable, one of life's natural victims, born to end up here, unaware of my gaze or Usupov's instruments. The sort of woman who continually walks into doors, especially when the doors have been drinking, until one hits her too hard and shuts her out of life.

But she looked more at rest than Chinara had, when her sisters wrapped her in a burial cloth and placed her on the right side of the yurt, the woman's side, for her last night on earth before the men carried her down to the graveyard overlooking the valley.

I could smell her guts, the reek and iron taste of her as if I'd had my head between her legs, lapping at her during her period, and I had to swallow hard. Then, reluctantly, I looked at the wound.

'My God,' I muttered.

But if there is a God, I was pretty sure he was off duty when this had been done.

'Interesting, isn't it?' Usupov said, as calmly as if he was admiring the bouquet of a fine wine, or appreciating the craftsmanship of a hand-blown glass vase. 'I honestly can't say I've ever come across anything quite like this before.'

Most wounds I see are haphazard, tentative, a prod here, a nick there, taking several terrified attempts before they finally kill. Or they're driven by ferocity, a hatred boiled up out of cheap vodka, kids who never stop crying, a wife who long ago stopped caring. The cuts are random, ripping and slicing, the blade or bottle or axe hacking away, the work of amateurs, of people who woke up that morning never expecting to change their life or steal another's. This one was different. Determined, accurate, precise.

Usupov once told me that the most practical way to wield a scalpel in an autopsy is to imagine you're drawing a razor blade through soft balsa wood. The skin peels back slightly, opening up so you can slice through the meat, the fat and the muscle, down to the bone beneath.

'You'll notice, of course, that the initial wound was inflicted with a single cut. No hesitation. Someone knew what they were doing, before they got stuck in and started hacking about.'

'So I should consider you a suspect, Kenesh?'

Usupov looked affronted at my tone. I've never known whether he thinks death is no laughing matter or he just doesn't have a sense of humour.

'I'd have made a better job of removing the uterus,' he said, parting the two raw slices of her pudendum with his thumbs as if peeling an orange for dessert. 'Not bad, you understand, but you need practice for this sort of thing. Medical school, I would imagine, a gynaecologist perhaps; you wouldn't get the skills needed to perform a hysterectomy on the killing floor of a slaughterhouse.'

I wondered what sort of world Usupov thinks we live in, a place where carving a woman open and taking home the trimmings is considered good work experience.

'So you can't tell if she was sexually assaulted?'

'Well, if he did, he took the scene of the crime away with him, so to speak.'

Usupov gave one of his rare chuckles, a phlegmy snort that rattled in his chest.

'That's not what's interesting; every sex killer from here to the Urals can carve up a woman's *pizda*. But look at the way he's sliced a transverse cut above the edge of the bladder. Beautifully done, he's laid her open perfectly, with the minimum amount of damage. If your wife was having a baby, this is the man you'd want to do her Caesarean.'

He peered into the gaping wound like a bridegroom watching his wife undress.

'Beautiful, perfect work of its kind. Although she'd never survive the blood loss from the other wounds, of course,' he added. 'You'll notice that he opened up all of her womb to view, like using a can-opener, so he could peel back the lid and peek inside.'

I tried not to look into the raw mass of gristle, veins and arteries that was once a young woman. I could see the curled foetus lying on its side was that of a boy, knees drawn up to the chest, paper-thin fingers clenched into fists.

'How long had she been pregnant? How old was the child?'

Usupov looked at me, the lights flashing off his glasses once more.

'I don't think you quite understand.'

He waved a latex-gloved hand at the body in the cabinet. I looked away from the wound, from the butchered girl, from the child murdered before being born.

'Maybe the father of the child did this. Or her husband, if someone else had got her pregnant. We can trace him, once we identify her. Clinics will have records, or a doctor might recognise her.'

'You'll be wasting your time.'

'Mine to waste, Usupov. The White House still pays.'

Usupov merely grunted: everyone knows what he thinks of the government. It was Usupov who had to autopsy the bodies of the protesters gunned down by the riot police in Ala-Too Square during the last revolution. Waving placards and demanding the President's resignation, the demonstrators stormed the parliament building. It was then that the shooting by both sides started.

I'd been investigating the sudden death of a young man in Tokmok, a few miles east of Bishkek, when I got the call to head back to the city and go to the morgue. I pushed my way through the crowd, mothers and fathers, daughters and sons, surrounding the building, weeping, demanding the return of their loved ones, the arrest of the president who'd given the order to open fire. In the lobby, dozens of the dead lay stacked in the random pattern that death brings, bodies ripped apart and shredded by heavy-calibre bullets, the floor slick with puddles of blood. The stink of cordite and dead flesh was sour in my nostrils.

Bent over the body of an elderly man whose shirt was a flowering splash of crimson, Usupov didn't look up at my arrival.

'I don't suppose you'll be arresting anyone in connection with this, Inspector?'

I said nothing, and my silence hung in the air like an admission of failure.

'These people didn't want much,' he added, and his voice was thick with grief, 'just a decent meal every once in a while, schools for their children, hospitals for the sick, decent roads. A government that would help them, not rob them of every last *som*. Too much to hope for, when there are foreign villas to buy, luxury cars to drive and international bank accounts to fill.'

Usupov had the old man's shirt open by now, and was probing into the fist-sized hole in his chest.

'Cause of death?' he said. 'Hoping for a better tomorrow, don't you think?'

He didn't look up as I left the room, unable to disagree with him . . .

'A waste of time,' Usupov repeated, his fingers tapping on the side of the drawer.

I was intrigued. He might not be a man I'd want to share a half-litre and a few *zakuski* snacks with, but Usupov knows what he's doing, and he rarely says anything without the science to back it up.

'If you look closer, you'll see that there's no sign of a placenta, no widening of the pelvis, a narrow canal where her uterus was. It all adds up to something most unusual.'

I peered in, as instructed. But all I saw was a swamp and turmoil of butchery and, in the middle of it all, the dead child. I turned away and raised an eyebrow at Usupov.

'This woman's never been pregnant,' he declared. And Usupov is never, ever wrong when he uses that tone of voice.

I stared, as if he'd lined up the pieces of a puzzle and I still couldn't make them fit. Usupov peeled off his gloves, and meticulously polished his glasses on the hem of his lab coat. There was a splash of dried blood by one of the pockets.

'This child isn't hers, Inspector. She wasn't pregnant. Someone killed her, sliced her open, hollowed her out, and then placed another woman's foetus there.'

Chapter 3

The light was fading, or at least the grey sludge that passes for light in a Bishkek winter, and it was starting to snow again by the time I unlocked the steel outer door to my apartment, and then the wooden inner door behind that. Most apartments here have the same system; when you don't have much to steal, you guard what you do have with a passion. Anyone who breaks in here is welcome to the old TV with rabbit ears or the Chinese microwave. I couldn't care less, as long as they leave the box of photos. I put my gun in the small lockbox by the front door, turned the key and retreated into the kitchenette.

I pulled the window open and checked that the half-litre I had left out on the sill was still there. I could have kept it in the freezer of my fridge but there's something pleasing about the thought of vodka chilled by the elements rather than electricity. Not that I drink any more, not since Chinara died. I fished out a tumbler from the chaos of the sink, rinsed it, poured a good-sized shot. I stared at the glass for a long time, remembering the days when I drank, the reason why I stopped. A sort of penance, I suppose. Then I tipped it down the sink, rinsed the glass once more, took three steps to the bedroom and lay down.

Years of turning up at crime scenes hadn't made me stamp on the bottle cap; I'd wrestled with the odd nightmare, sure, the occasional double take as someone walked past me on Chui Prospekt who I could swear I'd stood over the week before, shot, stabbed, kicked to death. And there were nights drinking beer in some bar with other detectives, telling war stories, and hazy memories of getting back home. Putting the dead at arm's length. But I told myself I had to do that to keep my edge, to stay on the side of the angels, one of the good guys, an avenger.

Until the day Chinara came back from the hospital.

I knew it was bad from the way she thrust a glass of vodka into my hand before I could sit down, wouldn't look at me, stared out of the window at the play area below. The rusted slide and climbing frames had been embedded in concrete, but any metal parts that could be stripped had long since disappeared. It looked like some ancient skeleton half unearthed and left to bleach. But the children still found a way to play there – tag or hide and seek – living in the moment, not worrying about crime or where their next meal would come from.

When she finally spoke, it was almost a whisper, so I had to strain to hear.

'They say it's a growth. In my right breast. Cancer.'

The vodka seared the back of my throat; I felt anger, confusion and finally fear. Years of visiting apartments at all hours, saying the facts that no one wanted to hear, watching the reactions of others to unexpected death: none of it had prepared me for when death picked the locks and tiptoed into my home.

'They must be wrong. We'll get a second opinion. The X-rays must have been mislabelled, it happens all the time . . . they must be wrong.'

Chinara shook her head, and the curtain of long black hair folded back on itself like a crow's wing. She still didn't look at me, but continued to stare out over the ravaged playground. I wanted to hug her, shake her, anything to make this all go away.

'But what if they're not?'

Her tone was almost resigned, even worried that I might blame her for being sick.

'They're wrong, I'm sure. You've never even smoked. We ought to go to Moscow, see specialists. I'll ask about emergency leave tomorrow.'

'And how would we pay them? On what you earn? With what we've saved?'

I didn't speak. I couldn't catch my breath; my heart jerked and kicked in my chest like a terrified animal. I could call in favours from all over town, from other cops, from politicians I'd helped out of a jam, even mafia I'd dealt with. But there was no negotiating with the third person who had just joined us in the room.

'I saw the X-rays. The tumours. A lot of them. The doctor said he'd stopped counting.'

The sunlight in the room was very bright, so strong my eyes watered. I could hear the children in the park calling out to each other, shrieking with laughter, and I wanted to open the window and yell at them to be quiet. Because my world was collapsing in on itself, because I was afraid, because it seemed so unfair that anyone in the world should be happy.

'They want to operate this week. Remove what they can.'

I sat down beside her, my arm around her shoulders. I tried to turn her face towards me, but she stiffened, and looked away.

'You're going to be OK, it happens to a lot of women . . .'

I heard my voice tail away. Somehow, I couldn't conjure up the same air of reassurance that I'd used so many times before scared, shocked, devastated faces.

'*He'll turn up safe and sound when he's hungry.*'

'*He's in the operating theatre now.*'

'*We'll find whoever did this.*'

And sometimes we did, and sometimes we didn't.

I set my glass down carefully, as if the slightest noise might set off some terrible explosion, and hugged

Chinara from behind. Her hands came up at once to cover her breasts, as if to protect them from my grasp, or to prevent me catching some awful contagion. Strange what goes through the mind at such a time. All I could think of was that, a week from now, there would be nothing there for me to hold and caress.

'I'm sorry.'

'I know, it's all right. It'll be fine.'

The words we use to reassure ourselves that it's not yet time to join the long procession, not our turn to fall off the conveyor belt and into the darkness.

I moved my hands up to her shoulders. I could tell by the way they trembled that she was silently crying.

The rest of the evening was a blur, and then a blank. Glass after glass, tears, self-hatred, empty reassurances. Passing out, the half-full glass spilling out on to the rug. A role model for being supportive, there when Chinara most needed me . . .

I locked the memories back into their cupboard, shut my eyes and focused on the dead woman lying in the snow under the trees. And on the dead child stowed away inside her. I'm not overly sentimental about children. Chinara had had an abortion not long after we got married, when we were still living out at Alamedin, in a decaying cement slab of an apartment block, the kind of place where I'd spent most of my career kicking in doors, gun in hand. We're not ready for this, she'd said, career first, then family, there'll be time later. But there wasn't.

I don't bang a drum about a foetus having a soul, but I don't believe in contraception by abortion either, the way a lot of people do. If my job is about anything, it's about protecting the vulnerable from the predators, the ones who circle around the herd, waiting for a stray to be separated before they pounce. And I can't imagine anything more vulnerable than an unborn child.

Maybe I'm a fool to take on responsibility for people I never knew in life, and who reveal their secrets only in death: the wardrobe full of shoplifted clothes; the hidden stash of porn, straight or gay; the empty vodka bottles stashed under the bed. I've found them all. Sometimes I tell the relatives, more often I take their weaknesses away with me, burying them in files that gather dust in the Sverdlovsky basement. That's if the death isn't suspicious, of course; any hint that it is, and all bets are off. You can't shame the dead with their past, but you can make damn sure that the living don't join them.

I opened my eyes, stared up at the ceiling. No chance of sleep, and I'd work to do. I pulled myself to my feet, looked at myself in the mirror on the front of the wardrobe door. A face as rumpled and creased as my clothes. One that's won a few fights in its time, but started none of them. Stocky, not tall, black hair cut close to my scalp, black eyes staring out from under thick eyebrows. You can see a hint of my mother's Tatar genes in my cheekbones, higher and more slanted than the average moon-faced Kyrgyz. My grandfather, her father, was Uighur, and I've inherited my flat, impassive stare from him.

'Don't show your character,' my mother used to say, whenever I got cross or unhappy. 'Don't reveal any emotion or weakness, keep it to yourself, lock everyone else out. What they don't know can't hurt you.'

She'd watched, not a hint of any feeling on her face, as they carried her father's body and, years later, that of my father, out of the three-room apartment we called home. Not a tear, not a clue that she was feeling anything. None of my colleagues, even the ones who prided themselves on their powers of 'interrogation', could have got my mother to talk if she'd decided to stay silent.

For weeks after Chinara died, I could smell her perfume, her shampoo, her neck, on the pillow next to mine. I'd lie there telling myself she'd just gone to the bathroom, that she was away for the weekend visiting her brother, making one of her endless cups of *chai*. And sometimes it would work and I'd drop off to sleep, my arm reaching over in the night to seek a warmth that wasn't there.

But then, in the morning, a split second of happiness before it hit me like a speeding, out-of-control car. Dead.

Dead.

I stared out of the window. The rusted climbing frame was invisible in the darkness, but I knew it was there. Just as I knew Chinara lay under a mound of earth, in the grave her brothers laboured over for hours, smashing the frozen soil to make her bed.

Chapter 4

Unable to sleep, I decided that anything was preferable to a night of memories and silence. My work doesn't keep office hours, so I locked the door and headed out into the dark.

The far end of Chui Prospekt was deserted as I crossed the road and headed towards the Kulturny Bar. It was after midnight, no one around, my boots crunching on newly fallen snow. That part of town, snow's pretty much the only virginal thing you'll find. All the trees on the side of Panfilov Park have had their trunks whitewashed, so they seemed to float in mid-air, as if being lowered into place by an invisible crane. A Ferris wheel flickered through the mist, like the memory of a long-past spring.

I'd stopped off at the Metro Bar and watched some drab local girls playing pool, their arses stuck up in the air in case an off-duty Marine from the US base happened to wander in. That got old fast, so I decided to walk back to Ibraimova by way of the Kulturny.

The name, in case you don't know, is Russian for 'culture'. But *kulturny* has a much wider significance

27

than art, music and literature, important though they are. It's a way of behaving, an attitude to life and other people, of graciousness and appreciation of the finer things in life. If you can quote Pushkin, hum Rachmaninoff and drink your *chai* from delicate porcelain cups, then you probably count yourself as *kulturny*.

Of course, Russians love a paradox, particularly the cosmic sort, which reassures them that they alone are the butt of some universal joke. How else could they have convinced themselves for eighty years that they were privileged and superior to the West, as they stood in line for hours to buy bread or milk or shoes, or whatever was at the sharp end of the queue? Which is why they also recognise – and appreciate – *antikulturny*, low life at its most uncompromising.

The Kulturny Bar is one of Bishkek's best jokes, and one of its best-kept secrets. No sign, no welcoming neon, just a battered steel door, scarred and scuffed from years of being attacked with boots, spade handles and, on one memorable occasion, a petrol bomb. Nothing as elaborate as CCTV to screen would-be drinkers, just a Judas hole and the knowledge that the bouncer inside is probably drunk, violent and armed.

I unfastened my jacket, tapped my hip, felt the reassuring heft of my gun. Not the standard issue Makarov pistol, but a Yarygin I liberated from a hash smuggler over in Karakol. More kick, and seventeen rounds in the magazine. *Kulturny.*

I stared at the door, gave it an experimental kick and waited. Nothing: silence bounced off the snow. I raised my hands in the air, and beckoned for the door to be opened. Still nothing. I pantomimed looking at my watch, shrugged and made a cutting gesture across my throat. But just as I was about to head to the station and return with a sledgehammer, the door swung outwards. With it came an unholy reek of piss, fried *pelmeni* dumplings and stale beer.

A shaven head emerged, dotted with blue-black cobwebs – prison tattoos. Steroid-built muscles coiled and wriggled down arms bare in spite of the cold. A ripped T-shirt and greasy camo pants. Almost two solid metres of thug. Mikhail Lubashov, 'of interest to Sverdlovsky Police Department', as they say in court.

I'd sent him down once before for administering a beating that left an Uzbek gang member in a coma, so Mikhail wouldn't have taken kindly to me tapping on his door. But he'd have more sense than to keep me out, if he wanted the bar to stay open. Losing money wouldn't sit well with his masters, and a coma of his own would be the least he could hope for if I shut the place down for a week or two.

'Inspector –'

'*Past' zahlopni, packun!*'

Mikhail didn't take kindly to being told to shut his mouth, or to being called a little prick, but I thought I could live with the disappointment. Being pretty *anti-kulturny* myself when I choose to be, I decided it was best to let Mikhail know what was what from the off. I didn't mind him hating me, as long as he feared me.

'The usual collection of *alkashi* downstairs?'

The naked Madonna on Mikhail's biceps flexed her tits as he shrugged. Not one to give anything away, Mikhail settled for giving me the prison-yard stare. He liked to hint that he had been involved in the kidnap and disposal of Chechen mafia boss Movladi Atlangeriyev in Moscow a few years ago, but that was strictly to impress the punters. The cobwebs on his skull might have boasted to the world that he was a murderer, but Mikhail kept the tattoo on his belly that told the world he had a thing for kids well hidden. You don't want everyone to know you're a sex criminal, especially if you're a paedo.

I looked around and down the street. Empty, no one to witness any trouble, and that suited me just fine. I pulled my jacket open, let Mikhail see that I was on official business and tooled up. I knew about the baseball bat behind the door. And he knew I didn't fuck about, not any more.

'Mikhail, don't take the piss.'

He still said nothing, but stepped aside. The stairs down

into the bar looked as inviting as a trip into the sewers. No lights; the darkness gaped like a broken mouth.

'If any shit comes my way, Mikhail, I won't take kindly to it, understand? Especially from an aborted shit like you. A single turd and I'll cut you a new hole.'

Mikhail pondered this for a moment, as if studying a particularly hard sentence about dialectical materialism, then nodded.

I pushed past and headed downstairs into the dark, like falling into a nightmare.

At the bottom of the stairs, a corridor that stank of piss and fear led towards another battered door, this one half open and as tempting to enter as an old hooker's mouth.

I went in.

Two of the five overhead lights were blown, and another two simply lacked bulbs, so the atmosphere reminded me of my office back at the station. But my office didn't boast a collection of thugs, alcoholics and prostitutes. Well, not every day, at any rate.

A ripped and torn poster showed the ravages of drugs on a young girl's face, her front teeth missing, blackened stitches above one eyebrow, deadness in her eyes. The headline read: 'BEFORE KROKODIL, I HAD A DAUGHTER. NOW, I HAVE A PROSTITUTE.' Underneath, someone had written in a shaky hand: 'SO I'VE BEEN ABLE TO GIVE UP THE DAY JOB.' Very *kulturny*.

There were several mugshot faces dotted about the room, and a couple of hookers stroking a drunken civilian's hair, but I finally spotted the guy I was hunting. Even in this light, leaning by the bar, glass of bootleg vodka in hand, Vasily Tyulev wasn't difficult to pick out. Half the Kumtor gold mine's annual output hung around his thick acne-spattered neck or pushed his stumpy fingers apart.

'Vasily, how are you, whoreson?'

Now the funny thing was that Vasily really was the son of a whore, but he preferred not to be reminded about it whenever we met. So I saw it as part of my official duty to protect the public by citing him on every occasion as an example of the awful consequences of unsafe sex.

Vasily kept up his mother's tradition by running a string of second-rate girls out of a run-down apartment over on Jibek-Jolu, but until the last revolution he'd also had a neat scam, telling the gullible he was the nephew of the president, a fixer without compare, the man to make magic happen and problems disappear. Not true, of course, but I was always amazed how many people would hand over a bundle of *som* in the hope it would buy some favours. Of course, after the last revolution – when the president fled the country, taking only a dozen large suitcases and the country's savings with him – Vasily got a fair number of threats

32

from people who suddenly wanted their money back. Which was why he kept Mikhail Lubashov around, as a head bodyguard and thug.

Vasily was a pretty shitty human being, but he kept his ears to the ground, his eyes open and his mouth shut, except when I wanted answers.

Which is what he did then, as he took a final drag of his *papirosh*, dropped the butt to the floor, ground it out with his heel and spat on the floor. He looked over at me, one bushy eyebrow raised, and jabbed at his mouth with his thumb. I nodded at the unspoken question, and snapped my fingers at the barman as he reached for a particularly dodgy bottle.

'*Nyet*, top-shelf stuff, the Vivat.'

The barman reached for a half-empty square bottle, and I shook my head.

'Unopened.'

The barman nodded, and put a full bottle in front of me. He didn't ask for money; there was never any question of me paying in there. In dives like the Kulturny, the house 'vodka' is one part petrol, one part piss, two parts poison: with an unopened branded bottle, you stand a slight chance of making it home before cirrhosis or blindness set in.

I picked up the glass before the barman had time to pour, gave it a wipe with my shirt tail, holding it up to the light, checking for smears. I took my time, reminded everyone who was the boss around here. We do things my way, in my time, or we all pay a visit to the tiled and soundproofed room in the basement of the Sverdlovsky Station.

I poured a glass, left it untouched; it's not been unknown for someone to slip a knockout into a likely punter's drink, then roll them once they've passed out. I ran my finger round the cold rim of the glass and looked over at Vasily. Expensive leather jacket, Versace jeans, spotless white Nikes. But he still looked like a third-rate thug, the 'roid-rash covering his neck, the gold-coin rings rapping on the bar as he raised his glass and put the contents down with one swift, practised swallow.

'So, Inspector, a social call?'

I rolled my eyes, poured him another shot.

'I heard about your wife. If you ever need, you know, a spot of physical relaxation, just call me. On the house.'

I winced at the thought of fucking one of Vasily's skank hookers, and resolved to rip his tongue out with pliers if he ever mentioned my wife again. Vasily mistook my look for one of anguish at my loss, and tried to look sympathetic.

'It's about a girl.'

Vasily shrugged.

'It usually is when you come to see me, Inspector.'

'Murdered.'

'If she was strolling down Sovietskaya without a care in the world, you wouldn't be looking me up, would you?'

A hint of cheek, which I lost no time slapping down.

'A prick up your arse, Vasily.'

'The girl on Ibraimova?'

I nodded. Whatever else Vasily was, he was well informed. Maybe from a squealer back at the station, given a bonus every week for a few bites of information here and there.

'Nasty.'

I nodded again, waiting for Vasily to volunteer more, but he just shrugged again.

'Not good for your business, a killing like that.'

'It's got my girls worried, I can tell you that. I'm giving Mikhail a few extra *som* to keep an eye on the place.'

'You're all heart, Vasily.'

'A businessman is all, Inspector.'

He paused and looked at me more closely.

'Not a regular sex killing, then? We don't usually see the police as concerned as this when a crazy guts a *moorzilka*.'

'Someone else been asking?'

'No.'

But the way he hesitated before speaking made me think that I wasn't the only one on the trail.

'The word is that she was cut up bad, real bad. So you're looking for her killer?'

'No, not yet.'

'Then what are you looking for?'

'The other victim. Another woman.'

Vasily looked knowing. About the woman not being a regular street girl. About her gutted womb. And the foetus dumped inside her. Vasily's squealer deserved an extra wad of *som* that month.

'Who told you?'

I was getting very tired of Vasily's shrug. Disrespectful. And more important, wasting my time.

'Word gets about, you know how people gossip.'

I decided it was time to hunt down Vasily's little blabbermouth, and tweak his tongue. Then Vasily surprised me.

'Have you thought there may not be another victim? Maybe the baby was newborn, unmarried mother decides to dump the shame, killer finds it and decides it's time to start cutting?'

I lit another cigarette, gave myself time to consider.

'Maybe she was his girlfriend, he wants kids, she won't give him a son, he goes crazy, they fight, it gets out of hand, and she ends up under the birch trees.'

No, I'd already convinced myself that this wasn't a spontaneous murder, no blood-stained knife thrown away in a panic, no tyre tracks or footprints to give us a clue. There was someone out there who loved the power; the resistance and give when you took the knife that you've lovingly whetted and honed and drew it across someone's flesh. But there was no reason why Vasily needed to know that.

'Save the detecting for me. You hear anything? Anybody kinky giving your girls a weird feeling?'

Vasily half laughed, revealing a set of teeth that were half grey, half gold.

'My clientele as killers? It's the best they can do to get a stiff one most of the time, they're so drunk. I swear, when they come, it's not spunk, it's *pivo*.'

He paused, remembered and started to reminisce.

'There was a guy, couple of years back, he had a thing for Irina – you know, the Uzbek from Jalalabad, the one with only one tit? Wanted to bite her remaining nipple off. Total crazy. Offered to pay, took out a roll of notes big enough to stuff a cushion. But I said to him, what use is damaged goods to me? Didn't like that, tried to cut up rough.'

'This pork-chewer, you know his name? Where he is?'

'First question? No idea. Second? You know the runway extension out at Manas Airport? The one for the transport planes at the US base? Couldn't say where exactly, but he's under it. Happy digging.'

'Vasily, you're as much use as a split condom. But if

I hear that you know something, and you decide to keep it all to your shit-rotten self, then *zhopu porvu margala vikoliu*, understand?'

Vasily nodded, sombre. When an Inspector promises to rip you a new arse and then poke out your eyes, it tends to focus the mind. Vasily slipped another mask on to his face, the one of genuine concern and community duty.

'It's terrible, terrible, that murders like these happen,' he said. 'That poor girl.' He shook his head at the iniquity of the world, before the mask slipped. 'Besides, it's bad for business.'

'You're all heart, Vasily,' I said, and pinched his cheek, not like a *babushka* with her favourite grandson, but hard enough to make his eyes water and his head twist forward. For a second, I thought I'd provoked him enough to kick off, and I slipped my hand towards the Yarygin. He saw my move, and settled back, rubbing his cheek.

'Always a joker, Inspector, always good to see you.'

I gave him the hard stare until his gaze broke, and then walked to the door. My shoulder blades itched, but he didn't have the balls to try anything. Not that day, at any rate. But I didn't feel really comfortable until I was up the stairs and out on the street. There was no sign of Lubashov, never a bad thing, and the freezing air tasted sweet and clean.

It had started to snow again, and the tracks I'd made earlier were already half hidden; a couple of hours, and it would be as if I'd never existed. I thought of the young woman under the trees and the soft white flakes that bloomed on her body, of Chinara and the earth that covered her face, and my cheeks were wet with snow, or perhaps tears. For perhaps the thousandth time, I wondered how I could carry on in a world where love always ends. And for the thousandth time, I told myself that no one really dies until there is no one left to remember them. All any of us can do is try to weather each storm, and help the ones we love to do the same.

I spat to flush the bar's rancid stink out of my mouth, and started trudging through the snow towards home. But I'd only walked a couple of blocks from the club when I heard the crunch of footsteps behind me, not quite a run, coming up fast.

The Yarygin was already in my hand, safety catch off, as I swung round to face my future.

Chapter 5

I was a split second away from aiming and pulling the trigger when I saw that it wasn't Lubashov or one of his *droogs* about to deliver a coup de grâce.

'For fuck's sake!'

The kind of squeaky voice you hear when a grim middle-aged slag tries to convince you that she's young and desirable, despite the overwhelming evidence. At least this one was young, but you'd have needed a lot of vodka on board to find her desirable. Skirt just about covering her moneymaker, thick legs turning blue with cold, trowelled make-up and a cleavage of plucked chicken skin. She started to walk towards me, reaching into her handbag.

'Staying right where you are will do just fine,' I said, all too aware that I'd been about to blow a teenage prostitute out of her fake leather boots. I holstered the Yarygin and put my hand in my pocket, where she couldn't see it shake.

'And you can take your hand out slowly,' I added. Most of these girls carry razors, and more scars are something I don't need. Her face revealed annoyance and fear as she took out her cigarettes, tapped one from the pack and waved it at me for a light. I ignored it so, with a melodramatic sigh, she rummaged in her bag for her lighter. Smoke mingled with her breath on the air, making her head disappear into a thick blue fog for a brief second.

'You don't remember me?'

As she drew deeply on her cigarette and plumed the smoke upwards, I looked at her. Something about her was familiar, but she could have been a thousand working girls I've seen over the years, defiant outside, broken and cowed inside. The same lacklustre hopes beaten out of her by poverty, drugs and the fists of a hundred men.

Her eyes stared back at me, black and unreadable, marbles in the pallor of her face.

'Shairkul? You remember? You helped me a couple of years back?'

I shrugged.

'Outside Fire and Ice at closing time? Some bitch tried to stab me, when her punter decided I'd be the better ride. I punched the cow out, and you stopped me doing worse.'

A memory surfaced. I vaguely remembered taking a knife out of some girl's hand, throwing it in the gutter and telling her to piss off before I took her down the station. I'd given her a few *som* and bullied a reluctant taxi driver into taking her home. Maybe this was her, but maybe not. Shairkul, meaning 'joyful', but there was nothing very joyful about her.

'You could have arrested me, but you didn't. So I owe you.'

I stayed silent. Gratitude isn't something you generally expect from a working girl. Life throws enough shit at them without them having to drop to their knees at the memory of a good deed, or do any favours once they're there. She might have had something to tell, but I didn't expect her to volunteer the information.

'I saw you talking to Vasily. In the bar.'

Now I placed her. One of the two hookers in the corner, getting a punter to rise to the bait.

'You were asking about the murder up on Ibraimova, weren't you?'

'And if I was?'

'I might be able to help you.'

'You know who she was?'

'No.'

'You know who killed her?'

'No.'

Shairkul smiled, revealing a wide-gapped row of golden teeth. Business had obviously been good, once upon a time. She knew she had my interest now, and I was waiting for the squeeze.

'I left that pisshead back there to come and talk to you. That's got to be worth something.'

I nodded, and her smile got wider. A mistake; a couple of her teeth were missing, and it didn't add to her charms. She stepped forward and put her hand on my sleeve.

'It's fucking cold. Maybe we can go somewhere?'

I removed her hand, and nodded again.

'I've got a spare bed you can have. Down the station. You might have to share with some ninety-kilo bull-dyke dreaming of breaking in a sweet little slut like you, but hey, it's all girls together, right? And in the morning, when you've rinsed out the blood, we can have our little chat.'

Her face hardened, and she turned to spit.

'You're a bastard, Inspector, I bet you have to pay to fuck your wife. Everyone else does.'

She took a step back at the look on my face, and held up her hands in apology.

'OK, sorry, start again? I can help you. With the killing? There's a reward going, maybe? For information? And Vasily doesn't have to know, right?'

Suddenly I felt old, washed up, as if I'd been listening to the same lies, self-justifications and greed all my life. I nodded my head towards a doorway, to get us off the street. She took a final drag of her cigarette, flicked it away and stumbled after me.

Out of the wind, her cheap perfume burnt my eyes. The top must have come off the bottle.

'She was cut up, right? I mean, badly cut up? And someone shoved a baby inside her belly?'

'You've got big ears, and someone's got a big mouth.'

She pouted. This wasn't going the way she'd planned; grateful cop gives her a handful of notes and a Get Out of Jail card. She fumbled through her bag for another cigarette, found only an empty pack, crumpled it up, dumped it. I offered her one of mine, and she leant forward as I lit hers and mine. True romance. I could almost hear the violins.

'My friend Gulbara told me a girl had been killed.'

'And she knew, how?'

I didn't expect that she'd tell me. Gulbara, if she even existed, wouldn't be likely to share her informant at the station with anyone. But you have to ask, make sure they don't think they can get away with anything.

'I wasn't sure if I should believe her or not. But then Vasily told us as well. Said not to worry, that we could keep on working, that this guy wasn't interested in working girls.'

Typical Vasily. As long as the *som* came in, he wouldn't give a fuck if his whole stable got slaughtered. Plenty more where they came from.

As if she read my mind, Shairkul took a final, lung-bursting drag from her cigarette, threw it away.

'He would say that, right?'

I nodded.

'So what should we do?'

I shrugged again.

'What did Gulbara say?'

She took a step back, took a fresh look at me.

'You don't give a fuck either, do you?'

'What do you want me to do? Give you money to catch the bus back to your village? Call out the army to give you twenty-four-hour protection? You know how it works.' I threw her the tough-but-honest-cop stare. 'You tell me what you know, I find the dickhead, book him in at the no-star hotel, and we all go back to work as normal.'

Shairkul seemed less than reassured by this, and gestured for another cigarette. At this rate, it would be lung cancer that laid her out on Usupov's slab, long before any crazies got to her.

'She wasn't one of us, not a regular working girl. But you already know that, right?'

'I know what we know. What I want is what you know.'

Even though the street was deserted, Shairkul looked over her shoulder before speaking.

'She wouldn't have lasted three hours without a pimp, you know how this town's carved up.'

I winced at the word, remembering the frozen stare

gazing out past the trees towards uncaring stars, the uncoiled tangle of guts, the half-clenched fingers of the foetus.

'So she was an amateur, that's what you're telling me?'

Shairkul smiled; there'd be a price for her information.

'Is there a reward?'

'For you?'

I stopped for effect, reached for my cigarettes. Shairkul grinned, the money already as good as in her handbag.

'Let me explain. I saw the body of a young woman hacked up worse than I've ever seen, and I've seen plenty. Some other woman, if she's still alive, is mourning the death of her unborn child. So my patience is not just wearing thin, it's non-existent. And I'm in a hurry.'

I grabbed Shairkul's jacket and pulled her to me, so close that anyone passing by would think we were lovers, oblivious of the cold. I lowered my voice to the gentle, persuasive murmur that I've always found more menacing than a shout or a snarl.

'Unless you start talking, I'm going to tell Vasily just how talkative you can be. You know how pimps feel about girls that use their mouths for something other than giving a customer a blow. And then you won't be talking at all, will you?'

I smiled with my mouth and not my eyes, and gently tapped her cheek.

'Gulbara found her,' Shairkul gabbled, face white under the caked *prosti* make-up. 'She thought she might find some drunk up for a short time in their car, on the way home from the Blonder.'

'Go on,' I said, and tapped her cheek again to refresh her memory.

'She saw the girl's handbag. Good quality, designer. She figured there'd be money, a mobile, maybe even car keys.'

'She didn't think to be a good citizen and call us?'

Even terrified, Shairkul smiled. We both knew that nobody does anything to help the police in this town, unless there's something in it for them.

'So Gulbara's got a fancy new handbag. What about it?'

'It's what's in the bag that's important.'

'And now you'll take me to Gulbara, as long as you get your piece?'

Shairkul nodded.

'You want to get the bag sooner rather than later, *da*?'

I couldn't fault her logic.

'We'll go see Gulbara, and discuss it all later, OK? One hand washes the other.'

I used my mobile to call a patrol car. When we got in, Shairkul gave an address on the far side of Osh bazaar. The patrol car's flashing lights bounced off the hard-packed snow, the colour of blood, the colour of death.

'Stop here,' Shairkul said, 'I don't want police shaming me in front of my neighbours.'

Which just about sums up how most Kyrgyz, decent or otherwise, feel about us.

'You didn't say you lived with Gulbara.'

Now it was Shairkul's turn to shrug.

'You didn't ask.'

Having an idea what was in store, I borrowed a torch from the reluctant uniform, who grumbled about its return, and then we walked round the corner, towards a dilapidated *khrushchyovk* apartment block.

The city is full of these relics of our Soviet days, solid, durable, ugly and practical, named after the former Soviet premier who'd had them installed across the Union. You'd never describe them as stylish, but they're an improvement on the shacks or yurts that we lived in before, especially when the winter sets in and the snow descends from the Tien Shan.

The building's five-storey cement prefabricated panels were stained and cracked, and some wit had spray-painted HILTON above the entrance. The metal door hung open, and we pushed through into the dark. You never find a *khrushchyovka* where the communal lights work, so I switched on the torch and we walked up the litter-covered stairs towards the lift. By some miracle, it wheezed into life and we rode in silence up to the fifth floor.

Outside the apartment, Shairkul started to speak, but I held my finger up for silence. I didn't want any surprises on the other side of the door, and that meant not alerting whoever was inside. She unlocked the heavy-duty steel door, and then the ornamental wooden door inside, and I gripped the Yarygin.

We went inside.

Someone had been smoking *travka*; the thick sweet smell was everywhere. But the apartment was clean and neat, cheaply furnished. Whatever failings Shairkul and Gulbara might have had, slovenliness wasn't one of them.

The bedroom door was ajar and, from the sounds inside, Gulbara was obviously hard at work. Reluctant to interrupt anyone's pleasure, I peeked round the door. Plain walls, a couple of worn rugs on the bare concrete floor, a couple of half-drunk beer bottles on a bedside table. The ideal setting for an erotic tempest. The bed was creaking like an old ship in a storm, and Gulbara was moaning and groaning as if about to be shipwrecked.

'*Da, maloletka, da!*'

Gulbara might or might not have been a little slut, but the man thrusting between her legs was certainly a fat pig. Coarse black hair spread like a rug across his shoulders and down his back and on to the top of his arse. He was doing his best to push the bottle-blonde beneath him through the thin mattress, his head buried in her hair, nuzzling her neck.

Gulbara's eyes widened at the sight of me, and I put my finger to my lips as I tiptoed to the bed.

I waited until the punter's grunting accelerated, then placed the front sight of my Yarygin against his arsehole.

I didn't know if that triggered his orgasm or simply gave him a heart attack, but he squealed, yelled and farted all at once. He rolled off Gulbara, at some considerable pain to both of them, and covered his rapidly dwindling erection with both hands. Gulbara was less modest, probably as a result of fucking strangers morning, noon and night, and simply reached for her cigarettes on the floor.

I did my best not to stare, and motioned Shairkul in the vague direction of the mattress. My smile was not guaranteed to inspire confidence in any of the trio.

'Let's all make ourselves comfortable, and then we can have a little chat.'

Chapter 6

'Let me put my fucking trousers on!'

This from the fat pig; Gulbara didn't care who checked out her goods as long as there was a cash purchase. He reached for his clothes, and I shook my head, waved the Yarygin, and he sat back up. I'm not an admirer of the male nude, especially when it's fat, furry and about thirty kilos overweight. But you never know what people have in their pockets; a four-centimetre scar down my right forearm taught me that the difficult way. Besides, being naked with a gun pointing at you loosens the tongue. Not to mention the bowels.

'Name?'

'Who the fuck are you? Don't you know who I am?'

'If I did, I wouldn't be asking, would I?' I said in my most reasonable voice. He was recovering now, and wondering what the play was. I could see him reasoning he'd already be dead, if this was a hit. Maybe he believed he was important enough not to get robbed by some street hood. And I wasn't working the irate husband badger game with the girls. So just who the fuck was I?

I decided to confuse him a little further.

'You're a good citizen, right? Helping this unfortunate young woman back on to the straight and narrow, right?'

He answered by leaning over Gulbara and spitting on to the floor.

I leant forward and gave his kneecap a little tap with the Yarygin. His reflexes were OK, I had to give him that.

'Dumb arsehole!'

I shook my head and looked disappointed.

'I'm not dumb, I'm the one with the gun. And as for being an arsehole, well, we've all seen yours. So I'll ask again. Name?'

He remained silent, and my patience was shrinking faster than his prick. We could have gone on playing tough guys all night, but I'd better things to do.

'Relax, I'm law. Murder Squad. I don't give a fuck if you get her to give you a blow in the centre of Ala-Too Square. I want to talk to her, not you. Your name, then you can fuck off.'

Pride meant he didn't want to tell me. The Yarygin and being bollock-naked meant he would.

'Gasparian. Khatchig.'

Armenian. That accounted for the furry back. And the attitude. We Kyrgyz don't hate the Armenians as much as we hate the Uzbeks or the Uighurs or the

Kazakhs or the Tatars or the Russians, or, to be honest, anyone who isn't Kyrgyz and most people who are. But there are a couple of gangs from Yerevan working the heroin routes from Afghanistan into the American military airbase, and our home-grown bad guys don't care for foreign competition.

'So what is this? You're looking for a sweetener?'

He mimed cash with thumb and forefinger, and reached down for his trousers.

'Empty your pockets. Slowly. Finger and thumb. The other hand. And if anything naughty comes out, you've just had your last come.'

He nodded understanding. A wallet thick with *som*. Car keys: he drove a BMW, judging by the fob. A fancy mobile. And a switchblade with a pale horn handle. His ID said he was telling the truth, at least about his name.

'Kick the knife over here.'

He did so, and I looked around for something to pick it up with, to avoid smearing any fingerprints. The only cloth near to hand seemed to be Gulbara's panties. I'm not a fastidious man, but sometimes this job makes impossible demands. I dropped the panty-wrapped knife into my pocket, smiled, and then tapped Gasparian on the knee again. This time, not gently.

He roared, the bellow I'd come to associate with his sex life, and clutched at his knee. He tried to stand, but had to grab at the wall for support. Gulbara sniggered, the sort of laugh you'd expect from a naked woman with a tattoo of a monkey climbing into her pubic hair.

'You'll need to go to a hospital with that knee,' I told him. 'Should keep you out of trouble for a few hours.'

'Cunt,' he muttered, but I could tell his heart wasn't in it.

I picked up his clothes, walked out into the hallway, and flung them through the open door. He took the hint and limped past me, his knee already starting to swell. He tried the dead-eye stare, which impressed me about as much as his dick did, and waited until he was in the safety of the hallway before he snarled, 'This isn't over.'

I smiled politely, shut the doors and bolted the inner one. Someone back in Sverdlovsky would have his record; it wouldn't be hard to find him if I needed to.

I turned back to Gulbara, who still lay sprawled in the wreckage of the bed.

'Get dressed.'

'You've got my panties. Going to sniff them when you get home?' She spoke with a thick country accent; Osh, or maybe Naryn. Come to the big city to make her fortune.

'I'm sure you've got another pair for best. Get dressed so we can talk, or you can come down to the station as you are. It's cold enough out there to freeze the nipples off a whore. Given your job, I wouldn't run the risk.'

Once Gulbara had slithered into a red dress short enough to delight a gynaecologist, we went into the sitting room. Shairkul reached into a wall cupboard and brought out a bottle of Kyrgyz brandy and three small mismatched glasses. I nodded and watched her pour three shots. I waited until the two women had downed theirs before I sniffed at mine. Rough, raw, perfect for weather like this, for a case like this. I raised the glass to my lips, pretended to join them, then put it down, untasted.

'I won't beat about the bush,' I began, 'especially not with the monkey that lives there. Its bite might be poisonous.'

Neither woman smiled. Judging by a couple of track marks in the crook of Gulbara's left arm, that wasn't the only monkey she was carrying around with her.

'You found a dead woman last night. Found her handbag as well. And that's what I'm here for. Anything else you do outside of that, I'm not interested. Understand?'

Gulbara nodded, and Shairkul refilled the glasses. They drank again. Companionable silence.

'I had nothing to do with her dying, you understand?'

I waited for her to continue, my eyes never leaving her face.

'She was dead when I came past. I was heading for the bridge over Ibraimova, looking for a taxi. No business, too cold. And then I saw her.'

Gulbara gave a theatrical shudder at the memory, and held out her glass for another drink. I shook my head at Shairkul; I didn't want Gulbara pissed before I'd had a chance to hear her story.

'You saw her.'

Not a question. I nodded my head.

'I thought at first it might be one of the regular girls. An occupational hazard. But not the way she was dressed. Too smart for a tart. And too pretty.'

Suddenly Gulbara looked like the frightened, vulnerable woman just out of her teens that she was behind the harsh make-up and the cheap nylon dress. She knew there was a killer out there in the dark, maybe waiting for another woman, maybe looking for a prostitute to slice and hurt and scar and maim, looking to turn her into so much cooling meat. Death comes to all of us, and the best we can hope for is that it's painless and quick. All too often, it's neither.

'I could see there was nothing I could do. And too many trees there, too much cover, no one around. He could have been hiding, waiting for the next one. Maybe five minutes earlier and it could have been me.'

She waved her glass again at Shairkul, and this time I let her drink, a single long swallow that left her breathless.

'So you took the handbag and legged it?'

'What would you have done?'

'You didn't touch the body?'

'You are joking. I just grabbed the handbag and I was away on my toes. Didn't even look inside until I was in a taxi.'

'Any money?'

Gulbara looked at me as if I was a *myrki* peasant straight up from the village. I sighed.

'I need to know if she was robbed as well. If it was about money or about something else. So I want to know, right?'

Gulbara muttered something I didn't catch.

'How much?'

'A thousand dollars. New notes. Hundreds.'

'And where is it?'

She looked away.

'You fed the *krokodil*?'

She said nothing, but glanced down at the tracks on her arm. My only witness a junkie, any hint at motive snug in a dealer's back pocket, and snow starting to fall again. Christ.

I snapped my fingers.

'Bag. Now.'

Shairkul reached into the wall cupboard and pulled out a smart shoulder bag, the sort a woman might wear to an exclusive party, drinks in the 191 Bar, a job interview at one of the embassies. To my eyes, it looked expensive, but I'm a man, what do I know?

Chinara would have been able to tell me the label, the date, the price from across the room. Her handbags, her jewellery, even her shoes, still in the wardrobe, waiting for me to find the courage to get rid of them, dispose of her presence. For a second, I could have sworn I could smell the perfume she wore, as if she'd entered the room, was standing behind me. And then I remembered she'd gone.

For ever.

I took the bag from Shairkul and gently put it down on the red rug that was the concrete floor's only covering. Rich, soft cream leather. Ornate gold metal clasp. A logo saying 'Prada'. If it had said *Pravda*, I might have been better informed.

'A good-quality bag? Expensive?'

The two girls looked aghast at my ignorance.

'Maybe fifteen hundred dollars. And the real thing too. Not bought here, but abroad, maybe GUM.'

I couldn't help sighing. GUM is the ornate building that sits on Red Square facing the Kremlin, probably the most expensive cluster of boutiques in the world. Anyone who could afford to buy there was bound to have influence, people who would demand quick results and a head on a platter. And if I couldn't find a killer, I knew whose head it would be.

'You take anything else besides the money?'

Gulbara shook her head and watched me open the bag. BlackBerry, keys, lipstick, a pair of gold hoop earrings and, tucked into a zipped pocket, the thing I'd hoped to find. An ID card.

The face I found under the trees stared back at me. The same calm, the same detachment. The face lying in a drawer waiting to be claimed.

I read the name.

And realised that I was in a world of shit.

Chapter 7

I was in a patrol car, on my way back to Sverdlovsky Station, the windscreen wipers struggling against the snow with a dull, relentless screech. Pretty much what I expected to hear once I saw the Chief. I'd put in the call before I organised a ride, knowing that he'd been overjoyed at being woken up and asked to meet me at the station. No one could ever mistake a Tatar for a sunny day, but my boss lived in an almost permanent state of rage.

The cop at the wheel swore almost constantly as the car slithered and slid through the snow: at the weather, at the authorities for failing to clear the roads and, under his breath, at me for hauling him halfway across the city. As we passed the memorial to the dead killed in the last revolution, the floral tributes were almost invisible under fresh snowdrifts, just as Chinara's grave up in the mountains – and the grave someone would dig for the girl under the birch trees – would be hidden. I considered asking the *ment* to stop so I could get a hundred grams of vodka to warm me up. But then we were pulling into the forecourt, waved in by the officer on guard, stamping his feet for warmth, gun slung over his shoulder.

It was no warmer inside the building than it was outside, one more thing that wasn't going to endear me to
the Chief. I made my way up the chipped and cracked
concrete steps and along the corridor to his office. I
passed Urmat Sariev, one of the old guard, famous for
being the clumsiest cop in Bishkek: at least, more
prisoners had accidents while in his care than anyone
else's. We'd never been openly hostile to each other, but
Sariev knew I thought he was a shit-sucker. And when
he wasn't doing that, he was pouring it on the heads of
everyone else. Being better at politics than policing gave
him the inside track on what was going on.

He gave me a gold-toothed grin.

'It's the Clever Wolf, come to teach us all how to
catch the bad guys!'

I should explain: my given name is Akyl, which
means 'clever', and my family name contains the word
'boru', Kyrgyz for a wolf. So Clever Wolf is the joking
name I've carried around with me ever since rookie
days at the academy. Pretty much a job description, I
suppose, if you're planning to survive in a job where
even the people on your side might be enemies.

Sariev smiled again and drew a finger across his
throat, so I knew it wasn't good news. I gave him a
wink of confidence that I was far from feeling, and
rapped on the wooden door.

The rest of the station may have been a shithole, but

no one could have accused my boss of lacking civic pride. He knew that he had the spotless reputation of the police to uphold. That explained the colourful *shyrdak* felt rug on the wall, the polished wooden floor, the car-sized desk with a bronze half-size hunting eagle perched on one edge. Of course, it helped that it was all paid for out of the police budget, probably with a little extra commission in place for him.

As I walked in, the Chief was pouring himself a drink. I noticed that there was only one glass. He threw it back, poured another one.

'*Zatknis' na hui!*'

Told to shut the fuck up, before I'd even opened my mouth. Not a good sign. The Chief sat back in his chair and looked at me disapprovingly with red-rimmed eyes. A big man, a champion wrestler once, running slightly to fat after too much *plov* stew and Kyrgyz-brewed *pivo*. The round moon face of a Tatar, black eyes impassive, unwilling to give anything away. But he was shrewd, a tough bastard and a good cop. He wasn't a political appointment either, so his tongue wasn't lodged up any politico's arse.

He'd seen out both revolutions since independence, even managed to get promotion after the second one. He knew where the bodies were buried, had probably put a few there himself. He was a survivor. But I didn't know whether I would be, once I told him what I knew.

'Two o' fucking clock in the fucking morning, this had better be important. Otherwise, they're looking for traffic cops up on the Torugart Pass.'

Torugart. Four thousand metres up in the Tien Shan Mountains down in the south, the border pass into China, impassible in the winter, through snow or avalanches or both. The arse end of nowhere, with nothing to do but watch lorries crawl past, laden down with cheap Chinese furniture. With the Chief, it wasn't an empty threat. It never was with him. He always made sure to get his retaliation in first; it was what made him a force to be reckoned with.

'Illya Sergeyevich,' I began, hoping to appease him by using his patronymic, 'we've had some major developments in the Ibraimova case and, since you're the most senior and experienced officer we have here, I considered it best to keep you informed at all times.'

He grunted, and took a sip of vodka.

'I have some good news: we've managed to make a tentative identification, and I'll go to the morgue in the morning for further confirmation.'

I poured some water into a glass and raised it in a toast.

'*Na zdrovia.*'

I wondered how healthy I'd be once the Chief heard what I had to say.

We emptied our glasses and set them down.

'And the bad news?'

'As I said, we've managed a tentative identification.'

He nodded, impatient. But I wasn't about to rush into some indiscretion that could land me up in the mountains. And for all I knew, the Chief's office might be bugged, either with or without his knowledge.

'After extensive inquiries among various sources, I managed to recover the deceased's handbag.'

The Chief gestured, impatient, but I picked my words carefully, all too aware of their potential to come back and kick my arse later on. I didn't want any mis-understandings, misinterpretations. A shit-sucker like Sariev would be all too ready to pour poison in people's ears, and there are always people ready to listen. I explained about meeting with Vasily, about encounter-ing Shairkul and Gulbara, about retrieving the bag.

'You want the slapper brought in? A couple of min-utes in a cell with Sariev and she'll be begging to talk. Maybe a turf war between working girls?'

The Chief looked hopeful; low-life deaths don't make headlines or waves.

'I think our victim was in a different league. And she wasn't a hooker – at least, not as far as I know.'

'And this Gulbara ending up with the bag? That doesn't set alarm bells ringing?'

I braced myself; now was the time to come clean.

'I have no reason to think that the handbag was

anything other than an opportunistic theft on her part, unconnected to the murder.'

The Chief looked up, picking up on my words.

'You've established a motive? Inspector.'

Reminding me just how thin was the ice on which I stood. I shook my head and quickly added, 'But we do know who she is. Was.'

'Will you for fuck's sake just tell me?'

'Yekaterina Mikhailovna Tynalieva.'

I paused, and waited for the news to sink in.

The Chief reached for the bottle and poured another shot, a big one, and without waiting, threw it back. His face was serious, worried.

'Whore! Why couldn't the bitch get herself sliced in someone else's district?' he snarled.

'Wouldn't make any difference. We're Murder Squad. Ends up on our desk one way or another.'

'Your desk.'

I shrugged.

'Get one of the uniforms to drive you. And be discreet. No flashing lights, sirens, any of that crap.'

He looked at me, at the crumpled suit, the wrinkled shirt, the snow-sodden boots.

'Could you look any less like a cop?'

Personally, I thought that's exactly what I did look like, but it wasn't the time to say so.

'You want me to go home and change?'

My one good suit, unworn since I threw a handful of dirt on to Chinara's shroud. Appropriate, maybe, for another grieving family, another woman dead before her time.

'No. Better get it done with. He won't appreciate you putting on a tie to bring him this shit.'

'If he wants to know the details? Do I tell him about the cutting, the mutilation? The foetus?'

'If you had any discretion, I'd say use it. But we'll get more shit pissing him off by hiding stuff. If he doesn't ask, he doesn't need to know. We don't need to make this *pizdets* any fucking worse.'

I nodded.

The Chief looked slightly more relaxed, knowing the burden was sitting good and square on me. I knew he was already working out how to minimise his exposure to the shit storm.

'He's not going to want to wait until morning. Get Usupov to open the morgue.'

He poured another drink, then looked surprised to see me still standing there.

'Now fuck off. And for fuck's sake, tread softly.'

I shut the door behind me, and walked back towards the entrance, wondering just how exactly I was going to break the news that his daughter had been murdered to the Minister for State Security.

Chapter 8

The State Service for National Security plays by its own rules. Its people are never photographed, quoted in newspapers, hauled before Parliament. Think of them as smoke, or morning mist on the water of Lake Issyk-Kul, drifting, intangible, impossible to pin down. They're the elite, the Kyrgyz equivalent of the Russian *Spetsnaz*, hand-picked and trained to eliminate any threat to the welfare and security of the state. The problem is that, all too often, the welfare of the state means the welfare of the top men. So anything that's bad for them is bad for the country. And Mikhail Tynaliev was the kind of man who refuses to let anything bad happen on his watch. He would take the news I was going to bring him very badly indeed.

As we pulled up outside his town house, motion-controlled lights flashed on while we parked. An armed guard in a secure sentry gatehouse kept a close watch on the street; the blue flickering light across his face told me that the cameras around the grounds weren't just for show. This was one of Bishkek's smartest roads, private houses set back, secure, regularly patrolled.

I got out of the car slowly, my hands well away from my body, my ID card already in my hand. This was not the time or place for any sudden moves. From the other side of the glass, the guard beckoned me further forward. I smiled, doing my best to look harmless, my boots skidding on the packed ice.

'How's tricks, comrade?' I said, holding up my card.

The guard didn't take his eyes off me, but pushed a sliding tray from his side of the glass. I dropped my card in, and waited while the guard scrutinised it. Obviously, I wasn't his comrade. Eventually, I passed muster.

'What are you here for?' he asked, his voice mechanical and hoarse through the loudspeaker set into the window.

'I'm here to see the Minister. Police business, official.'

'Does he know you're coming?'

'*Nyet.*'

This was where it could all go to shit. Maybe the guard wouldn't admit me, in which case Tynaliev wouldn't find out about his daughter until the morning, which wouldn't please him. And if I told the guard my reason for coming, it would be all over the city in an hour.

The guard pondered his options, then made a call. A couple of moments of conversation, his face turned away so I couldn't lip-read, then the decision was made.

'Someone will be down from the house.'

'Can you open the gate? We'll park outside.'

The guard shook his head. No matter that this was a police car, that he'd seen my ID; the risk of a suicide car bomb was too great. I stamped my feet to keep warm, until a side door in the main gate opened. Two more guards waved me forward towards a scanner, but I stopped, held my jacket open to show the Yarygin. No point in giving anyone an excuse to show how fast and decisive he could be when guarding the boss.

They took my gun away, walked me through the scanner a couple of times, and then the senior of the two guards led me towards the house.

'This had better be important,' he said. 'No guarantee he'll see you.'

'My Chief sent me personally. It's to do with a case.'

The guard looked at me, curious, but I wasn't about to volunteer any more information.

'You'd better hope he thinks so.'

I trudged down the path, my boots crunching in the newly fallen snow. A wave of tiredness drifted over me at the thought of another death to announce, another person's grief to observe. The door swung open as I arrived, and I was shepherded into the hall by yet another guard. He patted me down again, clinically and thoroughly, and then took me through into a study to wait for the great man. I could feel sweat starting on my forehead, so I removed my fur hat and stood bare-headed. The room was stiflingly overheated, but that wasn't the only reason I was sweating. I knew my career could end right there.

'Inspector.'

I turned round to see Mikhail Tynaliev standing in the doorway. Shorter than I'd imagined from his pictures, but with the typical Kyrgyz build: broad shoulders, a bull neck, powerful hands. Easy to imagine him interrogating a prisoner in the basement of his headquarters, standing too close, the casual punch, the backhanded slap that loosens teeth and lashes blood across the floor.

'Minister.'

'It's very late for an unscheduled visit.'

'My apologies. I wouldn't have come at this time of night had it not been a matter of the utmost urgency.'

I stood to attention, spoke formally, tried not to let a tremor enter my voice. Because this man had seen and heard the sounds of fear a thousand times, knew them all.

'Which is why I'm seeing you now.'

The Minister crossed over to one of the leather sofas that stood against the far wall and sat down. He didn't invite me to join him.

'I find it hard to imagine that there's a threat to the state that the police would know about before my people.'

'It's not a political matter, Minister.'

'No?'

I saw that I'd caught his attention. Not terrorism, not organised crime. Then what? His eyes were on my face now, cold and black as the ice outside.

'A personal matter. A family matter.'

His voice, when he spoke, was harsh, flat.

'Go on.'

'Early yesterday morning, the body of a young woman was found off Ibraimova Street. We were unable to make a preliminary identification at first; there was no ID on the body. But further information came into our possession within the last couple of hours.'

I paused, but the Minister simply stared at me, his face unreadable.

'I very much regret to tell you that our inquiries suggest that the young woman may be your daughter, Yekaterina Tynalieva.'

The Minister looked at me.

'On what basis do you suggest it's her?'

'We recovered an ID card in her name, in a handbag taken from the scene of the crime.'

'So it is a crime, then? Not an accident?'

'I'm afraid not. We're treating it as murder.'

I reached into my pocket and pulled out the dead woman's ID card. He stood up and took it from me.

He stared as if unable to make sense of what he saw, and I reminded myself that, right then, he wasn't one of the most powerful and dangerous men in the country but a man faced with what must be the most terrible news a father can receive.

'That's her, that's my Katia. But there must be some mistake. Her handbag stolen, or . . .'

His voice trailed away. I said nothing but took out the head shots that Usupov had prepared for me in the morgue a thousand endless hours ago. She looked calm, no expression of surprise or terror, just that indefinable stillness that separates the dead and the living. He took them from my hand, looked at them, nodded.

'*Da.*'

One of the photographs fell to the floor, but neither of us moved to pick it up. When he spoke, his voice had aged, suddenly weary, an exhausted man at the end of his tether.

'Did she . . . ?'

'As far as we can tell it was very quick.'

I chose my words carefully. The normal phrases of condolence seemed less than adequate, an insult almost.

'Was she . . . ?'

'We don't think so. But the pathologist was unable to tell if she'd been raped. There were . . . post-mortem wounds.'

Tynaliev pursed his lips, a gesture so slight he might almost have been turned to stone. He reached for a crystal decanter on a nearby table, poured a drink, downed it, poured another, and then, after a moment's thought, one for me. I nodded my thanks and took the glass.

'Tell me.'

'I don't think that we need to go into details, Minister. I realise this has been a terrible —'

'Tell me.'

His voice cold, flat. An order.

So I did.

I hid nothing, not the hacking away of his only daughter's vulva, the gouging out of her belly and womb, the uncoiling and unwinding, the final insult of the foetus dumped inside her like some backstreet abortionist's garbage can.

The only thing I didn't tell him was how the snow had settled on her face like the veil of a bride, how quiet the night was beneath the birch trees, how I thought of my own dead wife newly laid in her grave.

Tynaliev gave a long sigh, of resignation almost, at the prospect of a difficult but necessary task about to be undertaken.

'You'll bring him to me.'

Not a question, not a request. An order. I put my glass down, untouched.

'As yet, we don't have a suspect –'

'This is not a matter for the security forces, Inspector. But I don't want every incompetent *myrki* policeman stumbling his way through this. I want you to handle this case personally, no one else. When you catch him, you bring him to me. Don't worry, I'll clear it all with your Chief, and tell him you're handling the case alone. I'll see you have your back covered, a roof over your head. And I'll owe you.'

I understood why the Minister didn't want the department involved; a hint of weakness and his image as a hard man would be threatened. In Kyrgyzstan, to be seen as weak is to invite your fall, from power, from office, perhaps even from life. And political protection from a man like Tynaliev wasn't something to be tossed away lightly. But at the same time, I knew that handing a suspect over to him would mean taking part in torture, agony and, only after a long time, death. Then the remnants to deal with: a couple of torn fingernails, splintered teeth, a puddle of blood for the cleaners to mop away. Tynaliev might owe me, but he'd also own me, and I knew enough about how things worked to know it all gets called in, sooner or later.

'We'll obviously keep you informed of the progress of the investigation. But right now, I must ask you to come with me. For formal identification, you understand.'

'Now?'

'I've had the morgue opened for you. At a time like this, the family's wishes are paramount.'

I didn't mention his wife, Yekaterina's mother. It was common knowledge in the department that she lived in the *dacha*, the country cottage near Talas, while Mikhail Ivanovich occupied himself with an ever-changing line-up of ambitious young women.

'Very well.'

He paused, placed a hand on my shoulder, gripped it uncomfortably tight.

'But let me repeat, Inspector, you bring him to me.'

This time, not an order. A threat.

Chapter 9

Impassive, Mikhail Tynaliev stared down at the face of his dead daughter. I'd warned Usupov of our visit, so the body was laid out in the inspection room rather than tucked away in a refrigerated drawer. A sheet covered the body, so that only her face was visible, but nothing hid the sour stink of dried blood, the harsh smell of raw meat.

I cleared my throat, gave a preparatory cough.

'Mikhail Ivanovich Tynaliev, are you able to make a formal identification of the deceased?'

'This is my daughter, Yekaterina Mikhailovna Tynalieva.'

His voice level, unwavering. My God, this bastard was strong. I'd seen some of Bishkek's toughest break down in this room, scream, yell, weep, threaten the world with blood and fire. But not this man.

He reached out for the sheet, and I took him by the wrist.

'Honestly, Minister, there's nothing to be gained by that.'

He looked at me, his eyes as blank and unstoppable as a rockfall, and I had to turn away from his gaze.

'She's my daughter.'

'The courts will be very severe with a case like this. The maximum sentence.'

I paid lip service to law and order, but we both knew that was never going to happen.

I left the room, left him to the carcass and ruin of a daughter he had once cradled and bathed, sung to sleep, kissed, danced with at her graduation, where she wore the class sash and rang the last bell.

In the lobby, I tried not to hear Tynaliev's howl of pain and anger. When he emerged, ten minutes later, he was all business, calm, efficient. The autopsy completed, I saw no point in holding the body, and we arranged for its removal in the morning.

'I want to thank you, Inspector, for the delicacy you've shown in this matter.'

I nodded. Only the Chief and I knew who the dead girl was, although Usupov must have had some suspicions, having seen the Minister arrive.

'As I said earlier, you're to handle this personally, no involvement from my department, official or otherwise.'

I nodded again. The Minister hadn't survived two revolutions by not knowing exactly where power lay at any moment, and how best to use that knowledge. If his daughter's death had any political resonance, he would keep silence until the best moment to strike and avenge her.

Tynaliev wrapped his scarf around his throat, pulled on his gloves, glanced over at the door where his driver and a bodyguard were waiting. He strode towards them, saying nothing. He didn't need to. I had my orders.

The sound of their boots was still echoing off the walls when Usupov appeared. He cocked his head in the direction of the door, and raised an eyebrow. I nodded in answer.

'Shit,' he muttered, 'you'll have to dance carefully, Inspector. You're amongst the wolves now.'

'You think so?' I asked, fumbling for a cigarette to soothe my nerves.

'So now you know who she was?'

'Not was. Is.'

He shrugged but, to me, it made all the difference in the world. Once her killer was caught, once her death was accounted for and laid to rest, then she could silently slip into the past. Until then, I wanted to think of her as an unseen presence, spurring me on, watching from the sidelines. Chinara always said that I wanted the world to be explained, understood, a place where the dead could rest appeased. I wanted to understand Yekaterina's death, but I didn't believe in the solace of explanations. Not any more.

I shut my eyes against the glare of the overhead lights and tried to remember when I had last slept properly. Almost forty-eight hours, but it was my soul that was exhausted. Anyway, I'd have for ever to sleep, once I joined Chinara and Yekaterina, and all the others I've attended over the years.

'Here.'

Usupov was shaking my shoulder, and I realised I'd been dozing on my feet.

'Why don't you go home, sleep for a while? Even Tynaliev can't expect you to work without a break.'

I shook my head.

'That's exactly what he does expect,' I replied, rubbing my face as if to massage the weariness out of it. I remembered the pills stashed back home, pharmaceutical speed. Just enough to keep me up for a few more hours, to try to work out where I might find a lead, something to report back to the Chief, and for the Chief to tell the Minister.

I shook Usupov's hand, told him what time the undertakers would arrive, and took a copy of his report away with me. I decided to walk back to the apartment; another dawn spent trudging through the snow, trying to work out a pattern, sifting my thoughts to see what links I could make.

Usupov shut and locked the morgue door behind me, and I looked around to see what the new day would bring. The snow had stopped, the wind had died down, and it was brutally cold, in the minus twenties, at a guess. I didn't want to imagine how cold the Torugart

Pass would be. It was early yet, but I'd be able to buy a couple of chicken *samsi* on the way home. The thought made me realise how hungry I was. A case like this, I might go for days without a hot meal, but wherever you turn in my country, there's a bottle of vodka to tempt you.

It was getting light when I got back to my *khrush-chyovk* apartment block. As usual, the main entrance door was ajar. People either forget the security code or can't be bothered to use it. The lift wasn't working either, so I climbed the three flights of concrete stairs, past the rubble and clutter that communal spaces always acquire. What wasn't so usual was that the doors to my apartment were open. I stopped, waited to get my breath back, listened. The TV was playing, which was strange since I live on my own. I took off my boots and unholstered my Yarygin, wondering why I always seemed to enter a room with a gun in my hand. I pushed the wooden door further open, and peeked in. The kitchenette was empty, but the steam rising from the kettle told me someone was making themselves thoroughly at home.

I walked towards the main room, my stockinged feet making no noise on the wooden floor. I reached the door, and braced myself to dive through and start shooting.

'Come in, Inspector, I'm in here. And put the gun away.'

I decided to disobey the second part.

'I know they pay you cops fuck all, but there's no excuse for drinking this shit pretending to be tea. And surely you can afford a decent samovar?'

'Hello, Kursan,' I said, putting my gun away. 'Since when did you become a tea drinker?'

'Since I couldn't find a proper drink anywhere in this dump.'

Kursan Alymbayev grinned at me, his white felt *kalpak* hat tilted at a jaunty angle on his head, gold tooth glinting, stubble white along his jaw. A face as creased and stained as an old waistcoat, seventy something years old, still strong enough to lift a horse, punch a hole through a door, coax the dress off a reluctant *babushka*. First Tynaliev and now Alymbayev: it was my week for encountering hard men. But while the Minister is firmly on the side of law and order, Kursan hasn't done anything legal since long before independence. Smuggling meat from China, marijuana to Uzbekistan, BMWs stolen to order from Almaty, Kursan knew every border crossing, every mountain pass, every corrupt guard. I couldn't help admiring his talent for survival. And since he was Chinara's father's half-brother, he was family as well.

Kursan jabbed a grimy thumb at his mouth and raised an eyebrow. I opened the window and brought in the bottle that had been sitting on the ledge. Kyrgyz hospitality always overrules tiredness. I handed him the bottle and a glass, and watched as he took a good shot, then lit a foul-smelling home-made *papirosh*.

'You?'

'Not this morning.'

'Getting old, brother. This stuff keeps you young, strong. Ask the young girls.'

He cupped his balls and leered, before pouring another shot to follow the first.

'Word gets around fast. I assume you're not just here to finish my vodka.'

'Well, if you insist. Sure you won't?'

I shook my head. Seeing my face, Kursan's expression changed to one of concern.

'Of course. Forgive me. You don't get over a death like that in a hurry.'

The memory of the dead woman rose up before me, the unborn child curled up inside her, a question mark without an answer.

'I know you loved her, brother. The way you love once in a lifetime.'

I realised with a shock that Kursan was talking about Chinara, and felt sick to my belly at the way she'd been supplanted in my thoughts. Kursan walked over to the wall unit and picked up the one photograph of Chinara that I had on display. Taken a couple of summers ago, from the top of the Ferris wheel at Bosteri, by

Lake Issyk-Kul. Laughing, her hair caught in the wind, sunlight dazzling off the lake. Joyous and carefree. Alive.

Kursan stared at the photo for a moment, his face unreadable, and then carefully replaced it on the shelf.

'I'm here to help you. About the Minister's daughter.'

First Vasily, now Kursan; they must both have a squealer at the station with a mouth working overtime. I sometimes wonder if I'm the only law not on the take.

'It's not what you're thinking. It's been a long time since anyone at Sverdlovsky told me anything other than to fuck off.'

He grinned lopsidedly, and poured a small shot.

'Well, Kursan, if it's not a uniform looking for breakfast money, what do you know that I don't?'

He put the glass down, without taking even a sip, walked towards me, put his massive hands on my shoulders. I could smell his sweat, the sweetness of vodka, the tang of his *papirosh*. He stared at me, unblinking, his face as serious as death. When he did speak, it was in a whisper so low I could barely hear him.

'I can tell you where the dead child came from.'

Chapter 10

Late morning, and Kursan and I were on the road to Karakol, pretty much the other side of Kyrgyzstan, an eight-hour drive at the best of times. Which, being winter, it wasn't. We were crawling along, Kursan driving, which was fine by me.

'Relax, I know what I'm doing, there was one time I brought a cargo of furs in from Tashkent over to Osh. No paperwork, you understand. The snow was as thick as an Uzbek's neck; I couldn't see out of the windscreen, so I just stuck my head out of the window. Try driving like that for five hours!'

We'd passed Bosteri about an hour ago, so we were skirting the northern shore of Lake Issyk-Kul, about halfway to Karakol. I'd grabbed a couple of hours' sleep, left a cryptic message for the Chief, then we'd set off. A *ment* drove us as far as Tokmok where, at Kursan's insistence, we changed cars, into an elderly but serviceable BMW.

'They all know this car, believe me. Don't worry about the traffic filth, I hand out enough *som* all year, we won't get stopped for speeding.'

I thought that the likelihood of us going any faster than a brisk walk was pretty remote, but I didn't want to stop Kursan in full flow.

'I love a good mystery, but maybe you can tell me why we're going to Karakol? Only so that, when they drag me up before the disciplinary board, I can give them some half-arsed excuse. Before Tynaliev's men drag me up in front of him, and I lose my arse altogether.'

'Brother, I'm family, remember. Would I let anything happen to you? Don't forget, I know people.'

He grinned, and lit another of his stinking *papirosh*. Somehow, I didn't think that Kursan's 'people' would want to take on the might of the State Security Office, but I kept my doubts to myself.

'You know a little about my business, *da*? How I can get things at the right price for the right people, without those wolves in the White House taking their piece and leaving nothing for honest folk? Fuck your mother, that's what I tell them!'

He looked round at me, genuinely indignant. I smiled at the thought of Kursan telling a set of strait-laced bureaucrats about his assignations with their mothers, and pointed in the direction of the windscreen, just as a gentle hint about his driving. He gave a dismissive snort.

'Don't worry, only an arsehole would be out driving

on a day like this. Me, I know this road like I know my old woman's tits.'

He wrenched at the wheel as a giant truck loomed out of the whiteness, and I bounced against the door as the wheels locked and skidded. I had visions of us being dug out of a snowdrift in about three months' time, but Kursan set us back on the road, and brought us to a halt.

'Fuck off!' he yelled into the blizzard, then turned to me and grinned. 'Told you I could drive, *nyet*?'

Despite myself, I had to grin back.

'Anyway, I do a little trading, a little bobbing and weaving, you understand. Takes all sorts. A little weed, it grows by the side of the road around here, and it's herbal, natural. But you know I never touch any of the hard shit. You sell *krokodil*, to me you're scum. Same with pimps. Arseholes!'

Kursan's always told me he doesn't handle pills or injectables. And unlike a lot of smugglers, he's totally opposed to trafficking; it's the reason I've been able to turn a familial blind eye to his activities for all these years.

'There's other shit I won't touch as well. Parts.'

'Parts?'

'Animal parts, you know, all that stuff those slant-eyes over the mountains take, to make their little yellow dicks stand up.'

Cross over the Tien Shan Mountains into China and head to the market in Urumchi, and you can find all sorts of strange medicines. Everybody knows about the belief that rhino horn cures impotence, and tiger bones help with arthritis. But that's just the start of a long list of ingredients in traditional Chinese medicine: syrup of bile extracted three times a day from captive Asian bears, dried seahorses crushed into a powder, bitter herbs used to make tea, and who knows what else.

I sensed Kursan was hinting at something. But although I was family, I was also *ment*, and it went against the grain to tell a cop anything. I said nothing; I've always known the value of patience. When he was ready to tell me, he'd talk. There was a reason why he was dragging me out towards the mountains. And so far, he was the only lead I'd got. I stared out at Lake Issyk-Kul over to my right; even this high up in the mountains, it never freezes, which is how it gets its name, 'Warm Lake'.

In the summer, the place is packed with holidaymakers enjoying the clear water and clean air. Expensive sanatoria are filled with Russians coming to take a health cure; the bureaucrats stay in government-owned *dachas*. By the roadside, the locals sell buckets of glistening cherries and apples picked fresh from their gardens. Headscarved women stroll up and down the beaches selling smoked fish. You might even glimpse a two-humped Bactrian camel, trudging gloomily along the shore, a couple of screaming children on its back.

Winter, though, that's a different story. In the sour grey light, with the wind blasting down from the Celestial Mountains, the old stories about sacred rocks and rivers, ancient armies riding through the night, the sack of villages and the slaughter of the locals, seem only too real. The only sensible course of action is to hole up somewhere warm with a bottle of vodka and wait for the spring to stumble back in four months' time. The Kyrgyz winter reminds us that the past is never dead, simply waiting to ambush us around the next corner.

'The thing is,' Kursan continued, 'I know this Uighur, from Urumchi. Not a bad type, not a shithead like most of them are. We've managed to do a bit of business in the past. He called me up a couple of days ago, and asked if I'd heard anything about girls being shipped over the border into Bishkek. You know there's lots of demand in Dubai, not so much in Moscow, but why would you drag someone all the way over the Tien Shan in this weather? Plenty of young bitches in Panfilov Park, if that's what you're after.'

'And?'

'Well, he was a bit concerned about this woman because he said she was pregnant, long way gone, and with her time almost due, when she disappeared.'

I began to get a very bad feeling about this.

'And when you heard about the murder?'

'And the baby in the belly, right, I wondered if there was a connection.'

'We're on our way to meet him?'

'Right.'

'A phone call might have been easier.'

Kursan laughed at my naivety.

'Get a smuggler to talk to the filth on a mobile? With State Security and the Chinese Border Police tracking every call? Sure. Nothing he'd like more than fifteen years in Bishkek Penitentiary Number One catching TB from all the lifers. Or a bullet in the back of the head, depending which side of the border they catch him.'

'So where are we meeting him?'

'I know where. So you don't need to.'

And with that, he turned his attention to driving through the blizzard, peering to see the road ahead, while I stared into the murk and gloom for any idea where the case was going.

Chapter 11

For the last hour, I'd been blindfolded, at Kursan's insistence, bouncing from side to side as the car drove over what was clearly no more than a dirt track. I was bruised, sore and pissed off. My gun was locked in the trunk, 'to be on the safe side'.

Finally, I sensed the car slowing to a halt. Some shouting outside, then Kursan removed my blindfold. I blinked, and looked through the windscreen. Fuck knew where we were; it was hard to make anything out, with the falling snow. I suspected I'd fallen off the edge of the earth. Two men, both Uighurs and clutching Makarov semi-automatic pistols, beckoned me out of the car. They both looked as if you could beat them with a scaffolding pole for a day and still not get anything out of them. I opened the door slowly, making sure my hands were always in view. It was freezing, and I pulled my fur *ushanka* tight over my ears. Right then, a vodka would have been very welcome.

The thug on the left, whiskery and sullen, reeking of garlic, patted me down, then pointed to the black Mercedes parked nearby. Kursan and I made our way over, the rear window sliding down as we approached.

'Abdurehim Otkur,' Kursan made the introduction, reaching out to clasp the hand of the man in the back seat. I noticed no one wanted to shake my hand. Abdurehim Otkur was one of the great poets of the Uighur language; clearly I wasn't supposed to know the real identity of the man in front of me. Reassuring, in a way; if he'd wanted to have me killed, he wouldn't have bothered with a false name. I watched as he got out of the car, fastening his coat as he did so.

' "We were young when we started our journey",' I said, quoting the only line of Otkur I remembered from school.

' "Now our grandchildren can ride horses",' he finished the quotation. 'I'm impressed, Inspector, I wasn't expecting a man of culture.'

I did my best to seem modest, while looking Otkur up and down. Burly, above average height for an Uighur, dark, expressionless eyes, with a long face made longer by a knife scar running from his left ear to the corner of his mouth. He noticed my gaze, and drew his index finger down the length of the scar.

'You won't find my picture in your files, Inspector,' he said, 'and you won't find the son of a whore who gave this to me, either. Not in one piece, anyway.'

The grin he gave wasn't reassuring, his scar twisting across his cheek.

'I wasn't planning on looking for your mugshot, not if you can help me out. Anyway, I assume some obliging squealer back in the Prosecutor's Office managed to spill coffee on your dossier?'

'Law, always suspicious,' Otkur said, turning to his thugs, who smiled obligingly. 'Who can say how these unfortunate accidents occur?'

'The case I'm investigating wasn't an accident,' I said, my voice harsh. Back to the business in hand. I was cold, hungry, and my arse felt like I'd been thrashed after eight hours on the road. My gun might have been in the boot of Kursan's car, but I was still an Inspector, Murder Squad, and people shouldn't ever forget it.

Otkur's face grew serious. He would be a ferocious enemy, cunning, implacable. But then there were plenty in Bishkek Number One who might say the same of me.

'Inspector, Kursan and I do business together now for many years. I don't like Kyrgyz, he doesn't like Uighur. But we understand each other. No drugs except for weed, no girls. It's straightforward, business. But sometimes, shit happens you can't ignore. That's when you stand up, be a man. Make sure the scum, the low life know their place, bottom of the shitpile.'

He paused, and we lit cigarettes. He plumed the

smoke out, and I watched the cloud flood through the snowflakes. I guessed we were somewhere the other side of Karakol, up towards the Kazakh border. Before we headed back to Bishkek, perhaps I'd have time to visit Chinara's grave. Maybe permanently.

'You know Chinese medicine.'

It was a statement, not a question. I looked over at Kursan, who nodded.

'Only what Kursan tells me.'

'You fuck a Chinese pussy, they go crazy because you've got a dick like they've never seen before. So, naturally, they complain about their men. So after they've given their bitches a touch of muscle to quieten them, the guys start wondering about medicine.'

'Rhino horn, tiger bones, that sort of shit?'

Otkur laughed, and dropped his cigarette on to the snow, where it hissed for a second.

'Shanghai? Beijing? Maybe you find the genuine article there. Urumchi? The arse-end of China, Inspector, so they make do.'

I stayed silent.

'Remember, people want to believe. Tell them something is good, it might even be true, if they believe it hard enough. And something they really want, they pay good money for.'

'And they want what?' I asked, having a good idea of the answer.

'Remember what Genghis Khan said? "There is no greater joy than conquering your enemy, riding his horses, taking his wives and daughters." Nothing changes; we all want long life, stiff dicks and many sons.'

I looked over towards the mountains, where the last sunlight was turning the snow blood orange and red.

'What has all this got to do with a murder in Bishkek?'

'You can't get rhino horn or tiger bones for sex, you go for the next best thing. Something you can harvest, with an endless supply, something that proves a man's strength.'

Otkur paused.

'In the border villages, they believe nothing's as powerful or as virile as an unborn baby boy. Energy untapped, un-drained. Harvested fresh while the heart still beats, mother's blood flowing through its veins.'

I thought back to the morgue, the unborn child ripped from its mother's womb, his eyes accusing me of betrayal, and my mouth filled with bile. When I spoke, I sounded weak, incredulous.

'Human foetuses, you mean? Children?'

He paused and spat. When he looked back at me, his face was grave.

'Women don't go missing around here. They're always close to home. Unmarried, they could be bride-stolen. And once they're wed, they're a symbol of their husband's strength, his property.'

The thugs nodded in agreement. Kursan swore under his breath. Then silence, except for the wind.

'A pregnant village girl goes missing. The other side of the country, the daughter of a member of the *nomen-klatura* is murdered, and another woman's dead child is dumped in her womb like so much trash. I don't see the connection.'

Otkur nodded his head, as if in agreement. The scar on his cheek stood out livid against the bitter cold. I blinked against the snowflakes and turned my collar up, but nothing could warm me against the sour feeling in my gut.

'And you'd be right, Inspector.'

Otkur's face was unreadable, his eyes never leaving mine.

'Except?' I asked.

'The village girl isn't missing any more. But her unborn child is.'

Chapter 12

Otkur told me the story, leaving out no details, his voice calm, measured, but with anger apparent in his eyes.

Her name was Umida Boronova. Nineteen years old, married just ten months, to Omurbek Boronov. He'd been at school with her, and had asked her out repeatedly, always being refused, unable to stop hoping. So one evening, he and his best friend drank a litre of home-made for courage, drove his battered Moskvitch to the edge of the village, waited for two hours until Umida appeared.

They grabbed her, screaming and kicking, and drove to Omurbek's house, where his mother and three sisters were waiting. The women helped Omurbek wrestle the girl out of the car, and dragged her into the single-storey house with the whitewashed walls and pale blue window frames. All evening, they told her what a good catch Omurbek was, how he'd inherit the farm when his father died, about his kindness to his sisters, his respect for his mother and aunts. All the time, Omurbek waited outside in the car, finishing off a second bottle and wondering if the scratches on his face would leave a permanent scar.

Umida fought, wept, begged the women to let her go home. Again and again, they told her how lucky she was, tried to put the white scarf over her hair to show her acceptance of Omurbek as her husband. They pointed out the fine china, the white linen, the elaborate brass samovar. And finally, worn down, terrified, wanting nothing more than her ordeal to end, Umida agreed.

And now, a year later, she'd faced something much worse. Missing for two days. The whole village turning out to look for her, knowing that an eight-months-pregnant woman out in a Kyrgyz winter stood no chance of surviving the night. Then the finding of her body, face down in a snowdrift, already half shrouded, arms and legs frozen into position. Lifting up the body, hearing her fingers snap like twigs, blood half frozen into a thick black puddle beneath her, squelching like a boot being pulled out from thick mud. And then seeing the belly sliced open, the gaping wound and absence, the placenta torn, amniotic fluid spilling out in a grotesque imitation of birth.

Even before the police were called, the word reached Otkur. An important man, a *chelovek* who could organise the hunt, track down the killer, bring him back to the village to face a justice more determined and brutal than anything a cynical uniform would hand out.

'Can you find out if she'd seen a doctor? Maybe her blood group is on file?' I suggested, knowing that it was unlikely. Umida was a poor girl from a poor village, with no money for doctors; her mother and the old women would have cared for her during her pregnancy. If you die in childbirth in this part of the world, that's just how it is.

Otkur shrugged, walked away a little, made a call. When he turned back, it was to shake his head. There was no easy way to find out if the dead child in the Bishkek morgue was Umida's foetus.

I called Usupov, telling him to liaise with the local authorities, to drop Tynaliev's name into the conversation, terrify the police into action. We were a long way from Bishkek, but not as far as Tynaliev's reach.

'If you find the man who did this, call me. I'll make it worth your while,' Otkur said. So now the Head of State Security and the boss of the Uighur mafia were both after the same man. I would have felt sorry for him if I hadn't been the one stuck in the middle, with both sides ready to look for a scapegoat if the killer wasn't found.

There was no point going to look at the woman's body. The local custom is to bury someone as soon as possible, and I didn't need to offend any more people by suggesting an exhumation. The effort of digging a grave in weather like this would have been immense; lighting a bonfire on the hard earth, raking it back to scrape away a few inches, then starting all over again. And the cold would keep the body preserved until the spring thaw; time enough to get someone else to dig her up, if necessary.

I thought of Chinara, just a few miles away, and winced at the thought of a carelessly handled spade smashing through her cheekbones, or severing the one breast that remained.

Otkur went back to his car, got into the back seat. His thugs climbed into the front, their Makarovs still vaguely pointed in our direction. A snake of dirty blue exhaust smoke plumed upwards. The number plates were smeared with mud and unreadable; Otkur took no chances.

'What do you think?' Kursan asked as we got into our own car. He started the engine and turned the heater up, but it had minimal effect.

'The business about harvesting foetuses for traditional medicine? You ever hear of anything like that?'

Kursan opened his door and spat.

'The slants? Those fuckers will eat anything. I don't put anything past them.'

'It's a clever theory, but I don't believe it.'

'No?'

Kursan turned to me, interested.

'We've got one dead child. And no one would have known whether it was a boy or a girl until after the . . . harvesting. One baby boy isn't going to build you an international illegal drug empire, is it?'

Kursan muttered something about his dick being big enough to stiffen the resolve of the entire Chinese nation. I ignored his bravado and looked out of my window. The snow was falling faster now; our footprints were hardly visible. Maybe there were more dead children out there, harvested and then discarded, open mouths silently screaming as they filled with snowflakes. It was a terrible thought.

'Kursan, let's fuck off out of here before we end up being found in the spring.'

It was too far for us to drive back to Bishkek, but Kursan knew a woman in Karakol who'd happily give him a bed for the night.

'Listen, and you might pick up a few hints,' he grinned. The idea of listening to Kursan's sex life didn't fill me with relish. But if we didn't get out of this cold, the only thing that would get stiff was us. Kursan set off down the rutted track.

'No blindfold?' I asked.

'Weather like this, you'd never find this place again. Why I chose it. No distinguishing features.'

Unlike the two dead women that I knew about, I told myself, and closed my eyes against the glare of the headlights reflected off the falling snow.

Chapter 13

It was a long drive back to Bishkek the next day, but the snow had stopped, and the light was dazzlingly bright, splashing off the Celestial Mountains over on the far side of Lake Issyk-Kul. I'd spent the night dozing on a *shyrdak* carpet while Kursan drove some elderly lady to vocal heights of delight in the room across the hall. The daylight might have been clear, about the only thing in this case that was. For a moment, I wondered why I put myself through the shit of trying to improve a world beyond redemption or relief. Then I remembered Yekaterina Mikhailovna, forever without a child of her own, snowflakes settling on her upturned face, her belly opened to an indifferent world. Her father, sitting behind a walnut desk that no longer had any grandeur, nor the power to bring his daughter back, cognac after cognac failing to blur the memory of her frozen face on the morgue slab. And fast following, like an autumn storm battling across the Tien Shan Mountains, I thought of Chinara and her last dreadful days in hospital, soiling the bed linen I carried in to replace the hospital's threadbare sheets, recalling the soup and *lepeshka* flat bread I took every day that she was too weak to eat.

Towards the end, as she asked, I brought the embroidered cushion that her grandmother had made as a wedding gift for us, the vivid colours and traditional pattern a dramatic splash against the white sheets and Chinara's equally pale face. She would run her fingers over the intricate needlework, as if tracing our history together, tentative, the way a child or a blind man touches an unfamiliar face. It seemed to offer a comfort I was unable to provide.

Every day of her final week, I held her hand, hoping she would squeeze mine, show that she knew I was there, that she recognised me.

That she loved me, remembered me, even as she slid from her life into my memory.

It crossed my mind to find the killer, watch his brains turn to fine red mist from a bullet in the back of his head, then turn the gun on myself, put an end to all this. But there'll be other Yekaterinas, other Chinaras, other unnamed children. And if I'm dead, who is there left to speak for them, to fight for them?

'You need to find yourself a woman,' Kursan announced, unexpectedly, after an hour of silent driving. 'It's not good to be alone for too long.'

'And what would you know about that? Half the children in Tokmok are probably yours.'

Kursan grinned at this compliment to his virility, then turned serious.

'Chinara wouldn't have wanted you to stay single. A man needs a woman, more than a woman needs a man.'

'Enough.'

'I'm only saying.'

'OK, and now you've said.'

My temper wasn't improved by the landscape we were passing through. On our right, empty fields stretching towards the Kazakh border; on our left, the cold slab of the lake. Dotted every few miles were the graveyards that served long-abandoned villages, the memorial stones and brick arches slowly crumbling under the assault of summer heat and winter cold. Sepia photos of *babushki* in headscarves and old men in black and white felt *kalpaks* fading under glass roundels, thin strips of weather-faded cloth flapping in the wind. Most of the graves were surrounded by railings, a small metal crescent moon at each corner. Chinara was buried in just such a place, on the outskirts of her village, on a stony outcrop overlooking the river below and the valley that stretches out before rising into the mountains separating Kyrgyzstan and China.

A peaceful place, if you chose to see it like that.

Kursan dropped me off at Sverdlovsky Station, but it was well after nine, so the Chief wouldn't be in his office, and I'd nothing much to report anyway. A dead daughter of one of the top *nomenklatura* trumps a dead peasant girl from Oblast Issyk-Kul any day. The Chief wasn't a bad cop in his time but, at his level, the only thing that counts is politics. I didn't want a drink, but I also didn't want to be alone. The Metro Bar was too far, and I didn't want to go to the Kulturny, in case I met Vasily and his crew, and gave them a couple of smacks. But tiredness kicked in and I decided it was time for home, then bed. One thing about the winters here: everything stays preserved, not just the corpses. I knew that, in the morning, I'd drag myself out of bed, hope there was enough hot water for a shower and a shave, reluctantly pull on all the layers of clothing I could find, and set out once more. Or I would if I knew where to go.

I was halfway along Chui Prospekt, walking in the road, when the black BMW pulled up. That kind of car, that time of night, I knew it wouldn't be a *myrki* lost in the big city and looking for directions. My Yarygin was hopelessly inaccessible, under two layers of tightly buttoned clothes, so I didn't even think of making a move for it. Instead, I took two quick paces back and threw myself over the piled-up snow at the roadside. At least, that was the plan, but my foot skidded and, instead of an acrobatic leap, I tumbled and lurched into the slush by the pavement. The snow softened my fall, but not by much, and a massive flash of white light burst inside my head. For a split second, I wondered if I'd been shot, if I was dead, but the icy dampness against my face reassured me.

What was less reassuring was the diplomatic corps number plate about three feet from my head. Or the slam of the car door and the big black boots that halted next to me. Expensive boots, thick military soles, steel-capped footwear that could administer a terminal kicking. I shut my eyes and screwed my face up against the blow that would smash my nose and cheekbones into a bloody mass.

'Not much of an ice-skater,' a voice said from some-where above me. 'Not much of an inspector, either.'

I cautiously opened one eye and looked up. The legs went on for ever, and they were wearing army camou-flage. Summer pattern, though, so they stood out like an accident in a paint factory. Or brains on snow.

I levered myself up on to one elbow, shook some sense into my head and the snow out of my hair. No damage done, not yet. I was halfway to my feet when Army Camouflage stepped closer and pushed me back down.

'Not planning anything foolish, I hope, Inspector? I hear that Yarygin of yours has a very light trigger.'

The previous year, I'd had an unfortunate exchange of words with a murder suspect, followed by a fortunate exchange of bullets. Fortunate in that he missed and I didn't. He was fortunate too; my bullet only clipped his spine. So now he's spending the next fifteen years lying in the bottom bunk of a communal cell in Bishkek Number One, a cell bitch waiting for the block boss to choose the evening's hole.

I raised my hands to show that my intentions were pure. A meaty paw grabbed my arm, hoisted me to my feet, pulled me towards the car. It was the second time in twenty-four hours that I'd had to deal with a stranger in an expensive car, and I was beginning to dislike the experience.

'Turn round, face away from the car.'

I was reluctant to do so, but Army Camouflage twisted my arm around and the rest of me followed. The window hissed down, and I braced myself for an execution bullet.

'You'd be well advised to take some compassionate leave, Inspector. It's been, what, three months since your wife died? And not a day off since then? The mind needs time to rest, to forget about the everyday stresses of work, and to focus on healing, repair, recovery.'

I'd been expecting threats, bribes, pain, not advice and consolation. Or a voice like honey poured over ice cream.

A woman's voice.

Chapter 14

'No, don't turn round,' the voice continued. 'I wouldn't want to see you get hurt.'

'Well, if you don't want to hurt me, and you don't want to show me your face, what do you want?'

'For you to take the advice I've just given you.'

Army Camouflage tightened his grip on my arm. It was a very persuasive argument.

'Everyone gets depressed this time of year. The cold, the snow, the dark. And of course, in your case, your unbearable loss. You should get some sunshine.'

I could recognise a hint, but that didn't mean I would take it.

'No fun going away on your own. And anyway, I can't afford it.'

'You should consider it. Head for the sun. Bangkok is very pleasant at this time of year.'

'I've got sensitive skin. Ten minutes in the sun here and I burn. Thailand would fry me to a crisp.'

The voice took on an edge of steel.

'There are worse ways to go. As you know.'

I decided it was time to remember I was an Inspector, Murder Squad.

'I don't know why you care so much, but you know I can't come off this case. And maybe I should make it my business to find out why someone riding in an Uzbek Diplomatic Corps car is so concerned about my welfare.'

'Inspector,' the voice said, and this time there was a note of world-weary impatience, as if explaining to a toddler for the tenth time why he can't have a biscuit, 'you're a shitty little cop who solves shitty little murders, nobodies killing each other over a half bottle of cheap home-made vodka, or who fucked who. You are so far out of your depth in this one. Believe me, you don't want to solve this case.'

The voice paused, and I stiffened, thinking maybe the last sound I would hear was the snap of a trigger. Army Camouflage gripped my arm a little tighter, and kicked my feet further apart. He pushed his hand deep inside my coat pocket, took out my apartment keys, threw them into the snow.

'Think about it, Inspector, how many more enemies do you need?'

Army Camouflage kicked my right leg from under me and, even as I tried to regain my balance, shoved me sprawling back into the slush. The car window whispered shut, the engine started up – a smooth purr that said money, and lots of it – followed by the crunch of tyres on snow as the car pulled away. Only then did I start hunting for my keys.

Back in my apartment, I fished what Kursan had left of my vodka from the window ledge and looked at the bottle for a long time. Harsh electric light reflected off the edges, reminding me of my decision not to drink, a test to overcome, like everything else in my life.

There's no love lost between the Kyrgyz and the Uzbeks; we've had too many riots and too much killing over the last hundred years for that. But here in the north, we're a long way from the Fergana Valley and Osh, where most of the Kyrgyz Uzbeks live. Blame Stalin; he wanted to keep everybody at each other's throats, divide and rule, so he carved up Central Asia like a blind man cutting up a sheep. Everybody got a bit that they didn't want, and somebody else got the slice that they did. And before independence, the Russians were top dogs anyway, so it didn't matter what we ethnics thought. Once we got independence, it was all up for grabs, and you fought your way to the top of your particular pile any way you could. And like all wars, if there isn't very much to fight over to begin with, the battles are all the bloodier.

The apartment wasn't just warm, but hot; in the winter, all the old apartments are heated by an elaborate system of giant hot-water pipes a metre in diameter that criss-cross the city. Sometimes it works, sometimes it doesn't, and if you've fallen out with the *babushka* who manages your block, you might find your heating turned off, whether you've paid your bill or not.

I dug my hands deep into my coat pocket and found an unfamiliar shape, slim, cylindrical, evidently put there by Army Camouflage. I took it out: a bullet for a Makarov, wrapped in paper. These were not subtle people. I read the note scrawled in pencil.

> You have a pain in your head from thinking too much. Here's some strong medicine to clear your brains. Don't forget that you're in our crosshairs. So think this through.

At least it wasn't signed 'from a friend'.

I tossed the note on to the table, and weighed the bullet in my hand. A Makarov is the terminator of choice in our part of the world; light, reliable and virtually untraceable. I'd have more luck chasing snowflakes than ever tracking one down.

There was no point in having the bullet checked for prints; in weather like ours, you wear gloves all the time, and the people I was dealing with weren't amateurs.

I walked towards the wall unit, to drop the bullet into a drawer, then paused. Something was wrong, out of place, missing. For a few seconds, I couldn't tell what, then I saw the gap on the shelf, the thin dust-free mark. Chinara's photo, the one taken on the Ferris wheel, laughing, carefree, wind in her hair.

Gone.

Someone had obviously managed to pick both locks without me noticing anything out of the ordinary. As I said, not amateurs.

I stood the bullet upright in the place where the photo had been, and stared at the glint of light shining off the brass. Whatever was going on, one thing was now very clear.

Someone, somewhere down the line, was going to pay.

Chapter 15

I woke up to find two messages on my mobile. One from the Chief, one from Tynaliev. Both asking the same thing: where the fuck have you been, and what the fuck have you found out? Hard to know who to call first, so I decided to ring neither of them. Instead, I hunted down a contact in Motor Vehicle Registration and, for the promise of a couple of bottles of the good stuff, he agreed to check on the BMW. He got a bit twitchy when I told him about the diplomatic plates, but he finally agreed to get back to me in a couple of hours. I decided to pass the time by wandering over to the Uzbek Embassy on Tynystanov Street, just round the corner from Fatboys. If nothing else, I could get a decent breakfast, and then loiter outside the embassy to see what that stirred up.

An hour later, I was stamping my feet outside the embassy and thinking about getting fed and watered. I'd had a less than discreet word with the uniforms we keep parked outside, and made sure the security cameras on the gate got a long look at me. For good measure, I went and peered through the railings a couple of times. After half an hour or so, I got called over to the police car; there'd been an official complaint from the embassy. I waved my arms about a bit, in case I hadn't attracted enough attention, then sauntered back towards Chui Prospekt. I didn't know if the BMW would come by, but the Yarygin was in my coat pocket, nice and tight in my hand. I tried to look casual, but I listened hard for the sound of a car engine behind me.

I turned into Chui Prospekt and took a seat on the decking outside Fatboys. It was too cold to sit out there for long, but I was interested to see who might come round the corner after me. I pulled a copy of today's *Achyk Sayasat* out of my pocket, and pretended to be engrossed in the lead article. A close observer might have noticed that the newspaper didn't quite lie flush with the table top, might have speculated about what the bulky metal object underneath could be, wondered why my hand was out of sight.

Coffee and a full horse sausage and egg breakfast arrived, together with a complimentary hundred-gram shot of vodka, which I pushed to one side. I was keeping an eye on the corner, sipping my coffee with my left hand, so I was caught off guard when I heard a familiar and unwelcome voice behind me.

'Inspector. The vodka's on me, please, I insist.'

I sighed and twisted round in my seat.

'Vasily, I hope for your sake that this is a coincidence. You're my least favourite whoreson.'

Vasily Tyulev smiled, my insult of no consequence to him. Anything that didn't cost him pain or money, it was merely snow melt slipping into a raging mountain stream.

'Inspector, there's no such thing as coincidence. Not in your line of work or mine.'

'Vasily, the only time our paths ever cross is when you're up to some shitty little scam, or selling some underage pussy, and I find out about it and come after you. If you're fucking me around, we'll go for a little dance in the basement at Sverdlovsky. I catch you giving me grief? We'll waltz the evening away, my little bitch.'

'I may be your bitch, Inspector, but that doesn't mean I can't be useful.'

'Talk.'

'About money? Sure, I help you, you help me, a few *som* changes hands, maybe, or a file gets mislaid. Lots of ways for mutual help, right?'

I sighed. Vasily's roundabout tango always took time, but he'd delivered in the past. I needed to keep him balanced between knowing who was the boss and making sure he talked to me before anyone else.

'No mislaid files, Vasily. You know I don't work that way.'

He held his hands up in surrender.

'The folding stuff is always good.'

The waitress looked out of the door to see if the two madmen sitting outside in the cold needed anything else. Vasily jerked his thumb towards his mouth, and she nodded and disappeared back inside.

Once the glasses were in front of us, Vasily raised his as a toast, and knocked it back. I left mine where it was.

'I'll come to the point, Inspector. I sort things out for a lot of people around town, a middleman, you might say. I do them a favour, I do you a favour, easier to get someone else to scratch your back, then you do the same in return, right? I got a call this morning from someone asking me to have a quiet word with you.'

'That someone being?'

'Well, right now, that's a confidential matter,' he smiled, rubbing thumb and forefinger together, 'but it doesn't have to remain that way.'

'No name, no green.'

'Hear me out,' Vasily said, looking hard at his empty glass. I pushed my untouched drink towards him and made a point of looking at my watch.

'I have a friend who works for a neighbouring country –'

'Uzbek,' I said, cutting him short, showing him he wasn't the only one with a clue or two.

'I couldn't say,' Vasily countered, taking a gulp at his vodka, 'but they know you've got a strong interest in the case of Tynaliev's daughter. They feel there may be certain international implications that it might be better to keep in perspective, to avoid unnecessary tensions.'

I gave Vasily my hardest stare, the one I wear in Svcrdlovsky basement.

'You're saying an Uzbek murdered two Kyrgyz women, carved the foetus out of one of them, and dumped it in the belly of the daughter of our Minister for State Security? And you want me to keep quiet about it?'

Vasily paled; this wasn't going to plan.

'Not at all, Inspector. No one knows who did this terrible crime, right? You just shouldn't leap to any hasty conclusions that might spark trouble in the wider community. That's all my friend is saying, *da*?'

The next bit was easy.

'What's in it for me?'

Vasily recovered himself, touched the thickest of the gold chains around his neck.

'My friend believes that good . . . no, great police work should always be rewarded. Where else would we honest citizens be without your finest endeavours? In shit creek, that's where.'

'Vasily, you know what I want? More than anything else?'

He smiled; he thought he had me, the hook firmly through my lips.

'I'm sure any sum within reason –'

He grunted as I threw a punch. Without much force, because I was sitting down, but enough to smack him in the belly and wind him.

'What I want, whoreson, is the name of whoever sent you. And of whoever they think killed those women. And why.'

Vasily opened his mouth, first to get his breath back, then to speak. But he didn't manage either, because his right cheekbone disappeared into a spray of thick crimson gobbets that splashed across the table. He gave a thin, high-pitched squeal as fragments of his teeth danced and chattered through the air, and the pressure from the bullet burst his left eyeball. A thin red drizzle hung behind his head.

As his body slammed backwards and down against the wall, blood splashing on the dirty snow, I'd already stood up and got the Yarygin out from under the newspaper, double-handed, looking out on to Chui.

Vasily's bodyguard, Mikhail Lubashov, was there, about four metres away, by the bus stop, holding a Makarov in that stupid sideways grip that wannabes learn from American films. The recoil can snap the bones in your wrist, it's awkward to sight and it makes a usually accurate handgun unreliable.

117

One of the surest ways to waste ammunition is to fire on the move, so I didn't hurl myself through the air, firing backwards over my shoulder in the hope of hitting someone. Instead, I locked my knees, crouched slightly, fixed my shoulders behind the line of the barrel. I looked down the gun's muzzle, centred on to Lubashov's chest, where diagonal lines from each shoulder to the opposing elbow would meet.

His next shot smashed chips out of the brick wall to my right, and I watched as the recoil pulled his arm to one side. Before he could regain his balance, I squeezed the trigger once, resighted, fired again, and then a third time, each shot hitting Lubashov in the sternum, driving spear-shaped fragments of bone tissue into both lungs. Never go for head shots or fancy 'shoot in the leg and watch him go down' tricks.

Centre chest, triple tap, each time.

Lubashov's mouth opened and a look of hesitation came into his eyes, as if he'd been asked a question to which he didn't know the answer. Each bullet punched him back half a step, until he hit the low fence separating the pavement and the road, and simply flipped backwards, his legs sticking up in the air like an abandoned shop mannequin.

I took a quick look around, saw no further threat. Then suddenly my knees abandoned me, and I sat back down heavily. With the clarity of adrenaline vision, I noticed that the splatter pattern of Vasily's blood fanned out in a triangle of splashes across the table, and the shoulders of my jacket were covered in dandruff. But when I tried to brush it away, I discovered that I was covered in fragments of Vasily's teeth and jaw.

That's when I started to vomit up my breakfast, thick mealy ropes of half-digested food, head down between my knees, while the whine and howl of sirens grew ever nearer.

Chapter 16

One of my shots had travelled through Lubashov and lodged itself in the shoulder of an irate Tajik carpet seller in town to visit his first cousin, so there was a lot of yelling and abuse going on when the Chief arrived. The Fatboys waitress, with admirable sang-froid, had cleared away the vodka and teeth cocktail I'd invented, and offered me a hundred grams on the house.

Lubashov's legs still pointed skywards, but I'd draped my copy of *Achyk Sayasat* over what remained of Vasily's head. His blood was soaking through a report of the killing of a plain clothes down in Osh. Poetic justice of some sort, I suppose.

The Chief was overjoyed, of course. Two pieces of shit scooped off the pavement, and a brutal crime with major political implications solved in just a couple of days. Better than his birthday.

'I'll contact the Minister right away and give him the good news.'

I was genuinely puzzled.

'What good news?'

'You've found the killers of his daughter, and they've been brought to summary justice,' the Chief said, defying me to contradict him. 'Of course, Tynaliev may not be too pleased that he didn't get to . . . question them himself. But it's clear you shot in self-defence. This piss-drinker pulled a gun on you,' he added, giving Vasily's newspaper-clad face a kick, 'and that shit-eater tried to shoot you, missed, hit his boss, and you cleared him away. Simple.'

'Vasily didn't have a gun,' I objected.

The Chief looked around, reached into his coat pocket and dropped an automatic next to the body.

'What's that, a pencil sharpener?' he said, and laughed.

'Motive?' I asked.

'Maybe Vasily thought State Security were on to him, wanted to get his retaliation in first.'

'Chief, Vasily Tyulev was a second-rate, no, a third-rate pimp, who couldn't get State Security interested in him if he chained himself naked to the gates of the White House and claimed he was Stalin come back to life.'

'Still waters,' the Chief said, and tapped the side of his nose. 'State secrets. Not for an Inspector, Murder Squad, to be party to.'

He looked around, and caught the eye of the waitress.

121

'Darling girl!' he beckoned, and she came over cautiously, looking worried. Another example of the healthy relationship ordinary Kyrgyz citizens have with their police force.

'You'll be wanted as a witness, of course, but it's just a formality. You've seen a hero of the Republic in action, and you can tell everyone how the police force is here to guard every law-abiding citizen, day or night.'

The waitress looked at me; hero wasn't exactly how she'd describe me right then, bloodstained, sweating and stinking of my own vomit. The Chief shook my hand again, and headed down the steps to his waiting car.

'He's a hero, mark my words,' he called out, 'bring him another hundred grams, shit, make it a bottle!' And then he was gone, the car doing a screeching U-turn against traffic and speeding back to Sverdlovsky.

I shook my head at the waitress, and sat back to wait for the clean-up crew. The Chief's theory had a lot of appeal. An end to the case, no irate boss or minister giving me grief. A neat solution. Or it would have been, if it had added up. Why those two women, separated by class and an entire country? Why the mutilations? And why the business with the foetus, assuming it's the same dead child transferred from one corpse to another? I would have loved to say 'case solved' and gone home. But I kept seeing Yekaterina's eyes staring up at the sky, the dead child inside her. And a terrified woman up on the border, begging her killers to spare her baby, as they close in with butcher's knives. And however hard I shut my eyes, those images weren't going away.

'Inspector?'

I opened my eyes, reluctantly. The waitress was standing in front of me, holding a piece of paper. For one ridiculous moment, I thought she was going to ask me for my autograph.

'The *chyoht*?'

She was right, of course; there's always a bill, and somebody always has to pay. I fumbled for a handful of *som*, which I handed over, waving away my change.

'Thanks,' she said, and daintily stepped over Vasily.

I started laughing then, and I was still laughing when the morgue waggon arrived to take Usupov's next two guests away.

A few hours later, I was showered and changed and thinking about going into the station when Kursan called me. The grapevine had been working overtime, and he wanted to know if the stories he'd heard were true. I told him that as shoot-outs went, it wasn't much to write home about; a total of five shots fired, rather than the eight dead and ninety wounded in the story going around town.

'They won't be missed. Low life, both of them,' he

told me, before adding that someone would step up to take their place straight away.

'One thing people will always barter: pussy,' he said. 'It's the way of the world. Men want to buy it, women want to sell it. What can you do?'

'Make sure nobody's forced to sell it, for a start.'

'Kids to feed, no husband, no money, what if it's all you've got to sell?'

Suddenly, I felt very tired. The aftermath of the shock, of course, but I was tired to my heart of all the crap, the politics, the unrelenting grime, the endless seeing people at their worst.

'Kursan, I really don't feel like a moral debate on hooking right now.'

'You want to meet up, have a few beers? You shouldn't be on your own tonight.'

Solitude was exactly what I did want, but there was no use trying to persuade Kursan, and we agreed to meet up later at the Kulturny. It was a good way of showing the regulars who the hardest bastard on the block was, that anyone who fucked with me would get what Tyulev and Lubashov got. I suspected Kursan was also pretty keen on the idea of a terrified barman supplying drinks on the house all night.

I saw I'd got a call coming in, a number I didn't recognise. The voice, however, I did. Honey drizzled over ice cream.

'I see I underestimated you,' she said, and her tone sent a shudder through me. The kind of shudder you get when a beautiful woman takes your hand and runs a slender finger across your wrist, a crimson nail raking your palm.

'Your boss must be pleased with you. Solving a brutal sex murder, making sure the villains can't do it again. You'll probably get promoted. Or asked to join the Ministry of State Security.'

Her voice was mocking, playing with me. And the idea wasn't entirely displeasing.

'I'd be delighted to. If I had solved it, that is. But we both know differently.'

She paused for a moment. When she spoke, her voice was edged with caution.

'Do we?'

'Those two couldn't organise anything other than selling third-grade whores and the odd shot of *krokodil*. Slaughtering a pregnant woman the other side of the country, getting the foetus over to Bishkek in the middle of winter, luring a senior minister's daughter to somewhere where they could kill her, and then dumping the body? No way. And even if they could have done all that, what's their motive?'

I listened hard for any clue to her whereabouts. But wherever she was calling from, it was as quiet as the grave.

'If your boss is happy that the case is solved, if Tynaliev is pleased that his daughter's killers are in a drawer next to her, you should be pleased.'

'I'm not happy that I killed a man today. Even if he was trying to kill me.'

'Are you sure it was you he was aiming for?'

I stopped. It hadn't occurred to me that Tyulev might have been the target, not me. But it made a sort of sense. Vasily was known to be happy to whisper in anyone's ear, if the folding was right. Meeting a Murder Squad inspector about a case that someone wants to quietly file away, what else could he be doing but selling information?

'You told Lubashov to take Vasily down?'

Her only answer was to laugh. Husky, seductive.

'You'll give yourself a terrible headache, thinking about things like that.'

I remembered the bullet on the other side of the room. The last of the daylight was shining off the brass.

'And you've already sent me the cure for that, right?'

Silence. And then a simple, cold warning.

'It's time for you to move on, Inspector.'

And then silence as she broke the connection.

Chapter 17

It was 1 a.m. in the Kulturny. Lubashov had been replaced on the door by some identikit tattooed thug, just as ugly, just as burly and just as stupid. The only difference was that this one had a pulse and eight pints of *krov* in his veins. Kursan was ready to give him the Saturday-night stare, but my new reputation preceded me because the *zalupa* let us in without a word. Down the stairs still stinking of fear and piss, and into the half-lit bar.

The barman narrowed his eyes when he saw me, but he put an unopened bottle of Vivat on the counter. A memory like that, he should be over in the Hyatt, pouring overpriced cocktails and fiddling the change of foreign businessmen. I pointed at a bottle of mineral water, and that arrived just as promptly.

Vasily's normal seat was empty, perhaps as a mark of mourning, so I went over and parked myself. The usual faces were still there; in fact, a couple of them probably hadn't stirred since I was last in. No Shairkul, though; maybe she'd got lucky and was being pounded into the mattress by some drunk with little money and less hygiene. I made a mental note to go and see her in

the morning, then focused on watching Kursan concentrate on draining the bottle.

I waved some *som* at the barman, and he shook his
head. On the house, after all. I wondered if they'd run
to a second bottle, in about fifteen minutes' time, the
way Kursan was upending his glass.

'Save some for later,' I said, as he poured his fourth
or fifth in as many minutes.

He grinned and nodded sideways at the room.

'This lot have probably been paying those two shitheads protection money for years. You want, they'll
club together and buy us champagne.'

I shuddered. Russian champagne is a taste you don't
ever want to acquire. As I finished my second glass of
water, I saw out of the corner of my eye that one of
the regulars was hovering nearby. Kursan half rose,
fists ready, but I restrained him and swung round on
my stool to face the newcomer.

He'd got his hand in his jacket pocket, and I didn't
like that. I pointed at his arm and he took his hand out.
Slowly. Once I could see he'd got nothing more lethal
in his hand than filthy fingernails, I nodded, giving him
permission to speak.

'We all heard about this morning, Inspector,' he
stammered, his eyes flicking between me and a very
belligerent-looking Kursan. 'They were pricks, and no
one will miss them.'

'You're mistaking me for someone who gives a shit what you losers think.'

He nodded agreement; a man of importance had given judgement. In his tiny vodka-sodden world, I was someone of consequence, while the Chief or Tynaliev could walk in and no one would have a clue about the shit storm they could cause.

'Of course, Inspector. But you ought to know,' and here he leant forward and lowered his voice, 'one person here was delighted to hear about those two.'

He paused for effect, saw I was less than impressed.

'You know the working girl that comes in here? The beautiful one?'

Genuinely puzzled, I shook my head. He made an hourglass shape with his hands, and then, just in case I hadn't got the picture, cupped his hands in front of his chest.

'Shairkul. You know Shairkul?'

I wondered just how much vodka you'd need to consume over one lifetime to see Shairkul as a Kyrgyz Venus.

'What about her?'

'She couldn't stop talking about how pleased she was.'

'You're surprised? Vasily probably kept ninety per cent of everything her pussy earned.'

'No, she said she was going to make a lot of money off what she knew.'

Now I was interested.

'Did she say what that was?'

The man looked abashed.

'Well, she was going to tell me, she said you'd pay her a lot, but then the bottle ran out, and I didn't have enough for another, so she went and sat with someone else.'

True love spurned; I was amazed we weren't both in tears. He looked longingly at the couple of inches that still remained in our bottle, so I prised it out of Kursan's paw, and held it out to him.

'How long ago did she leave?'

He reached for the bottle, but I kept it just outside his grasp.

'Maybe two hours ago?'

He looked so melancholy, I figured she must have left with company. I gave him the bottle, he smiled and scuttled away, pathetically grateful.

'We hadn't finished that,' Kursan complained.

He started to gesture for another bottle, but I shook my head, grabbed his arm, and started to haul him up.

'You want to go to another bar? What's wrong with this one?'

'What's right with it?' I wanted to ask, but just aimed him at the door.

'Where are we going?'

I pushed him up the stairs, past the thug and into the night air.

'We're going to pay a call on a hooker.'

He turned to me and grinned, gold tooth glinting, for all the world like a nineteenth-century bandit.

'*Da*? Now you're talking.'

And with that, he lurched off towards the pavement, to bully a *taksi* into stopping for us.

Chapter 18

The *taksi* stopped on the far side of Osh bazaar, out-side Shairkul's *khrushchyovk* block, Kursan loudly debating the cost of the ride, the driver's parentage and the prices his mother would charge her customers. The last thing I needed was for the world to know we were there, so I handed some notes through the win-dow and told Kursan to shut the fuck up. Amazingly, he did so without an argument. Without a torch, it was a slow job getting up the stairs, but we managed with-out making too much noise.

Once we reached the top floor, there was enough light to show me that both the ornamental wooden door and the heavy-duty metal door were ajar. I began to think that something very bad was about to come my way, and I gestured at Kursan to move down to the next landing. I listened at the doors, Yarygin in my hand. Not a sound. But while I was there, I recognised the sweet metallic smell coming from inside the apartment.

Usupov and I have argued about this one before. He claims that blood is blood, and it doesn't matter whether it's a sheep or a yak, a horse or a whore. But I believe there's something distinctive, unique, about the scent of human blood, catching at the back of the throat, electric, like silver foil on dental fillings. Of course, never having found a dead yak in a fifth-storey apartment, I don't have a really scientific comparison.

But I'd found enough dead people to have a pretty good idea what was waiting for me inside.

Shairkul was sprawled on the floor of the sitting room, legs apart, her knees raised, as if waiting for her next customer. Or perhaps that was how she'd been left by her last one. The red rug beneath her had changed shape, its edges irregular, as if the dye had run, smeared over the bare concrete. But it wasn't dye.

Like Yekaterina, Shairkul stared sightlessly upwards. But her face wasn't placid, calm, accepting of her fate. Her lips were drawn back in a scream that was half snarl, her gold teeth glinting under the harsh electric light.

I ignored the body for the moment and searched the apartment. I knew a *ment* who didn't check the scene of a murder; they feed him through a tube now, and his children stopped visiting the hospital a long time ago. So I checked the bedroom where I'd seen Gulbara hard at work, then the kitchen, the bathroom. I pulled back the shower curtain, expecting to find Gulbara's body in the bathtub, but the apartment was empty. I decided it was safe enough to holster my gun, and walked back into the sitting room. I was ready to call the scene-of-crime forensic boys, but first I wanted to get my own take on the butchery in front of me.

Shairkul had died hard, fingernails broken and shredded fighting off her murderer, jaw shattered by a punch. Her hands were covered in defensive cuts. Or maybe she'd fought back. The air was full of the stink of blood and sweat and shit and fear. I wanted to open a window, but didn't, at least until I got the say-so from Usupov's people.

I heard a noise behind me, a footstep, and I grabbed for my gun, ready to fire as I turned. A touch more pressure on the trigger and I'd have sent Kursan to wherever smugglers go when they die.

'*Ahueyet?*' he said, seeing Shairkul's broken corpse.

'Never mind "what the fuck?" – you almost joined her on the floor,' I said, tasting adrenaline and sour bile rising in my throat. 'You need to fuck off out of here, right now. I can't explain you away. And if the uniforms decide to arrest you, it won't be me dancing with you down in Sverdlovsky basement.'

Kursan took the hint; he's waltzed with Urmat Sariev before, and he wasn't keen to repeat the experience.

'Call me,' he said over his shoulder, already down the first flight of stairs.

Too late to tell him not to touch anything, but at least he was out of my hair.

'And don't say anything to anyone,' I shouted down the stairwell.

He was probably halfway to the Kulturny to spread the word. But I had more important things to worry about than Kursan's gossiping. I'd got a second – or should that be a third? – dead woman on my hands.

I used my mobile to take a few photos; forensics would take decent shots, but I couldn't wait the week or so that it would take to get a set into my hands. I could have used a cigarette, but I remembered the uniform up on Ibraimova littering the scene with butts, and decided to wait until I was outside.

I was deliberately avoiding looking at her stomach. That's where the killing blows would be. With a knife, they almost always are. Forget fancy knife play: if you know what you're doing, a thrust, a twist of the wrist, then pull back and you can disembowel someone faster than a gun will dim their eyes. So first I photographed her hands, the remaining nails scarlet with cheap polish, the other fingers scarlet where the roots had been wrenched out.

Then I photographed her face, trying to avoid the awful accusation in her stare. As always, I wondered if there could be any truth to the old story that you can see a murderer's face retained on the victim's eyes. Right then, if I'd caught sight of myself in a mirror, I'd look like her murderer. Or the man who didn't manage to prevent it.

Most of the victims I see are strangers to me, but the few minutes I'd spent in Shairkul's company turned her death into something more personal. Remembering the threats I made, the bullying to get her to talk, a wave of shame smacked into me.

And then it was time, the moment I'd been dreading. Shairkul was wearing her coat, unbuttoned but covering her belly. The material was slashed and torn, blood around the edges of the cuts. I had a good idea what was underneath, from the size of the bloody puddle on the floor. I used the muzzle of my gun to flip the coat open.

The smell of her death rose up to me, as I looked down at the grey coils and turmoil of her intestines, the diagonal cut through her stomach, her guts spilling out as if trying to escape the knife.

It's then that I saw why Shairkul was on her back, legs apart, knees raised. She wasn't lying in the position with which she greeted her customers, as I'd first thought. Instead, she'd been carefully arranged into a crude approximation of a woman giving birth.

Which perhaps explained the foetus nestling between her bloody thighs.

Chapter 19

I walked down the broken-tiled steps of the morgue and along the dimly lit corridor towards the racks of the waiting dead. Beyond the metal doors, the stink of chemicals and raw meat lingered in the air. The place was deserted, and the neon strip light above the dissection slab flickered with an intermittent high-pitched buzz, like a dentist's drill.

At the wall of storage drawers, I looked for Shairkul's name, but the label holders were all empty. I pulled out the nearest drawer, the runners giving their usual shriek of protest. The corpse inside was the *krokodil* junkie I'd watched Usupov dissect, what now seemed like months ago. The smell of iodine made my eyes water and I slammed the drawer shut. The next two drawers were empty. But the fourth drawer was occupied.

A woman, by the shape of the sheet covering the body. I pulled back the rough cloth, expecting to find Shairkul staring up at me, her mouth open in protest at the indignity of her penultimate home.

But the body wasn't Shairkul.

It was Chinara.

I stared, uncomprehending, unable to work out how my dead wife's body had been exhumed from her grave up in the mountains and brought there. A lock of her hair had fallen over her face, and I lifted it back and tucked it behind her ear. Her skin was smooth, unblemished; I could have almost believed she was asleep, if I hadn't helped carry her to the waiting hole in the ground. I put my forefinger on her cheek, stroked her face with the lightest of touches.

The final days in the hospital, Chinara was barely conscious for most of it, with ever stronger doses of morphine to dull the pain. I slept on a chair by her bed, in a room on our own because the Chief had pulled some strings. Sometimes working for a powerful man has its advantages. I would doze for an hour or two until her whimpering in pain, from the operation, from the tumours, would wake me. And finally, after eight days, as I sat watching her, she opened her eyes, half smiled, and drifted back into a final sleep. Too many memories, and all the good ones overlaid with the sorrow of what was to follow.

Then, as I looked down at my dead wife, she opened her eyes.

She stared up at me, her gaze unflinching, the way she'd always looked at me. For a moment, I realised with perfect clarity that her illness, her death, all of it was a dream, a hoax. And then with just as much knowledge, I worked out that I was dreaming. Even our loved ones never return from where we bury them. Except in dreams.

But I can't wake myself, return to the world where I live alone, surrounded by crooks and hookers, the warped, the stunted, the desperate amongst us. With Chinara is where I want to be. Even if that means in the grave.

She gazed at me, and I moved to one side, to face her properly. There was a question in her eyes, it seemed to me, or perhaps a warning. I wondered what she was thinking, even as the absurdity of imagining she could think at all hit me. Dead, decaying, buried under a harsh winter sky; that's my wife.

She used to interrogate me with each new case, forcing me to use logic, to think through the facts, lies, deceptions. Time after time, she offered directions, insights that helped me solve my cases. Nothing surprised her about human nature, but none of it soiled her.

I looked down at Chinara, her voice clear enough in my head; start finding the missing woman, start turning over rocks. Go back to being a detective again; I'm dead and that's not going to change. Go back to being the man I loved.

I shut her eyes with my fingertips and slid the drawer back into place, gently, not to wake her. Then I walked out of the room, and into the corridor, towards the morning light and the end of my dream.

I woke up, eyes raw from the light streaming through the window. It must have snowed during the night, because the air had that crystal clarity that presses like thumbs on your eyelids. I couldn't shake off the idea that Chinara had somehow been resurrected, even though common sense told me it was a case of wishful thinking. During the weeks after she died, I would hear her calling out from the next room, never anything intelligible, just sounds and notes that evoked her voice, summoned it from the dark of her grave. But the advice that she gave me, or rather, the advice my subconscious put into her mouth, held good.

I made coffee, lit and then stubbed out a cigarette, resolved to quit for the hundredth time, stared out of the window, wondered about my next steps.

I could have wandered down to the morgue to see what Usupov had dredged up about Shairkul's terrible last moments. But a nagging concern about my dream being all too real made the idea unappealing. I decided I could always call him later, no need to face the stink of antiseptic yet again.

First priority had to be finding Gulbara. Either she was dead, on the run as a murderer, or hiding from her flatmate's killer. She wouldn't be holed up with a wealthy client somewhere: she was strictly a fuck me and fuck off kind of girl.

It made sense to find Khatchig Gasparian, the Armenian last seen trying to whack Gulbara's monkey with his stick. Neither of them would be the other's dream date, but love can be blind, or at least blind-folded with banknotes.

I called Sverdlovsky to have archives pull his file, if there was one; the last revolution saw the Public Prosecutor's office burnt down, together with most of the files held on our career criminals. If all Gasparian had ever done was give a *ment* breakfast money to overlook his speeding, then I wouldn't be interested. But the odds were he was involved in something else. There's no big Armenian community here, no reason for him to be in Kyrgyzstan. Of course, he could have worked as Gulbara's minder, pimping her out to pay for his cognac and cigars and mobile, and keeping the punters docile in return with the promise of a slap or two. There was only one way to find out.

I was halfway down the stairs, fresh cigarette in hand, when I remembered that I'd decided to quit. Tomorrow, I promised myself, and pushed open the heavy steel communal door, emerging blinking into pitiless sunlight.

Chapter 20

'You're fucking my brain with all your questions!'

'Khatchig, why not try answering them? Or one of us will get tired of the dance, and you'd better hope it's not me. I might have to go out, have a little vodka, a smoke, something to eat. Of course, I can't leave you alone; got you booked in as a suicide risk. So one of my colleagues will step in, keep you company. Urmat Sariev, perhaps you know him?'

We were in the basement at Sverdlovsky. A morning of asking around had given me a lot of answers about Khatchig Gasparian, and I didn't like any of them.

He'd left the Armenian capital, Yerevan, in a hurry a few years ago, leaving behind a couple of dead small-time criminals, and headed down to Dubai, where he locked into a couple of property scams, selling apartments that weren't his to sell. When the Emirates got too hot for him, he headed north and east, ending up in Almaty. Marrying a Kyrgyz girl got him the right to live in Bishkek. She divorced him after refusing to go on the game and getting a smacking that put her in hospital for two months. She wouldn't testify, though;

swore she'd walked into a door. About fifty-three times, according to the photographs.

He'd got a lot of money in the bank, thanks to gullible Indians in Dubai wanting to climb the property ladder there, so he didn't seem to need a job. Maybe a bit of pimping, a little drug-running, or shipping a few weapons that fell out of either the Russian or the American military bases into the hands of our Islamist friends down south. But there was no hard proof, and he was small fry, too insignificant to interest Tynaliev's people.

Right then, I was having as much success at breaking him down as I would climbing Mount Lenina.

Gasparian pulled out his cigarettes, which I promptly confiscated.

'Fire hazard; don't want to burn the building down by accident.' I smiled, and lit one of my own.

'*Pizda!*'

'Cunt I may be,' I said, 'but I'm the one enjoying my smoke. Of course,' and here I looked solicitous, 'if the smoke is bothering you, I can always go outside.' I pushed my chair back and stood up. 'I'll just get Sariev,' I said, 'and he can show you what a real *pizda* is like.'

Gasparian just grunted, but I could smell the fear on him, like garlic on an Uzbek's breath.

I pushed his cigarettes over to his side of the table. It wasn't easy for him to light one, being handcuffed to a chain bolted into the floor, but he managed.

'Let's start again, about how you killed Shairkul.'

He sighed; we both knew he didn't do it.

'Why would I kill her?'

'Maybe you couldn't get it up? Maybe she started laughing? Maybe you lost your temper?'

He looked at me as if I was a peasant straight out of the village.

'You got money in the bank, Inspector?'

'I hope that's not an attempt to bribe an officer of the court, Gasparian.'

He looked alarmed, held up his hands.

'No, no. Just, you keep your money there so it's safe, so it earns you more money, right?'

'Go on.'

'Shairkul made me money. Why would I empty my bank account?'

I shrugged.

'Here's how it was. I was out with Gulbara. She was giving an American soldier a blow round the back of Panfilov Park, near the statue of Lenin. She gets a call on her mobile, answers it, which pisses the Yank off, what with her being paid to use her mouth for other things besides gossip. She gets up off her knees, comes over, says Shairkul's in trouble, we need to get over there. We leave the Yank swearing and pulling his pants up, and I drive over.'

He paused, and pursed his lips, remembering the scene in the apartment.

'Well, you saw her. You know what state she was in. We never touched anything, I swear. I wouldn't even let Gulbara see the body. That sort of thing, it can put a girl off her work for ever.'

'You're all heart, Khatchig,' I said, taking the cigarette out of his mouth and stamping it out on the concrete.

He didn't recognise the anger in my voice, and nodded agreement.

'Someone has to look after these girls,' he said, a defensive note in his voice.

'Well, you did a fucking bad job with Shairkul, didn't you?'

'You're the law, you're supposed to keep the maniacs off the streets.'

I didn't have an answer to that, so I tugged on the chain, forcing his head down on to the table.

'So where's Gulbara?'

'Don't have a fucking clue. That slut was down the stairs faster than piss down a drunk's leg.'

'What were you just saying about keeping your money in a bank?'

'So?'

'Gulbara and her performing monkey keep you in the good life. You're going to let her disappear?'

He shrugged, the timeless Levantine answer to any difficult question.

'She's gone back to Osh? Or you've stashed her away, ready to get back on her knees when this all blows over?'

No answer, just an insolent stare. Both made me decide it was time for more forceful measures.

'I think you could be more helpful than this, Khatchig,' I said, and tugged on the chain again.

'I told you all I know. I'm just an ordinary citizen.'

I heaved a deep sigh, to show Gasparian how disappointed I was.

'That law you punched when we tried to bring you in?'

'Plain clothes, how am I supposed to know he's one of yours? Self-defence, plain and simple.'

'Well, you bounced his head off the wall, and now he's in the hospital, in a coma.'

'And that's my fault?'

'Well, his uncle thinks so.'

Gasparian sneered.

'So get his uncle to sue me.'

I smiled, mirthless, stood up, put my cigarettes back in my pocket, crushed his pack in my fist.

'He might want to be more direct than that. I'll be upstairs if you suddenly remember where Gulbara's hiding out. You talk things over with his uncle.'

I paused, my hand on the door, turned back to face Gasparian.

'The officer you hit is called Kairat Sariev.'

I opened the door. Urmat Sariev was standing there, smiling at the prospect of a brief encounter with the man who put his nephew in hospital. Usually he uses a bag of apples; leaves lots of spectacular bruises, and you can rupture a spleen with one swing. But nobody would be too worried about Gasparian having a bruise or two. Not in his line of work.

As I trudged upstairs, I heard the flat thud of the first blow.

That's usually all it takes.

Chapter 21

The winding mountain road to Osh climbs to almost 4,000 metres between Bishkek and Jalalabad. I've done the journey countless times; I don't trust the flights between the two cities, and the driving relaxes me, lets my mind dig around for answers while being half distracted. The uncoiling road is a kind of hypnosis, using all my concentration while the pieces in my head form patterns of their own accord. But doing that journey in the heart of winter would be suicide, quick or slow, depending on whether you skid over the first bend or spend the next three months snug and immovable in a snowdrift, getting further buried with each snowfall.

So I flew, using all my energy to concentrate on keeping the plane aloft, which was more than I suspected the flight engineers had done.

Finally, I thought I might be getting somewhere on the case, thanks to Urmat Sariev and his fruit persuaders. I hadn't even stubbed out my first cigarette before they called me down to the basement. Gasparian was sitting on the floor, manacled hands shielding his head,

148

back to the wall to protect his kidneys. He'd been crying, and there was a thin river of blood dribbling from one nostril. Sariev wasn't even breathing heavily.

'This bitch won't last five minutes in Number One before some cell boss splits his arse with a big *yelda*,' Sariev said, and gave Gasparian shoe leather to reinforce the insult.

Gasparian started to mutter something, but Sariev has only ever been interested in coaxing a confession, not in actually listening to it.

'*Zakroy svoy peesavati rot, sooka!*' he screamed, spit landing on Gasparian's head.

'No, let the bitch keep his fucking mouth open,' I said. 'He knows what I want from him. Don't you?' And I gave a gentle toe-prod to Gasparian's ribs. It's a bad cop, worse cop thing.

Sariev shrugged, reached into the bag, selected an apple and took a massive bite. As an afterthought, or maybe as thanks for giving him the opportunity to dance in the basement, he offered one to me. I shook my head, and squatted down next to the prisoner.

'Khatchig,' I said, in my mildest tone, 'this could all have been avoided. We can stop it right now, or the sergeant can treat you to some more fruit. All I need is where you've stashed Gulbara. Just an address, that's all. For her own good, you know. We can protect her.'

Gasparian muttered something indistinct about us

not having helped Shairkul, and Sariev gave him another piece of fruit. Still in the bag.

Gasparian spat out a tooth, and looked up at me.

'You know you've got a squealer here in the station, don't you? Shit, you've probably got a dozen little birds all singing sweetly, the pay you get.'

'So?'

'Well, I'm not saying anything with anyone else in the room but you. Word gets round that I sing and I'll end up in the drawer next to Shairkul.'

I thought it over, and gave Sariev the nod to leave. He wasn't too happy about the idea, but headed for the door. He swung the bag at Gasparian's head one last time, pulling back at the last minute, so that the apples whistled harmlessly an inch from Gasparian's face, and grinned as Gasparian flinched.

'Just off down the bazaar, Inspector, pick up some apples. Nothing like a healthy diet, eh?' and he was gone.

I helped Gasparian to his feet and steered him towards the chair. He sat down, and blew a long string of bloody snot on to the floor. His wrists were raw and bleeding from where the chain had cut into him. I didn't feel proud of what I'd done, but there were three dead women who deserved answers, even if they weren't around to hear them.

'You know this is nothing, don't you, Khatchig?' I

said, in my most soothing voice. 'If I let him loose, there's no way he won't put you in intensive care, ruptured spleen, crushed testicles, burst eardrums, just for starters. Or he'll just dump you in the morgue, next to your two-legged bank account. You've hurt one of ours; you think anyone gives a shit what happens to you?'

He nodded, facing up to reality. Down in the basement, with flecks of dried blood sprinkled on the tiled walls, you have to be a bigger man than Khatchig to hold out. I offered him a wad of tissues, to wipe his face.

'So if I tell you where Gulbara is, I walk out of here?'

I shook my head.

'We've upped the stakes since then, my friend. If you'd sung before we came down here, you'd be back home having a little taste and wondering which one of your stable to fuck. Now, well, I've got other questions, and I want answers. And in case you're wondering, I'm not an animal like my sergeant. I don't like to just kick and smash and break.'

I took hold of Gasparian's jaw and wrenched his face round towards mine. His eyes dropped, avoiding contact.

'Look at me, Khatchig. No, look at me.'

He stared up at me, panic deep in his eyes. I narrowed mine, my face impassive, brutal.

'I don't like unnecessary pain. Make a note of that

word "unnecessary". But I promise you, any pain I think necessary will really hurt you.'

I pushed him back on to his heels, sat down in the chair. I lit a cigarette, held the burning end up, as if examining some kind of instrument. Which, in a way, I was. I blew on the tip, watched the glow burn brighter. I could smell the sweat on him, the fear.

'You've probably burnt yourself with a cigarette, by accident. Painful, but it heals. But not where I put it.'

I blew on the cigarette again, gave him my best mirthless smile.

'Left or right, Khatchig?'

He shook his head, puzzled, uncertain.

I explained.

'Left or right? Which eye do you want to lose?'

As the plane made its descent into Osh airport, I wondered if I would have actually blinded Gasparian in one eye, felt the burning tip of the cigarette push past the resistance of the eyelid, heard the sizzle of the eyeball's jelly, shut my ears against the screams. Of course, it didn't come to that. I learnt a long time ago that it isn't what you do, it's what people think you are capable of. Sariev just knows brutality; God help me, I know psychology.

As I'd expected, Gasparian gave up Gulbara's address straight away. Nothing in it for him but pain if he kept his mouth shut. So he talked. And kept on talking.

To my not very great surprise, it turned out he was a lightweight, at the very bottom of the Circle of Brothers, a foot soldier, expendable. He was terrified of the Circle. But the Circle weren't there in the basement, and I was, with Sariev lurking outside with a fresh bag of fruit.

I knew that before I left for Osh, I should have given Tynaliev the *malenkoe slovo* about the Circle of Brothers, the little word about their possible involvement in his daughter's death. For those who don't know, they're our very own home-grown Eurasian organised-crime group. After the collapse of the Soviet Union, a lot of the criminal gangs in the former 'stans' grouped together in a loose collective called the Circle of Brothers. Each of the countries has their own crime boss sitting at the table with their foreign counterparts, doling out territories, alliances, joint operations in information, not just in Central Asia but in Europe, Africa, Latin America and the Middle East, the UAE in particular.

Drugs are their big thing, as you'd expect, but they don't say no to robbery, prostitution, counterfeiting, smuggling, or anything else that can make money and isn't legal. And when it comes to ruthlessness, even the Russian gangs admit to being lightweight in comparison.

Devotion is absolute, unquestioning, irrevocable; break any of the rules and there's no question about what will happen to you, just how long it will take you to die, and how painfully. With the kind of power they wield, the resources they can call on, and the effect they have on the entire region's stability and economy, the Circle of Brothers are a serious problem, and one that Tynaliev would certainly be watching.

Which made my keeping quiet about Gasparian less than smart.

But I wanted this case for myself. If it went over to the security forces, particularly with Yekaterina as one of the victims, that's what the investigation would focus on. Nobody would give a fuck about a dead peasant girl or a butchered prostitute.

Nobody except me.

Not that I'm a holy guy. I've had my share of breakfasts bought by speeding motorists, known a bottle or two of good stuff come my way for a favour. But I owed it to the dead women, to Chinara. And of course, if I wanted to be sentimental, I owed it to myself.

I hadn't bothered to let anyone in Osh know that I was coming. If all this had a connection to the Circle of Brothers, then letting the cops know I was on my way was just setting myself up, either for a beating or a series of blank stares and shrugged shoulders. I clambered down the aircraft steps, setting my *ushanka* firmly on my head, turning up the collar of my coat. The Yargin was cold and heavy on my hip; no need to check it into the hold if you've got police ID. Sometimes, amazingly, the system works for you. It was only a couple of hundred metres to the airport terminal, but still cold enough for me to catch my breath, and shuffle a little faster across the hard-packed snow.

There's no such thing as car hire in Kyrgyzstan, so Kursan had sorted out transport for me. I wandered out into the forecourt of the terminal and looked for the oldest, most dilapidated car I could find. A burly Uzbek man stood by a Moskvitch whose multicoloured bodywork told me it was, in fact, several cars cannibalised and held together by string and bad temper.

After a series of grunts, we established that his name was Alisher, that Kursan had told him to take me wherever I wanted to go in Osh, and to find me somewhere to stay. I got in the front seat and strapped on the seat belt, which promptly collapsed around me. Not a promising start.

I gave Alisher the address for Gulbara that I'd coaxed out of Gasparian; somewhere off Lenin Avenue, not far from the Sulayman Mountain. The Moskvitch sneezed its way forward, the engine picked up, and we made our way towards the centre of the city.

It was the first time I'd been in Osh since the riots;

the streets with their burnt-out buildings, only smoke-blackened walls still standing, did nothing to improve my temper. People hurried along what pavements there were, wrapped up against the cold, avoiding eye contact. With everyone wearing thick winter coats and scarves, I couldn't tell who was armed and who wasn't. Best to assume everyone.

It was getting dark as Alisher steered us around the base of the sacred mountain. Everyone in Osh will tell you that Sulayman is buried there, near the mosque at the summit; good for tourism, I suppose. I climbed the mountain long ago, on a visit with Chinara. For a moment, memories came back: her long hair swept into turmoil by the wind, the same wind that snatched the words 'I love you' from her mouth and sent them scattering across the valley.

Alisher turned off Lenin Avenue and down a quiet, tree-lined street of one-storey Russian-style houses, all whitewashed walls and window frames painted a pale sky-blue. Very few of the houses had numbers, but we found the address that Gasparian had given me. Or rather, we managed to find where it had once been. Now, it was nothing more than a heap of torched rubble, crowned by remnants of the roof, which had collapsed in on itself. A chimney stack still stood in the far corner, a solitary finger insulting the sky.

I swore under my breath, and looked over at Alisher,

who simply shrugged, opened his door and hawked phlegm on to the snow. A gust of cold air blew in through the open door, bringing an acrid stink with it of charred wood and gasoline. I got out of the car, picked my way through the fallen timbers and corrugated iron towards the chimney stack. I placed my hand against the brickwork; it was still warm. When I picked up a blackened remnant of window frame, the soot and charcoal crumbled under my fingers. Whenever this house burnt down, it wasn't during the riots. Recently, not more than a day or so before my arrival.

So the new question: where was Gulbara? On the run, in hospital, or reduced to bones and melted fat beneath my feet?

I was wondering what my next move should be, when an unmistakable sound interrupted my thoughts.

The tap of a gun barrel against the car behind me.

Chapter 22

I raised my hands, shoulder height, turned round slowly, no hasty movement that could be misinterpreted. Alisher was already out of the car, his hands palm down on the hood, face turned away so as not to be able to identify anyone. The black eye of the Makarov pointing in my direction held my complete attention. Suddenly the air tasted extra clear and crisp, the sounds of traffic ringing in my head. I was about to die, and I couldn't even find it in myself to picture an alternative. A thought: would they bury me beside Chinara? Followed by: would there even be a body to bury, or would I end up in a ditch, a stream, a wood, unnamed, unmourned, a skeleton gnawed clean?

The black eye didn't blink. Whoever was holding it knew what they were doing. The hand didn't shake, its wrist supported by the other hand, classic military training. Or maybe police. A small hand, slim fingers, the nails a vivid red, the same red that would spurt from my chest if the Makarov's bullets tore into me. A woman's hand.

'Clasp your hands together behind your head, Inspector.'

The same honey-over-ice-cream voice. The same impersonal tone, cold, calculated, as warm as the dirty snow piled against the roadside. One consolation: I'd lived too long to die too young.

I tried to keep the tremor out of my own voice.

'It's my aftershave, right? So irresistible you decided to follow me all the way here?'

'Always the joker.' Her voice took on a faintly amused air.

But I still kept my hands tightly gripping the back of my neck.

'Not always,' I admitted, 'only when someone's planning on using my chest for target practice.'

'Use the thumb and forefinger of your left hand to take out your gun and – slowly – place it on the ground in front of you.'

I obeyed, the metal cold against my fingers.

'Now take three steps to the right.'

Smart thinking. Even if I'd been foolish enough to attempt one of those somersault rolls that you see in the movies, the gun was on my wrong side, giving her a lifetime to pull the trigger.

In one of the nearby houses, someone was cooking *pelmeni* dumplings, and the sweet scent filled my mouth with saliva. For the first time since I helped spade the earth over Chinara, I realised that life is sweet, that I didn't want to die.

The single eye of the Makarov blinked, turning its unrelenting gaze away from me.

'Just a precaution, Inspector, my apologies. You've got fast reactions and a careful aim. I saw what happened to Lubashov. You can't unpull a trigger, and I'd rather be safe than sorry. Or dead.'

I inspected the woman behind the gun. Slim, tall, long straight black hair falling to her shoulders. Eyes hidden behind wraparound sunglasses, crimson lipstick matching her fingernails. High, slanted cheekbones, and the kind of mouth the papers always describe as 'generous' – though, in my experience, lips like that are only giving when they want something in return. Long black leather coat, jeans tucked into shin-high lace-up combat boots. In a different place, at a different time, the type of woman it would be very easy to desire.

'Now we've established we're not going to shoot each other, I can put my hands down?'

I tried to give my voice a suitable air of amused nonchalance, but I wasn't surprised by the tremor in my voice. She nodded, and I put my arms down by my side. I looked down at my gun, and raised an eyebrow.

'I think we'll leave it there for the moment. Call it a first-date precaution.'

I shrugged, and looked past her to the black BMW with the Uzbek diplomatic plates, Army Camouflage standing there, arms folded, in his signature camo pants and steel-capped boots.

'You told me I was a shitty little uniform the last time we met. Doesn't sound good for a first date, does it?'

She stared at me, then pushed her sunglasses up on to her forehead. Her eyes were as black as her clothes, and just as unrevealing. A thin white scar cut through her left eyebrow, easy enough to conceal with make-up. The fact that she hadn't bothered made her more intimidating.

'I underestimated you, Inspector. But I can assure you, we're on the same side. Fundamentally.'

I puzzled over that for a minute, then shook my head.

'You tried to warn me off. All that crap about foreign holidays. Which wouldn't help me solve my case.'

'I didn't want you fucking up my case, getting in the way,' she said, holding her hand out in a vague apology, and taking a couple of steps towards me. 'I've put a lot of time and effort into this.'

There was a new scent in the air.

Perfume. Heady. Erotic. Maybe Kursan was right and it had been too long since I'd been anywhere near a woman.

'If you're Uzbek law, and I'm not sure about that,

you've got no jurisdiction here in Kyrgyzstan. Not even here in Osh. And why would you be interested in these murders, anyway? The victims aren't Uzbek.'

She nodded towards the limousine.

'Let's get out of the cold. We can talk there.'

I hesitated; there's nothing easier than to shoot someone in the back of the head as they get into the back seat of a car. The Makarov's 9mm bullet bounces around inside the skull, mashing up everything in its path and leaving only puree. If you're very unlucky, you get to spend a couple of decades having an impatient nurse spoon just the same sort of puree into your drooling mouth.

She spotted my reluctance, and gestured towards my gun.

'Pick it up, put it away, and I'll do the same. Illya, go and sit with the Inspector's driver, calm him down, keep him quiet.'

I took my time, using thumb and forefinger as before, but I felt a lot happier once I'd got the pistol snug against my body. And knowing that Army Camouflage called himself Illya didn't make him any less threatening.

'If it makes you feel any happier, Inspector, I'll get in the car first. No surprises.'

Once we were both comfortable in the back seat, she offered me her hand. The same hand with which she could have killed me. I noticed the square-cut nails, slim fingers, no rings, her strong grasp at odds with the scarlet polish. Her perfume was stronger now, sweet but with an undertone of something astringent, lemon perhaps. Maybe that was a hint, or a warning.

'You're wondering whose side I'm on, Inspector,' she said, never taking those eyes off me.

'Point a gun at me, and I'm pretty certain you're not on mine.'

She raised an eyebrow, and I watched the scar curve back on itself.

'The facts: you're Bishkek's top murder specialist, investigating the deaths of three women, and two unborn males. Nothing to connect the three women; they didn't know each other, they didn't share the same social circles, even come from the same city. A politico's daughter, a peasant girl, a prostitute. And you want to know what links them.'

Everything she said was accurate, but that didn't mean I had to share what I knew; we'd left the playground a long time ago.

'What I want to know is why you're interested. You're Uzbek, why should you give a shit about dead Kyrgyz? It's not as if there's much love lost between our two countries.'

While she decided what to confide in me, I pressed home my advantage.

'The two dead wannabes, the ones shot outside Fatboys. What's your connection to those two?'

She reached in the pocket of her jacket, smiled as I tensed, pulled out a packet of cigarettes, the cheapest, nastiest brand in all Central Asia, short of rolling your own *papirosh* from roadside tobacco.

'Cards on table?'

'Sure,' I said, 'let's see your hand.'

'You came down here looking for that prostitute? Gulbara?'

'She's a witness in my case.'

'Well, there's a problem.'

She lit up, opened her window, plumed smoke through the gap. Considerate. She gave me a hard, appraising stare.

'Do you want to fuck her?'

The question took me by surprise, and so did hearing her swear.

'Why would I want to do that?'

She shrugged, and took another hit of nicotine.

'Lots of men do.'

'Lots of men will fuck anything with a pulse, but I'm not one of them.'

'How long since your wife died?'

I didn't know how she'd heard about Chinara, but a slow anger started up, at her death being thrown so casually into the conversation.

'Being a widower doesn't mean I want to fuck a *krokodil*-shooting hooker.'

I didn't make an effort to disguise my rage, and she nodded slowly.

'She's worried that if you don't want to fuck her, there's only one thing you do want.'

'Which is?'

She stared at me, unblinking, those black impenctrable eyes never leaving my face.

'To kill her.'

Chapter 23

'See it from my point of view, Inspector.'

Gulbara was sitting across from me, clutching a cup of tea as if it was the only thing stopping her freezing to death. But the café was warm, and her shivering was due to coming down off the drugs. Her hair was scraped back and tied in a loose ponytail; she looked much younger, but maybe that was because she wasn't naked, and the track marks on her arms and thighs weren't on display. I imagined the monkey was still clambering into her *pizda*, though.

'I come back to the apartment, and I find . . . well, you saw what happened to Shairkul. The handbag led some very bad people to us. And you were the one who took the bag from me, who passed it on to someone. Who else knew about us, we were just working girls? The bag belonged to somebody rich, important. Someone who'd want their thousand dollars back.'

'How does that make me the one who killed Shairkul?'

Gulbara looked uneasy and sipped her tea.

'Maybe not you, but someone who could make the

police look the other way. A politico, maybe, one of the high-ups. What's a dead hooker to one of them?'

I sighed, and drank my own tea. Without asking, Gulbara added more to my cup, filling it halfway, the perfect hostess.

'You found a body, hacked and mutilated, with a dead foetus in her belly. Then you find your flatmate and work colleague in the same condition. You think I keep a store of dead baby boys just in case I want to make a murder more interesting?'

I reached across and pulled up her sleeve, the rotting *krokodil* greenish-brown against the pallor of her skin.

'How much of that shit are you shooting up?'

My voice had risen and I was getting curious stares from the people at the next table. Gulbara looked down at her cup, and I noticed that her fingernails were chewed down to the quick.

'Saltanat told me you were OK.'

I looked across at the other woman at the table. At least now I knew her name.

She nodded.

'You're one of the good guys, Inspector. Or . . .' Saltanat paused to consider, 'at least you don't mind killing the bad guys.'

'I don't want to kill anyone,' I said, and drank more tea.

'Doesn't stop you being pretty good at it, though.'

Her tone was mocking, as if I was a joke to which only she had the punchline.

I looked over at Gulbara. The cop banter wasn't helping her calm down. And then it struck me that I didn't know if Saltanat was law; I didn't know anything about her, except that she scared the shit out of me.

'Are you taking me back to Bishkek?'

I looked at Gulbara, tried to reassure her with a calm voice and an understanding gaze.

'You're not suspected of anything, there isn't a warrant out for your arrest. I just need your deposition. Give me some answers, and I'll see that there won't be any paper out on you, not even for fleeing the scene of a crime.'

Saltanat surprised me by nodding in agreement. I gave Gulbara my most winning smile.

'Tell me what you know, it ends here. No having to go back to Bishkek.'

'I don't have a minder any more, anyway, do I?' Gulbara asked, guessing that I'd given Gasparian the hard word.

Once back in the Kulturny, she'd be fixed up with a new protector in seconds, whether she wanted one or not, but I decided not to share that cheerful thought.

'Stay in Osh, maybe,' I suggested. 'Get off the *krokodil*?'

She looked defensive, and tugged the sleeves of her coat further down over her wrists.

'It's only every once in a while, to relax, for my nerves.'

We both knew she was lying; if the *krokodil* kept biting her, she'd got a year left, maybe two if she was really unlucky. But it was her call, and I was a murder cop, not a drugs counsellor, a father figure or a knight in tarnished armour come to the rescue. Gulbara knew that too, knew what lay ahead as surely as if I'd shown her a photo of a pile of freshly dug earth, with her name and face engraved on the headstone.

I gave up on the cheap advice, and got down to her statement. Saltanat listened intently, saying nothing, her eyes narrowed from the smoke of her cigarette. What Gulbara had to tell me was pretty much as I expected: no, she didn't know who Shairkul was meeting, didn't know anything about Vasily, or what he might have done to get Lubashov so pissed off with him. One thing she did tell me was that Shairkul was also working off the books, servicing clients she'd found on her own account. Which meant she got to keep the money, but risked a beating from Gasparian if he found out. But I already knew Shairkul's pimp wouldn't also be her killer.

'The dead woman, she was somebody important?' she asked, wondering if she should continue to be scared.

I thought about saying every murder victim is important, if only to their family and friends, but I knew both women would see that as the worst sort of lie. Yekaterina's father could turn Bishkek upside down to find his daughter's butcher, but I'd be lucky if I could get Shairkul anything more memorable than a cheap cotton shroud and a state-dug pit.

'Her father's a big guy,' I said, and left the rest unspoken. 'You know anything about Shairkul's family?'

I thought I could trace her easily enough, but it never hurts to save time when you're hunting a murderer.

'She's . . . was . . . from Tokmok,' Gulbara said, her face screwed up as if to help her concentration, 'but I don't know anything about her family. She said they didn't get on.'

I couldn't say I was surprised; not many parents are delighted when their darling daughter decides to start selling herself under the trees in Panfilov Park. It was time to push Gulbara a little harder.

'How did your house burn down?' I asked, throwing out the question as if the answer didn't really matter.

Gulbara fiddled with her tea, and I sensed a new tension.

'It's my mother's house, not mine. When the recent troubles came, well, we're Uzbek, and this is a Kyrgyz district. Mama lived through the killings twenty years ago; when it all started up again, she just grabbed what she could and headed for Doslik.'

We Kyrgyz call the Uzbekistan border Doslik, while the Uzbeks insist it's called Dostuk. Neighbours, and yet we can't even agree on a common name. It turned out that Mama had crossed into Uzbekistan and headed for relatives in Tashkent, fleeing the authorities on both sides. A lifetime's home suddenly in hostile territory, what else was she to do? Yet again, I felt weary despair at my country's endless acts of hate, stupidity, violence.

'But that was a while ago, and the ruins of your house are still warm. So, again, what happened?'

Gulbara looked over at Saltanat, but there was no help coming from that quarter.

'I've been staying there since I left Bishkek. A couple of nights ago, I'd gone out. Working.' She looked at me, defying me to criticise. 'I have to eat, don't I?'

I nodded. Whores get hungry too.

'I got back about midnight, and the place was alight. Nobody round here is going to do anything to help. I'm just an Uzbek slut, as far as they're concerned. Probably my fucking next-door neighbours. Some dickhead who thinks Osh belongs to the Kyrgyz.'

I didn't ask about insurance; it's as rare here as diamonds in the street.

'You don't think it had anything to do with what happened to Shairkul?' I asked, as gently as I knew how.

Saltanat flashed me a warning look, but Gulbara was

171

too busy thinking about the misery of her future to notice. I could see that she could use a *kosiak* right now, home-grown and hand-rolled, just to take the edge off things, but I didn't come all this way to listen to stoned ramblings. The thought that the fire might be a hit rather than some racist act wasn't the best thing to put in her mind, but better that than her stumbling into the sights of a Makarov.

'But I don't know anything,' she wailed, tears starting, face twisted, 'I swear I don't.'

'You've got somewhere to stay?'

'With my uncle and his family, near Gulcha.'

I nodded. Down south towards the Tajik border, far enough away from Osh to give her relative safety, I hoped.

'I'll see she gets down there without any trouble,' Saltanat said.

One last question.

'Your friend Gasparian? The fat hairy guy I caught teasing the monkey?'

'Him? Pays the rent on the apartment, keeps the local uniforms in breakfast money, we give him a slice of what we make. He visits me every couple of weeks. Can't get it in without swearing and yelling and calling me names. Not that there's a lot to put in.'

'Did you say anything about the first murder to him?'

She scrounged another cigarette off Saltanat. The air above the table was thick and blue, and I wondered if the café owners had ever considered turning it into a cancer ward. She sparked up, and blew smoke in the general direction of the kitchen.

'He mentioned it. Had I heard about it, was she a working girl, did I know her? That sort of thing. And then he got hard and climbed on. I didn't pay too much attention, too busy trying not to get crushed. And then you spoilt his party.'

I excused myself, and headed out into the relatively clean air outside. I called Sverdlovsky to tell them to hold Gasparian for further questioning, but he'd already been released. They asked if I wanted him picked up, but he'd either be laughing from the other side of a border, going about his daily routine, or dead. It could wait until I flew back.

Saltanat was making arrangements for Illya to drive Gulbara down to her uncle's farm. It was quite a drive, over two mountain passes that were going to be dense with snow, but the BMW should make it, if he took it slowly.

I scribbled my mobile number on the back of my card and gave it to Gulbara.

'If you think of anything more, call.'

But she probably wouldn't. And I was pretty sure I wouldn't see her again, unless it was round by the dark side of Panfilov Park, near the Lenin statue, or on Kenesh's morgue table.

Saltanat surprised me by kissing Gulbara on both cheeks, then hugging her; I had her down as an ice maiden. We watched as Gulbara walked down the street, Illya two paces behind. Alone, I turned to Saltanat. The sunglasses were back in place, even though it was now night outside. I reached over and removed them. She stared back at me, expressionless. It was clear that I wasn't going to get any information that she didn't want to give.

'I've got a few more questions,' I said.

'I rather thought you might.'

'Questions like: what's your involvement in all this? Who are you working for?'

I poured out the last of the tea into our two cups, added sugar, took a mouthful, savoured the flavour and the warmth.

'I'll answer your questions. Maybe. But first of all, I want a proper drink.'

Chapter 24

It was still dark when I woke up. But in a Kyrgyz winter, that can be almost any time before noon and after three. Out of habit, I reached over and checked that the Yarygin was still on the bedside table. A chair was propped against the door handle; I don't trust any of the flimsy locks in the kind of places I can afford. The guesthouse was not far from the city centre, just off Ak-Burinskya Street. I'd stayed there before, and the price was right, if you're law: free. Sure, I might have had to strong-arm an *alkash* if he'd been causing trouble, but it hadn't been a problem so far.

My piss smelt sour, and I could taste the pickled vegetables that had accompanied the *chai* I'd drunk while Saltanat made do with vodka. I remembered getting some straight answers from Saltanat, which made a refreshing change, until the tiredness creeping up on me slammed my head down on to the table. What I didn't remember was how I'd got back from the bar, exhaustion wiping my memory clean as effectively as a bottle of the good stuff would have done.

Or how Saltanat had ended up in my bed.

I'd still got my socks and underwear on, so maybe I'd played hard to get. There was no sign of any condom wrappers by the bed, and she didn't seem the kind of woman who took unnecessary risks about anything. I sniffed my fingers, but they stank only of gun oil and nicotine. I decided to postpone any sexual post-mortem for when I was feeling better, and settled down with a cup of tea.

Outside, a disillusioned sun was doing its best to struggle through a winter hangover. My watch said it was just after ten in the morning; time to work out a plan for the day, reprise the night before.

'You're going to offer me some?'

I turned round. Saltanat was sitting up in bed, braless; no modesty there. Small but perfect breasts, darker nipples than I would have expected. She pulled back the sheets and swung her legs out of bed. Black G-string, so I guessed we'd behaved like brother and sister last night. I didn't know whether to be stupidly grateful or truly pissed off.

'*Chai*, or . . . ?' and I held the vodka bottle up.

She gave a dramatic sigh, and ran her fingers through her hair. Whether or not she was intending me to see her breasts rise up, the effect was unmistakable.

'*Chai*. I'm not one of those cops who's half drunk most of the time, and all drunk the rest.'

I tried to look nonchalant as she swivelled round

and hooked herself into her bra with practised ease, as if she was alone at home. I pretended not to look; she pretended she didn't notice.

'So I'm the first woman you've slept with since your wife died.'

It wasn't a question. I rummaged through the blur of last night, wondering what exactly I'd said, how much of a fool I'd made of myself.

'No, don't worry, you didn't mention her, no tearful memories. I've seen your file. But it's hardly a state secret, is it?'

I wondered what this file was that she'd seen about me. Sverdlovsky's personnel file? A State Security dossier compiled by Tynaliev? Something the Uzbek police had put together? With both a Russian and a US military base in the country, the world and his mistress probably knew how many spoonfuls of jam I took in my tea. I thought about spy satellites tracking me, about people far more powerful than me with something to hide and no problem getting rid of me to do so. And just how much could I believe of what Saltanat had told me?

'In case you're wondering, you did ask me if I wanted to fuck you. Very politely, a real gentleman. And then, while I was making my mind up, you fell asleep.'

There didn't seem to be anything to say to that, so I finished my *chai* and headed for the shower. No hot water, a sliver of coarse soap, but you take what you can in these places. I got dressed while Saltanat showered. The look on her face when she came out of the bathroom told me that the water doesn't run cold for her too often.

Back in the café, we both lit up, and checked the menu. Mutton and rice. Eggs. Horsemeat sausage. Who could resist? I pushed the fatty yellow sausage to one side, just as the waitress brought over a hundred grams without me asking. The glass sat there and stared at me, telling me that if I was such a tough cop, it was there for the taking. Murder Squad cops have a name as hardened drinkers – goes with the territory, I suppose.

'Some of the details of last night . . .' I started, and then paused, uncertain what to say, 'maybe you can recap?'

'The embassy told me you were the best in Sverdlovsky's murder team, the one who uncovers the corpses. We got the whisper about Tynaliev's daughter; no way could anyone keep that hidden. And Otkur's been feeding us information for years, in return for the occasional blind eye at the border. So we knew about the peasant girl as well.'

I contemplated the burning tip of my cigarette, pushed the vodka to one side.

'So you've got good sources. With a psycho of a boss like yours, you'd have to.'

If she was at all annoyed at my insult about the Uzbek president, she wasn't showing it. But a man who has his political opponents boiled alive keeps his enemies close, because that's all he has. Children betray parents, husbands betray wives, and the secret police listen in at every door. Cross Islam Karimov and you wouldn't have to worry about planning for a secure old age.

'What I don't understand is why Uzbek Security would get involved. You are Security, I take it? All three victims were Kyrgyz.'

Saltanat continued to stare at me, unblinking. For once, I was on the wrong side of an interrogation, and I didn't care for it one little bit.

'You're right, they were Kyrgyz. Nothing to do with us, outside our turf. But the ones on our side of the border? They're very much our concern.'

For a second, I wondered if I'd misheard.

'How many?'

'So far? Eight. All found with male foetuses. Some theirs, some not.'

Light glittered off the surface of the vodka, whispering about the consolations in the glass. I don't mind not drinking, but I hate being tempted.

'So some kind of serial thing? A psycho?'

'We don't think so.'

'What else? Someone crossing the border, killing in both countries. Maybe going into Kazakhstan, Tajikistan.'

'We think it's political. Someone out to cause unrest, get the Uzbek people outraged at the lack of security, the failure of the police, maybe start our own version of your Tulip Revolution.'

I nodded; I could see why President Karimov wouldn't be too keen on demonstrations in the streets of Tashkent. But there was a serious flaw to Saltanat's theory, and I was quick to drive the point home.

'If the point of the killings is to destabilise your government, then why are there the same murders and mutilations here? And who's got the power to do that?'

Saltanat said nothing for a moment, looked into her half-empty teacup.

'We don't think there's a crazy guy roaming Central Asia looking to hack up women. We think it's your government trying to foment a revolution, maybe even revenge for the trouble here in Osh. And your dead women have been murdered just to draw suspicion away from your country.'

I said nothing; the idea was surely too far-fetched. But then I thought of the wave of killings and mutilations, the looting and burning that hit Osh during the last revolution, and suddenly I wasn't so sure. The Fergana Valley is the most prosperous, fertile land in the region; always has been, ever since the days of the Silk Road. Control that and you control the economy. And that means plenty of ways of wetting your beak, worth a little turmoil and strife, especially if it's somebody else's.

'If I'm so good, and it's all an elaborate plan, why would they appoint me to solve the cases?'

'You find some fall guy, pin it all on him, the killings continue in Uzbekistan, the people get angry that the Kyrgyz can find their killer and we can't.'

She shrugged.

'So why confide all this to me?'

'So I can make up my mind. Whether I'm going to carry out my mission, or not.'

She smiled at me, but the warmth never reached her eyes. I noticed that she had her hand in her bag, and I had a suspicion that she wasn't looking for her lipstick.

'I didn't come here to solve your case. I came here to kill you.'

Chapter 25

My Yarygin was on my hip, and I calculated how many bullets Saltanat could pump into me before I cleared my holster. About six too many to make it worth my while, and I suspected she would only need the one. I kept my hand well clear from my side, moved my arm slowly. If she was Uzbek Security, she'd have no hesitation in shooting if I made a threatening move. And if she was here to kill me, she'd have no hesitation at all.

This wasn't how it was supposed to end. Chinara, her long hair now grey, playing with a grandchild, while I watched approvingly. Long walks through the foothills above Karakol once the last snows of winter had melted away and the spring melt was cascading through the gorges. Quiet summer nights listening to her sleeping beside me, watching the morning light come up through the window.

'You wouldn't be telling me this, unless I've got a reprieve.'

'When we heard you'd been assigned to the Tynalieva case, we already knew of your reputation. Through Vasily.'

She nodded as I raised an eyebrow.

'Surely you're not surprised? He worked for us, for the Tajiks, the Kazakhs, for anyone who would slip a few thousand dodgy *som* his way. He said you were tough, reliable, good at carrying out orders. So we assumed you were on board to set this up as a race-hate crime: crazed Uzbek psycho slaughters Kyrgyz innocents, that kind of thing. While your government was also killing Uzbeks, to stoke the fires across the border.'

'Why go to all that trouble? Simply burn a few houses down, and everybody's ready to kick off, you know that.'

Saltanat shook her head, and I watched how the raven wing of her hair folded back across her cheek.

'Accountability. A riot is one thing, a coup organised by a foreign government is quite another. You need something to stir up terror, not just hatred.'

'That's why the mutilations? And the dead babies?'

'Of course.'

I lit another cigarette. There was a sort of mad logic to it, but I couldn't see my government organising it. Not when it took us all our time to get the electricity working. A thought struck me: could this be disinformation? What if it was the Uzbek government setting things up, to reclaim Osh?

I was wondering if aspirin would help, or only make

my headache worse, when Saltanat's phone rang. She stubbed out her cigarette, and walked towards the door. Too cold to stand outside, but I was clearly not meant to listen. I passed the time by remembering the curve of her breasts, and wondering if I was ever going to see them again. To have the woman you woke up with announce that she's been ordered to kill you is not a great start to the day. On the other hand, I wasn't lying face down looking surprised on the bedroom floor.

Saltanat came back to our table, her face grim.

'That was my Bishkek contact.'

'And?'

I searched her face for clues, but she remained impassive.

'Your pal, Gasparian. Your colleagues released him, took him up to Ibraimova Street, to the scene of the Tynalieva murder.'

I shrugged; nothing too unusual about that.

'For what it's worth, I don't think he did it; doesn't have the balls. I don't think he did Shairkul either. He's a liar and a pimp, sure, but he's no killer.'

Saltanat stared up at the stained and nicotine-yellow ceiling, watching her cigarette smoke ascend and melt into the general fug.

'Well, if he was, he surely isn't now.'

I got a sinking feeling. Maybe I shouldn't have left

him in the loving care of Sariev. A shitty day might be about to get shittier.

'What's the story?'

'Some genius decided that taking Gasparian to the "scene of his brutal crime" might spur a little remorse, perhaps even a confession and a plea for mercy. So they threw him in the back of a police car, headed up towards the Blonder Pub, and marched him down to where the body was found. He must have been guilty, because he headbutted his escort, put him on the ground and started running away through the trees.'

She paused, gave me one of her trademark hard stares.

I swallowed; I had a pretty good idea of what was coming.

'The enormity of his crimes must have driven him insane, because he ran all the way to the bridge over the carriageway. You know, the one with the two-metre fence on either side? And that's where he decided to end it all.'

I pulled a face. It's a long way down to the road, and nobody bothers too much about the speed limit there.

'On to the road below?'

'They're still scraping him off tyres between there and Tashkent. But he must have been really determined to kill himself. How many people do you know who could climb a two-metre fence with their hands cuffed behind them?'

I winced and ground out my cigarette, then waved to the waitress and pointed at my cup. I wanted something stronger, but I felt at enough of a disadvantage as it was.

'Sariev?'

Saltanat shrugged.

'Or Tynaliev's men, maybe,' she said. 'I can't imagine he'd be too happy with his daughter's killer getting three meals a day for the next fifteen years.'

Clearly Saltanat had never seen the inside of a Kyrgyz prison; a few months ago, the entire prison population of Kyrgyzstan sewed their lips shut with wire, protesting about the conditions inside. If the gangs didn't get you, the beatings or the TB would. But it still had to beat making a final Nureyev-style pirouette through the winter air before ending your days as roadkill.

I could see how the authorities would think it better all round if Gasparian was the killer, even if there was no evidence to link him to any of the crimes, let alone the ones in Uzbekistan. My boss would be happy, the word could go out that the guilty had been punished, and everyone could go back to filling their pockets. Unless the killings continued, of course, in which case, heads would roll — and I had a pretty shrewd idea whose.

I turned my mobile back on and, as if he'd read my

mind, a flock of calls from the Chief scrolled upwards. I didn't need to read them to know what he'd be saying. Fortunately, reception is pretty bad this side of the mountains, and my finger accidentally hit the 'delete all' button.

'What's your plan?' Saltanat said, watching me erase my career.

'I rather think it's time to call in professional help,' I replied, and sat back as the waitress poured more tea.

Chapter 26

'If you don't sort this shit out soon, the last massacre
down here is going to look like a cultural visit from the
fucking Bolshoi,' Kursan told me, and looked over at
Saltanat for confirmation.

As ever, she looked non-committal and blew smoke
into the air. We were sipping tea in our usual *chaikana*
tea room. Or rather, Saltanat and I were; Kursan didn't
believe in non-alcoholic refreshment.

Kursan had flown down at my request. No one had
his ear closer to the ground for any whisper, or kept
better contacts throughout the underworld of the
thieves of law. I knew that the usual investigations
wouldn't get me very far, and it was a case of grasping
at any thread that might turn into a rope. It might end
up hanging me, but I was willing to risk it.

Kursan looked around the *chaikana* and pulled a look
of disgust.

'Osh. I fucking hate it here. Nothing but stupid
myrki, ugly women and shit food. You owe me for
dragging me down here.'

I shrugged; I'd never known Kursan not to

188

complain about anything and everything, and if there was nothing to moan about, he'd complain about its lack.

'There was a riot in Talas last night,' he told us, in between gulps of vodka, mouthfuls of *plov* and lungfuls of smoke, 'with people marching on the police station, demanding that the "baby killers" be brought to justice. No shooting, just shouting, but it's only a matter of time. Same thing down here in Naryn. We're blaming the Uzbeks, and for sure they'll be blaming us. A couple more killings and the whole country explodes.'

That was worrying. Talas is where the last revolution began, and Naryn's the far side of the country. If Saltanat was right and this was a coordinated attempt at unrest, whoever was behind it was well funded and well organised. Forget mobiles or the internet; rumours carry between villages here within minutes, and they swell and get more impressive along the way. What's being gossiped about in Tokmok becomes eyewitness accounts in Tash Rabat the next day.

'So what are people saying?' I asked.

'Nothing in the papers, or on TV, of course. The White House won't want to start a panic. And those poor fuckers in Tashkent only get to hear about the President's latest exploits. Nothing as worrying as news for them.'

Saltanat nodded. Throughout Central Asia, you only

get told what the bosses want you to hear. Kyrgyzstan's a little more liberal, but I wasn't expecting to read a report of foreign baby killers any time soon.

'You know all this shit about baby pills from China turning up in South Korea?' Kursan continued.

I nodded. The story going around was that thousands of capsules from China containing powdered baby foetuses were being sold around the Far East as general 'cure-all' medicine. The story was given extra credence thanks to China's strict one-baby policy. Testing of the capsules was supposed to even tell you the gender of the foetus – usually female, since all Chinese families want to have sons rather than daughters. Naturally, we Kyrgyz are willing to believe anything bad about our neighbours. Was it true? Who knew? What mattered was who believed it, and what they would do about it.

'Well, they're saying that Kyrgyz boy babies make the best medicine. I told you that, right?' Kursan said.

I nodded again. I supposed the Uzbeks were saying the same about their sons.

'So this is a plot by the Chinese?' I asked.

Kursan looked at me as if I was half-witted.

'It's the Uzbeks doing it, and blaming the Chinese,' he said, 'stirring the shit until it's ripe, like they always do. So the trouble starts, and when the Uzbeks start shooting, it's all in self-defence.'

'Or it's the Kyrgyz doing the killing, and claiming we're doing it to discredit the Chinese,' Saltanat said, clearly not happy about Kursan's conspiracy theory.

'I'm not saying that your murders are trivial,' I replied, looking over at Saltanat, 'or that ours are. But are they really going to stir up a war?'

'By the time the rumours get around, it'll be whole orphanages and maternity wards massacred, you know that,' Saltanat answered, as Kursan pushed his plate away, belched and stood up.

'What did you do with the other hooker?' he asked.

'Gulbara? Saltanat has got her safely stashed away down south.'

'You don't think you should take her back to Bishkek? A witness to the last killing? Well, the last one we know about.'

He'd got a point, but I couldn't help feeling it would prove difficult to convince Gulbara that going back to the scene of Shairkul's murder was for the public good – or, for that matter, hers. So it made sense to get a more complete statement from Gulbara.

Kursan drained the last of his vodka, ditched his cigarette in the remains of his mutton stew, and we hit the road to Gulcha.

It was two hours later when Illya pulled up outside a whitewashed farmhouse on the outskirts of the village. Nondescript, like all the other villages we'd passed through, a huddle of single-storey buildings with pale-blue trim on the doors and window frames, net curtains drawn to keep out inquisitive glances. An occasional shapeless *babushka* in muddy *valenki* and patterned headscarf dragged a small trolley carrying a milk churn back from the village spring; stray dogs barked and chased the car before they lost interest and skulked back home. Those were the only signs of life we saw.

'This the place?' I asked.

Illya simply nodded. A man of few words.

We got out of the car and I led us across the road towards the gate. The place was pretty run-down, last painted about the time that Stalin was slicing up the country, with cracks in some of the windowpanes. There was a dog lying by the side of the house, asleep, not the best watchdog in town.

As we got closer, I wondered why the dog didn't jump up, start barking and snarling at us. And then I saw the red and grey puddle under its muzzle, dark against the mud.

If any birds had been singing, they were silent now.

I put one hand up to halt the others, and with the other hand I drew my gun. I didn't have to look round to know that Saltanat was doing the same.

The plain wooden door was scarred at the bottom

from decades of being kicked open by muddy boots, but that wasn't the reason why it was hanging off one hinge.

The usual farmyard smells of damp earth, sheep's wool and animal shit had an odd flavour overlying them, a sour, sickly stink that clawed at my nostrils. I pushed the door further open with my foot and moved slowly inside.

The smell was more powerful now, all too familiar. I thought back to my first killing, the old man butchered by his nephew in the one-room shithole, the walls smeared with blood, the entrails spilt out on to the bare concrete floor.

I could taste the blood in the air.

There's a game we play in Kyrgyzstan called *kok boru*. It's a kind of polo, where men on horseback battle to score a goal by hurling the headless corpse of a sheep or goat into a circle made of tyres. After an hour or so of being snatched up, dragged and trampled through the mud, the goat resembles nothing that ever lived, ripped and bloody, hoofmarks stencilled into raw flesh.

Which is what confronted me as I entered the main room.

Gulbara had defied the laws of physics and was in two places at once. Or rather, Gulbara's lower half lay in the doorway into the bedroom, while her torso and head stared at me from a chair facing the window. The decorative felt *shardyk* hanging on the wall was spattered with pale flecks and grey slivers of torn meat. The wooden floor was a sea of blood, starting to crust and blacken in the cold air. I got closer to the body. Gulbara's stomach was covered in a criss-cross and welter of razor cuts, none deep, none fatal, but enough to tell her that there was going to be no rescue. I hoped she was dead when her body was hacked in half, that her killer had been professional enough to see this as the next step in escalating the trouble, rather than a murder to be enjoyed and played over and over again in his head.

Gulbara died hard and slow, terrified and alone. And if I had anything to do with it, so would whoever did this.

A shadow fell across the floor, and I turned, raising my gun, ready to shoot. Kursan and Saltanat stood there, their faces numb with the room's stench and swill and stain. I've seen violent death at first hand so many times; I forget how much it shocks normal people. It's not something I'm proud of.

'Don't touch anything,' I said, reminding myself that I was Murder Squad.

Kursan looked at me as if I was mad, and he was right. If we called the local *menti*, we'd be there for days. And if they discovered we'd got a couple of

Uzbek Security people with us, the cell key might just get lost for weeks.

'We'll have to leave her,' Saltanat said.

'We can call it in from the road,' I said.

'What about her family? They could be back at any moment,' Kursan said, looking over his shoulder at the broken door.

'How did they find her?' Saltanat asked, picking her way across the floor, avoiding the worst of the pools of blood. 'She didn't have any information worth having. Why take this risk?'

'Scare a woman and you don't achieve much,' I said, 'but terrify a village and that gets the word out and about. She's a demonstration, the message that announces that nobody's safe, so do as you're told.'

'That doesn't answer my question,' Saltanat said, raising her voice. 'Illya. In here.'

The driver stomped down the path and into the house, eyes widening at the sight of so much blood.

'When you brought her here from Osh, were you followed?'

Illya shook his head.

'There was no one else on the road; I would have noticed.'

'So who did you tell?'

He paused, for half a second too long.

'No one.'

'You're sure?'

'I swear.'

But I could hear the fear in his voice, sensed the sweat on his palms. Saltanat stared at him, deadpan. She made a terrifying interrogator.

'Last time of asking, Illya.'

I could see that he was wondering which the least bad option would be, trying to make his mind up. Finally, he looked down at his steel-capped boots and mumbled something.

'I had a *pivo* or two last night. With my cousin. He was talking about the murders, about the missing kids. Maybe I said something.'

He looked worried. Saltanat took a step closer to him.

'I never said anything about bringing her here, honestly. I'm not stupid.'

'You mentioned her name, maybe. Heard about the hooker that shared an apartment with one of the dead girls? Nice tits. Comes from around here? Monkey tattooed on her pussy? Bitch called Gulbara. Is that how it was, Illya?'

'No, I mean, maybe I said her name.'

'And maybe your cousin told his pal, who told their best friend, don't tell anyone, keep it to yourself? And this is where we end up, Illya. Staring at something off a butcher's slab.'

Illya said nothing. The scorn in Saltanat's voice hung

in the air. She looked at him, and sighed. When she spoke, there was resignation in her voice.

'OK, Illya, question time over. We're through here. Time to go.'

As Illya nodded, Saltanat took another step closer to him, produced a gun from nowhere, and calmly pumped two bullets into the side of his head, just behind his ear.

Chapter 27

There was surprisingly little blood, though it wasn't as if the room needed any more. Saltanat had used a 9mm, so the two bullets rushed around inside Illya's head like hyperactive puppies, failed to find an exit, then rolled over and went to sleep. There were a few flecks and smears on Illya's boots and camo pants, but I couldn't tell whether it was his blood or Gulbara's.

I was too surprised to react, but Kursan reached over and forced Saltanat's hand backwards, twisting the gun out of her fingers with a single swift motion.

'What the fuck was that about?' he asked, slipping the gun into his pocket. Saltanat looked as unruffled as ever. Crazy bitch she might have been, but I couldn't help wondering if she ever felt anything, or whether she was ice queen all through.

'You believed that stuff about a family chat over a few beers? He'll have spilt everything he knew for a backhander,' she said. 'Illya told someone where Gulbara was, and this is the result. And if we don't leave now, we're in the frame for her murder, and now his. You think her butchers aren't coming back?'

I listened, suddenly attentive, for a car engine approaching, the stamp of feet outside. Nothing but a silence made ominous by the stink of fresh blood.

'We have a joke in Uzbekistan,' Saltanat said. 'We send Security forces out in threes: one who can read, one who can write, and one to watch the dangerous intellectuals. We don't even trust ourselves, let alone each other. I knew Illya would be reporting back on me; I just don't know who else he was whispering to.'

Even as she spoke, she stepped over Illya's corpse and headed for the door. Kursan and I looked at each other. He shrugged, and I followed her. Kursan gestured for me to carry on, before heading back into the kitchen. Saltanat got behind the wheel, and I slid into the back of the car, just as Kursan emerged and clambered into the passenger seat. We moved off back down the rutted track, the village as deserted as when we arrived.

'Nobody heard the shots?' I asked.

'No one who'll do anything about it,' Saltanat said, and the look on her face discouraged me from asking any more stupid questions.

'Where now?'

'Back to Osh, to the airport,' she replied. 'Better we get out of here before they find the bodies.'

'I took care of that,' Kursan announced, and didn't even flinch as the dull crump of an exploding gas cylinder boomed behind us. 'Hard to tell what's what when everything's been cooked to a crisp.'

Behind us, a watery spiral of smoke twisted upwards. I told myself it was my imagination, but I wondered if the roast meat I could smell on the air came from the bodies we'd left back there. I felt like an amateur in the company of two hardened criminals, but I told myself to focus on what really mattered. The dead women, the dead children, snowflakes settling on cold faces, bellies ripped into a confusion. Saltanat could take care of the politics, the intrigue, the corruption; I simply wanted to stop seeing Yekaterina Tynalieva's eyes staring into the dark.

Just for a fucking change, it was starting to snow; light at first, but I'd been caught in too many blizzards to expect it to stay that way. Sure enough, the weather got worse until, by the time we reached the outskirts of Osh, it was hard to see more than the length of the car bonnet ahead. There weren't going to be any flights out that day.

Saltanat's mobile rang, and she pulled over to the nearest snowdrift. I watched as she nodded, her face grim, listening, not answering. She rang off, and put the car into gear.

'Problems?' I asked, expecting and getting no reply, watching her profile as she stared ahead into the falling snow.

I consoled myself with the thought that anyone following us had to put up with the same whiteout, and the traffic boys were all safely tucked up in the station house counting their breakfast money. I figured we'd head back to the guesthouse off Ak-Burinskya Street, so I was surprised when Saltanat took the road that leads out to the airport. The car skittered and slid across the ice, but that didn't stop her putting the metal to the floor.

'There won't be any flights out, not in this,' I said, but she ignored me, and took a slip road away from the main terminal.

'You've missed the turn-off. The terminal's back there,' I added, not sure whether I wanted to be helpful or irritating. From the look on her face, I had a pretty good idea which one she'd settled for.

She sighed, as if dealing with a slightly dim child.

'We're not taking a commercial flight,' she said, spinning the wheel hard right and into the lee of a low building with a corrugated roof.

My heart sank; if there is one thing worse than trusting body and soul to an airline pilot, it is being flown in some rusting heap by an exile from the Kazakh air force over some of the highest mountains in Central Asia during the winter's most ferocious blizzard.

I looked over at Kursan for moral support, but he was slumped in his seat, eyes closed.

The snow battered against me as I got out of the car, and followed the others towards the hangar. I wasn't happy with what I found inside.

'We're going up in that?' I asked, shouting above the noise of the wind.

In front of me, pilot already in place, was a *krokodil*. Not a dead junkie, but a Mil Mi-24, an old Russian helicopter gunship, known as a *krokodil* because of its camouflage patterning. The Soviets used to call the gunship 'the flying tank', not because of its protection but because of its wallowing lack of manoeuvrability. As we clambered aboard, I couldn't help noticing that the metal of the door was scarred and torn, pocked and pitted with what looked like small-arms fire. Maybe the beast was a veteran of Afghanistan, one that had ended up being pensioned off cheaply to us. Or, more likely, at considerable expense, once the necessary *viziatka* had been slipped into the appropriate hands.

We sat down against the bare metal sides of the gunship, clutching at webbing straps as the pilot edged us forward out of the hangar and into the storm. The helicopter rocked from side to side as the winds started to buffet it, almost managing to drown out the belch and snarl of the engine. In weather like this, it was going to be a good four hours before we got back to Bishkek, and I needed a believable story to tell the Chief. Unapproved leave of absence was probably the least of my crimes, and the Torugart Pass looked ever more likely as my final posting.

The weather and the screams of the engine made it impossible to talk, even at the volume Kursan operated at, so we concentrated on getting as warm and comfortable as we could in a flying fridge. Kursan staggered to his feet and rummaged at the back, dragging out some canvas sheets and throwing one to each of us. I wrapped myself up, ignoring the smell of sweat and oil, and shut my eyes. And despite the noise and the endless shaking, I managed to doze off.

And dream.

Chinara's last few days were a flood of despair on my part and pain on hers. Morphine kept her asleep for most of the time, and when she was awake she often didn't recognise me. All her energies were concentrated on breathing, on hauling in the last few cubic centimetres of air, that final flailing to keep the flame alight. At times, her struggles would knock her embroidered cushion to the floor, and her hand would scrabble for it, her eyes frantic until she felt the familiar material under her fingertips.

Our hospitals aren't the best equipped, to say the least. Unwashed floors, broken windows, filthy bathrooms, even dirty operating theatres. Most families bring in a more comfortable mattress, favourite meals, home remedies to supplement the out-of-date fake medicines that the administrators buy from China. It's not always negligence or corruption; more often than not, it's just lack of money.

I took a month's unpaid leave of absence, although I knew I wouldn't need that long. Or rather, Chinara wouldn't. I spent all my time by her bedside, catnapping in the chair I'd bullied out of a ward attendant by flashing my police card, going home only to shower, shave and change when the stink of me got too much.

The days seemed to hurtle by; no sooner was it light outside than the sun was falling out of the sky. But the nights, they seemed endless, as if the same implacable force that had sown the tumours deep in her breast was determined to drag out the agony for as long as she could still gasp and scream when the morphine wore off.

Her hair had started to grow back, in some sick fucking parody of recovery, but the flesh was drawing back from the bones of her face, morphing into a shrunken head wearing a wig, eyes still glittering against skin worn sallow and smooth with exhaustion.

All I could do was hold her hand, smile when she surfaced from wherever the drugs had taken her, whisper to her over and over again that I loved her, that I'd never forget her, that I wished that it was me instead of her sliding towards the dark. The words became a tattoo on my tongue and I knew that, once she was gone, 'love' was a word I would never use again.

I would think of her on the shore of Lake Issyk-Kul, beyond the holiday towns like Bosteri, where we'd find some rocky spot, and clamber down to the shore to swim in its glass-clear water. In the darkest parts of the night, I would picture her, slipping away from my embrace, down deep under the surface, hair spread out around her, astonished eyes fixed on mine as she sank out of sight.

In one of her rare moments of lucidity, just a couple of days before she died, she repeated something she'd said to me over and over as we got past the initial diagnosis, the operations, the drugs, always hopeful of success.

'Only two things matter; the way you live your life, and the manner in which you leave it.'

I kept telling myself about her bravery, her stoicism, the way she never complained, even when the pain bit deep or when she saw the scar where her breast had been. And that just reminded me of my own self-pity, my own concerns about my future. She lived her life well, if for too short a time. And death stood in the corner of the room, ready to devour her.

She died just after sunrise, ten days after going into hospital for the last time. There were no final words, no parting glance, just the winding down of a machine worn beyond repair. I don't believe she knew I was there.

I drew the sheet over her face, found the duty nurse to tell her that it was finished, then walked home through the bright sunlight that burnt off the snow, finally facing the terror of being alone.

Chapter 28

I was woken up by a toe digging into my ribs. Somehow I'd managed to sleep through most of the flight and, judging by the look on Kursan's face, it hadn't been something I'd regret missing. I grunted and then snarled as another kick jabbed at me. The vividness of dreaming about Chinara was still with me, and I was reluctant to let go of anything that brought her back to me, however temporarily.

'We're fifteen minutes from Bishkek. The Russian airbase,' Saltanat told me.

'Why are we landing there?' I said, struggling to sit up.

From the look on her face, it was another stupid question.

'Who knows what sort of landing committee is waiting at the international airport?' she said. 'Who they might want to arrest?'

I nodded, although I still had no idea who had killed Gulbara or, indeed, any of the other women. In fact, my only murder suspect was crouched down facing me, checking her speed loader was prepared.

'There's one more reason,' she added, replacing her gun and buttoning up her coat.

My ears were ready to snap off with the cold, and I reached for my *ushanka*.

'There's been another murder, a bad one, over at Kant. The airbase there is the obvious place to land.'

I considered this for a moment. That explained the earlier call en route to the airport. Saltanat clearly had the sort of connections that reached right to the top. Yet another reason to be wary of her.

'We're still in Kyrgyzstan,' I said. 'You have no jurisdiction here. Shit, I don't even know if I have any more. You'll have to drop me off at the crime scene, and then you and Kursan disappear.'

'That won't be necessary. We're not going to Kyrgyzstan.'

I looked at her, puzzled, then over at Kursan, who simply shrugged his shoulders.

'The victim is Russian. And she was killed on the base. Russian diplomatic territory. So you've got no more right to investigate a murder there than I have.'

The *krokodil* gave a final lurch and bounced as we touched down. I fastened up my coat, checked the Yarygin was secure on my hip, and wondered – again – in what shit I'd found myself. Then the doors were flung open, and the full blast of a Kyrgyz winter descended upon us.

It wasn't snowing, but a bone-shattering wind hurtled down off the mountains and along the flat expanse of the runway. An open-topped military jeep was waiting for us, silhouetted against the landing lights. As we stumbled out of the gunship, headlights flared and the jeep raced towards us. A stony-faced driver in military garb sat behind the wheel and, in the front passenger seat, a *Spetsnaz* Special Forces soldier, dressed in black and with a woollen balaclava concealing his face, cradled a Kalashnikov AK-74 assault rifle lying ready across his lap. Once we were aboard, the jeep zigzagged across the tarmac and screeched to a halt outside a low-slung, drab and windowless building. As we clambered down, we looked like prisoners under guard. And perhaps we were.

The *Spetsnaz* pointed with his rifle towards a metal entrance door, and the three of us headed towards it to get out of the wind's howl. Inside, the noise dropped to a slightly more bearable shriek. We were inside a hangar, with half a dozen assault helicopters lined up. There was a stink of aviation fuel and machine oil in the air, a sharp smell that made my eyes water and burnt the back of my throat. But I wasn't surprised to find that a richer, familiar odour lay like an unsubtle perfume beneath that. My old friends: blood, raw meat and shit.

The woman's body lay face down in front of the

sliding hangar door, as if she'd been trying to burrow underneath it in an attempt to escape. The corpse had been carefully arranged after death; I could tell that much, even as we walked over towards it. Her knees had been tucked under her stomach, pushing her buttocks up into the air. She was naked from the waist down, and I saw that she'd been sliced open from vagina to anus, as if her killer swung an axe with the kind of power that splits wood for a winter fire. One quick blow, blade raised high, from someone who knows what they're doing. A pool of blood mixed with cement dust from the concrete floor spewed out of her and down past her feet.

I reached for my cigarettes, remembered how much inflammable stuff there was all around me, and put them back in my pocket. The memory of the sheep we had slaughtered at Chinara's commemoration flashed through my mind.

We stood around the body, like medical students watching a difficult birth, until the door slammed open and a Russian officer marched in. I knew he was a colonel, from the triple stars on each shoulder, and the look on his face told me he was a tough bastard as well. Kyrgyzstan may be a better posting than Chechnya, but the Russians know we have long memories for decades of humiliation, and there are plenty of Kyrgyz who

welcome any opportunity for a little retrospective dis-
cussion in a dark alleyway.

He walked over to us, his polished shoes echoing off
the concrete floor.

'Barabanov,' he stated. 'Which one of you is the
Kyrgyz investigator?'

From his accent, he was from the Urals, maybe Ufa,
far enough from Moscow to know we did things very
differently here. Saltanat jerked her head towards me.
Barabanov extended his hand. After a second's hesitation, I took it.

'I'm informed that you're a specialist in this sort of
crime?'

'I wouldn't say that, Colonel, but I'm Murder Squad,
currently investigating a series of murders . . .' I paused,
before adding, 'which may or may not be linked to this
woman's death.'

My qualified answer didn't satisfy Barabanov, and
his eyes narrowed as he stared at me. Terrifying if I'd
been a nineteen-year-old recruit. But I wasn't, so I gave
the stare right back.

'And what "may" link them, Inspector?'

'I really am not at liberty to discuss a matter of Kyrgyz State Security.'

Barabanov said nothing but reached inside his
immaculately pressed jacket, covered with a row of

service medals, and took out a sheet of paper, handing it to me.

I read the fax to myself:

> You will give Colonel Barabanov your complete cooperation in every particular, and answer any questions he may have regarding your investigation, holding nothing back.
>
> Tynaliev
> Minister for State Security

I decided to return a little friendly fire of my own.

'Colonel, the quickest way to work out what is and isn't relevant is for me to find out all the facts first.'

I could see he was reluctant to share information, so I decided to coax the answers out of him.

'The victim, who was she?'

'Marina Gurchenko, one of the health personnel on the base. Seconded here a year ago.'

'A jealous boyfriend? Enemies that you know of?'

'She was well liked by her colleagues, I know of no reason why anyone would wish to do . . . this.'

Barabanov looked over at the mound of flesh against the door, but his face showed no emotion. Not a man to face across a chessboard.

'A question. Was she pregnant?'

For the first time, Barabanov betrayed some emotion. He looked at me warily, as if I'd just produced a switchblade but wasn't quite sure how to use it. When he answered, I could sense the caution in his voice.

'Why do you ask? Is that relevant?'

'It's a common factor in the murders I'm investigating,' I stated. 'And I don't want to disturb the body before a Crime Scene team arrives.'

'This is a Russian airbase. Considered Russian territory. We will handle this matter ourselves. Your presence here is only due to the influence of your superiors.'

He tapped the fax to reinforce his point. But I could scent something else besides the bouquet of death.

'I ask again, was she pregnant?'

Barabanov paused before answering.

'Yes.'

'That may well be a motive, Colonel. A married colleague, having a fling? Worried about what his wife and children back home would think, what they might do?'

'That would hardly justify this ferocity, would it?'

Now we were on my turf, and I sensed his authority diminish.

'Colonel, I've seen people hacked into fragments over a bottle of *samogon*, cocks and breasts sliced off, brains blown out of both ears over a thousand-*som* loan. There's nothing humans won't do to each other, believe me.'

He nodded. He'd probably been in Chechnya, almost

certainly in Afghanistan. He knew what people were capable of.

'She was pregnant,' he said, 'but I'm certain that this wasn't the act of a married boyfriend afraid of the consequences.'

Saltanat spoke, for the first time, and I suddenly wondered why the Colonel hadn't asked who she was, or what she was doing there.

'And what makes you so sure, Colonel?'

'Because I am . . . was . . . the father.'

Chapter 29

As a Murder Squad, you learn pretty quickly which cases require priority solving. But I'd never been involved in the murder of a pregnant Russian army officer before; my first and probably best idea was to head to the Kazakh border and hole up for a couple of decades.

But Marina Gurchenko's murder put me firmly in between two of the country's most powerful men: the Minister for State Security, and a Russian Colonel with enough firepower at his disposal to drive us back to being nomads.

Both men wanted their respective victims avenged. Mikhail Tynaliev was expecting to see banner headlines about dedicated security forces hunting down a ruthless killer; Barabanov wanted the whole mess shipped quietly back to Mother Russia, and the case file accidentally shredded. Both men expected me to solve the crime. And failure wasn't going to be an option.

For a moment, I wondered if the Colonel could have organised the whole thing, had a few useless women slaughtered, so that when it was Gurchenko's turn, it would look like we had a serial killer prowling the land with a set of butcher's knives. But it would have been much easier for Barabanov to just arrange an accident; a lorry backing up without due care and attention, or an overdose and the shocking discovery that a member of the medical team abused drugs.

I walked over and crouched beside the body. Sometimes it's easy to forget you're standing over someone who only hours ago was laughing, making plans, wondering what to call her baby.

All of that had been taken away from her, stealing even her dignity as well as her hopes and beauty. Murder is the ultimate theft, leaving only a ransacked house, unfit for human habitation, ready to be razed back into the ground.

I reached out to turn the body over, but Barabanov pulled my arm back.

'We'll see to that,' he ordered.

'I can hardly help investigate this murder if I can't examine the body,' I said.

It was a battle of wills and, if I'd been in his regiment, I'd have already been doing punishment drill. But I wasn't, and he needed my knowledge more than I needed his. He reluctantly nodded, and I rolled the body over, away from me.

Marina Gurchenko slithered over, drying blood dark

and flaking on her skin. The first traces of lividity had begun, but there were no signs yet of rigor mortis. I'm no Usupov, but I guessed that she'd been dead less than three hours.

'How often is this hangar used?'

Barabanov looked thrown by the question.

'When the gunships are operational, or during regular servicing. The last time anyone would have had any reason to be in here was when the flight you came in on left here.'

'And the hangar isn't guarded?'

'This is a military base. No one gets past the wire, or the guards.'

'So your security was breached?'

Barabanov shook his head.

'I ordered a full search as soon as the body was found. Nothing, no gaps in the wire, no tracks in the snow, no vehicles came or left.'

It was time to ask some dangerous questions, the sort that you normally ask with a weapon in your hand.

'If you didn't discover the body until after the *krokodil* had left for Osh, why did it come for us?'

'I had orders.'

I waited. I'm very good at waiting. Sometimes that's all it takes. And he hesitated.

'I was told to give every assistance to a security agent of a friendly foreign nation.'

That would be Saltanat, then. Kursan and I had just managed to hitch a ride. I still hadn't figured out Saltanat's involvement in all of this. An Uzbek Security officer? A double agent for the Russians? On the side of the victims, or hunting with the killers? All I knew, from the way she'd executed Illya, was that she was quick-thinking, efficient and ruthless.

I turned back to Marina's body. The similarities with Yekaterina Tynalieva's corpse were unmistakable: massive damage to tissue and organs. But there were puzzling discrepancies as well. Where Yekaterina was precisely, almost surgically opened and her flesh peeled back, Marina's pelvis had been smashed apart by a powerful blow with an axe. Marina was naked and slaughtered indoors; Yekaterina was fully clothed and died in the open air. It seemed pretty certain that I was hunting more than one murderer.

There was no sign of drug use, no needle tracks, no bruising. I could sense Barabanov was anxious for me to be gone, so he could parcel his ex-lover up like joints on a butcher's slab, send her back to Mother Russia for burial without an autopsy. It was only at the last minute, as I heard the door to the hangar slide open, and a medical team arrived, that I spotted what might be a clue.

The Greek letter 'alpha', tattooed on her shoulder, was so small as to be barely noticeable. I didn't draw attention to it, just stored the information in my head, stood back as the medical team manhandled Marina into a black body bag, placed it on a collapsible gurney and wheeled her towards the exit.

The door clanged behind them, and all that remained of a life was a pool of blood. Barabanov jerked his head at one of the mechanics, who returned with a hose. Within ten minutes, Marina Gurchenko was rinsed away into the gutter, along with any forensic evidence.

Barabanov gestured us towards the door.

'My aide will escort you to the camp gates. One of your police cars is waiting to take you all back into Bishkek.'

He held the door open for us, but I wasn't quite finished yet.

'You spotted nothing unusual, nothing out of the ordinary happened this afternoon?'

My gut told me he'd got information he didn't want to pass on. So I held my ground, willing to outstare him, to wait as long as it took, while snow billowed in from the storm outside.

'The sentries stopped one car on the camp outskirts. A police car. The driver produced his police ID, said it was just a routine inspection, drove away.'

'And?'

Barabanov stared back at me, cold blue eyes giving nothing away.

'I was surprised when I saw your name on the gunship manifest, Inspector,' he said, 'although your reputation as a hunter of men precedes you.'

He paused for dramatic effect.

'You see, Inspector, the man my sentries stopped produced genuine police ID, no question of that. The odd thing is, the name on the card was yours.'

Chapter 30

As the Colonel said, a uniform was waiting for us at the main gate. Kursan climbed into the front, as if by right. He'd been in a police car before, but this was almost certainly the first time he'd not been handcuffed and chained to the D-ring on the floor. Saltanat and I sat on the back seat, as the driver turned the heat down to merely stifling, then headed towards Bishkek.

For the rest of the journey, I tried to work out how a police ID card with my name on it had ended up in someone else's hands. For a few thousand *som*, paid under the counter, it's easy enough to get false documents, birth and even death certificates, but no one would run the risk of producing fake police papers unless there was big money or a lot of influence behind it. And, of course, it would be all too easy to set me up if I got too close to something – or someone – I wasn't supposed to suspect. My ID found under another body, carelessly lost in a rage of lust, for example.

I decided that there was nothing I could do apart from report it, and switched on my phone for the first time in hours. For the next ten minutes, I endured a string of messages from the Chief, each one more hysterical than the last. They started off quite mildly with 'arsehole' and progressed to 'stinking fuckhead' over the course of a few minutes. It didn't seem like much of a promotion, but at least it showed he cared. I switched off the phone, and decided to surprise him. That way, we were less likely to have a reception committee waiting.

We were only twenty kilometres outside Bishkek, so I didn't bother trying to sleep. We bounced around quite a lot, what with the potholed road and the ice on what little tarmac there was. I made sure some of my bouncing included colliding with Saltanat. I was wondering if she'd want to retry the experiment of sleeping with me, but she wasn't giving off any encouraging signs. Then I pictured the hacked and mutilated woman back in the air force base, and felt ashamed of myself. I'd always sworn I'd never get desensitised to death, and I knew the pain of losing Chinara would never leave me. But the others? It was all too easy to see them as evidence of a crime, part of a puzzle to be solved, rather than ordinary people turned into victims against their will. None of us want to die.

I realised that I had no idea where Saltanat lived. Or, indeed, even her patronymic and family name.

'Where do you want us to drop you?' I asked, perhaps too casually.

'Anywhere you see a taxi,' was her reply, frosty as usual.

'No problem to take you home,' I said.

She simply threw me the hard stare, and I gave up. I decided to organise a plain-clothes guy to follow her, the next time we met.

Even though the storm had stopped, with just a few flecks of snow turning up late like drunks at a party, Chui Prospekt was deserted. The lights were still on at the Metro Bar, with a couple of hopeful taxis loitering with intent, hoping to overcharge a foreigner. She tapped our driver on the shoulder, and we pulled to a halt.

'I'll call you,' she said. 'Don't bother following me.'

So we followed her taxi down Chui as far as Tynys-tanov, where it did an abrupt right, in the direction of the Uzbek Embassy. As the tail lights disappeared, I wondered if I'd ever see her again.

'Some woman, that,' said Kursan. 'If I was twenty years younger –'

'And washed more than once a year, and didn't hang out with every crook in Bishkek, I'm sure she'd look at you with love in her eyes,' I said.

'Doesn't have to be love,' Kursan said. 'More than one way to get a *pizda* wet,' and he spat out a throaty laugh.

'You want to come and see the Chief with me?'

I asked, changing the subject and knowing that Sverdlovsky Station was the last place on earth that Kursan would want to be.

'Drop me at Ibraimova; I'll stay at your place,' he said.

I started to tell him I didn't have a spare key, then remembered Kursan's lock-picking skills. I sighed and nodded.

As we pulled up outside my apartment block, Kursan jerked his head as a sign for me to get out with him.

'I didn't want to ask when she was with us,' he said, and his face was serious, his voice almost a whisper, 'but what was it you noticed about the body?'

I debated about telling him, then decided he knew so much already, a little more wouldn't be a problem. We walked a few paces so the uniform couldn't hear us.

'A tattoo, very small, professionally done. A Greek letter A.'

Kursan sucked air between his teeth.

'*Spetsnaz.* Russian Special Forces.'

I nodded. *Spetsnaz* are the toughest, fiercest bastards in the whole Russian armed forces. If Marina had been one of them, whoever killed her must have been a stone-cold butcher. Every way I turned, this case got murkier and more dangerous. At the rate things were going, it wouldn't be long before I was lying next to

Chinara up in the mountains. Right then, that didn't seem like a bad idea.

I got back in the car and yanked the door shut against the cold.

'I'll see you when I get back from the station,' I said.

'If you get back,' he said, and laughed again, this time with no warmth in his voice.

'Just who the fuck are you working for? Is it that Uzbek bitch? Gave you the starry eyes, and a flash of tit? You're a fucked-up pussy-head!'

The Chief was closer to the truth than he knew, but that didn't endear him to me. I stood before his fancy landing-strip-size desk, and wondered how much the eagle statue had cost. He was pissed off with me for not declaring Yekaterina's death sorted, for getting the Russians mixed up in everything, for following a trail of death all over the country. But most of all, he was pissed off at the grief he was getting from the *nomenklatura* who held his career in their palms.

I waited until his rage subsided enough for him to pour a generous one and give me the nod to sit down.

'Have you actually found out anything while you've been on your winter holiday? I know you're an idiot, but you've never let a sniff of *pizda* hang you up before.'

I didn't know where he'd got the notion that I was a womaniser, but I supposed I ought to be flattered.

'What's interesting, Chief, is what I don't know.'

He tipped the bottle, nodded at me to continue.

'I know it's not a serial killer. Too many deaths, too many locations, too little time to get from one to another, especially this time of year. The murders are connected, but the pattern changes. These women have nothing in common, no social links, no friendships, not even the same nationalities. According to Usupov, Yekaterina Tynalieva's murderer had some sort of surgical training, but Marina Gurchenko's corpse looks as if a drunk had swung an axe in the dark. So not the same murderer; not the same psychologically driven modus operandi behind the killings.'

'"Modus operandi",' the Chief repeated, mock-impressed. 'You're a hunter of killers, not a university don. Spare me the fancy stuff.'

I ignored him, and carried on.

'There are the other deaths to consider. Gulbara, the girl in Osh; she wasn't pregnant. And Tyulev and Lubashov in the shoot-out outside Fatboys: what triggered that? And what made Gasparian take a header into traffic?'

Secretly, I was sure Gasparian's suicide had been one of those assisted ones, where two burly policemen throw you off a bridge, but I kept that thought to myself.

'The biggest puzzle? Find a motive and you usually

find your killer, but no one's claimed responsibility, no one's stood up and blamed the ills of modern society, or the Russians, or the full moon for why they did it. So that tells me it's about business, putting the frighteners on people; showing they can get away with anything, so get out of their way.'

The Chief nodded. He may well have thought all this through himself, but he was shrewd enough to know when a pat on the head would get him further than a kick up the arse.

'The Circle of Brothers?'

It was my turn to nod.

'Hard to see who else. The question is: why choose this way of sending out messages?'

'Drugs?'

'That's where the serious money is.'

An officer in the Anti-Drug Trafficking Department told me there are a couple of dozen drug cartels across Kyrgyzstan, mostly based on ethnic origins: Kyrgyz, Uzbek, Kurd, Gipsy, Chechen, Turkish, Armenian, Uighur and Tajik. Everybody wants a slice of our only growth industry.

'But they've already got their territories agreed upon and divided up,' the Chief said. 'So why kick up all this shit storm now?'

I sat back and watched him sip his vodka.

'Uzbek Security have a theory that it's political.

Someone stirring up trouble between our two countries. You know how Uzbeks always think that Osh should be theirs.'

The Chief pulled a sour face, as if his vodka was too warm, and pursed his lips. Osh is an enclave, housed on a narrow strip of land that lies next to Uzbek territory like a bridegroom's *yelda*. Half the population are ethnic Uzbek and resent being Kyrgyz; the other half are Kyrgyz and resent Uzbeks getting above themselves.

'Your girlfriend says there have been Uzbek women killed in the same way?' the Chief asked.

'She's not my girlfriend, but yes.'

'Deliberate misinformation, my guess,' the Chief pronounced, stumbling a bit over the words.

I figured he'd had enough vodka, and wearily poured the heeltaps of the bottle into his glass.

'But why?'

'If those Uzbek fuckers want a fight, they should come out into the open.'

'So you think it's about land, not drugs.'

'That's what I pay you to find out, fool.'

I stood up. The Chief stayed slumped where he was, eyes looking like boiled eggs.

'I'll ask around about any new alliances, fresh fallouts in the drugs trade, see if that gets us anywhere. But war with another country? I think you'd better talk to the Minister for State Security about that.'

I might as well have been talking to the eagle on the desk. The Chief's eyes were closed, and he was starting to whistle through his nose.

I put on my *ushanka*, buttoned up my coat and headed out of the building back towards Ibraimova, at a loss about what to do next.

Chapter 31

I'm not a fan of conspiracy theories. I believe the Americans did walk on the moon, there was nobody on the grassy knoll, and the shots fired outside the Kremlin at Brezhnev's motorcade came from an army deserter, not a deep-cover CIA operative. But this case was a line of distorting mirrors, each reflecting the truth away from me. There was a reason behind the killings; I just had to work out what it was.

I spent the next two days criss-crossing the city, putting the arm on pharmaceutical drug smugglers in Osh bazaar, giving a little muscle to a couple of Uzbek pimps working the parks, treating Alamedin's biggest heroin dealer to the sight of my Yarygin.

Kursan put me back in touch with Abdurehim Otkur; I told him what I needed and who I wanted to meet. At first he was reluctant to help, but I pointed out the benefits of peace and quiet for everyone on both sides of the border. Then I reminded him that Tynaliev could send a battalion of soldiers to make his life miserable; all it needed was a word from me in the

Minister's ear. Sometimes all it takes is a couple of hints here, a whisper in the right guy's ear.

Which is how I found myself back at the Kulturny, in the same chair as before, watching the *alkashi* drink themselves into a stupor not even the *moorzilki* can stir. I wouldn't have minded a glass of the good stuff myself, but I needed my wits sharp about me for the meeting I was about to have.

I checked my watch. Eleven. Already ninety minutes behind schedule. Maybe I should have posted some plain-clothes uniforms nearby, but I wasn't dealing with idiots like the late unlamented Gasparian this time. My Yarygin was safely locked up back home; for a meeting like this, carrying would be a sure sign I wasn't there just for the conversation.

Contrary to what a lot of people believe about the Circle of Brothers, all most of them want is a quiet life, free to pillage and loot and corrupt and steal. Killing each other might be good for business in the short term, but in the long term it gets in the way of the profit motive, and attracts unwanted attention. And the last thing you want to do is wipe out civilians. After all, they're your customers. That doesn't mean that the Brothers are good people to do business with, just that they won't kill you unless there's a reason.

The muscle who pushed his way through the door

looked like his weapons of choice were his bare hands. Blue prison tattoos danced down his fingers, and his palms looked dipped in ink. A church with three spires was tattooed on the back of his right hand, each spire representing a prison term; just as a church is the House of God, so prison is the home of the thief. From the way his shoulders stretched his leather jacket, when he wasn't spending his time away getting inked he was lifting home-made weights.

He might have been bulky, but he wasn't clumsy. He checked out the dazed clientele, spotted me, jerked his thumb towards the door. His boss wasn't going to walk down into any shithole like the Kulturny with only one exit, so I trailed behind the giant up into the night air.

No fresh snow, for a change, but what had already fallen crunched under my boots as we walked towards the SUV parked across the road, in the darkness under the trees. Street lights are a luxury in Bishkek at the best of times. But no muscle would ever give a rival a clear shot, anyway.

We stopped, he patted me down to ensure I wasn't carrying a piece or a recorder, and the rear window slid open. The man inside was invisible, but I could picture him from a dozen mugshots over the years. Old, bald, liver spots coating his head and hands like scorch marks. Eyes that gave away only cold calculation. A razor scar down one cheek, furrowing white and jagged into creased skin. And a voice like ice clawing across rock, the result of a bleach gargle administered by a rival now long dead and at the bottom of Lake Issyk-Kul.

The *pakhan*, the boss.

'Get in,' the voice dictated.

I shook my head.

'I'm Murder Squad, not some fucking baby uniform you own, not some cell bitch on his knees in front of you.'

'Big talk, Inspector. I've been asking around. What they all say about you? Good at putting down useless fuckheads like Tyulev and Lubashov. My mother could have taken those two. Me, I think that's all there is to you, talk. When you come up against real men? If you're trouble to me when you're sniffing around, maybe you should be head to toe beside your wife.'

It was the kind of threat I'd expected, just talk, dancing to show that neither of us was intimidated. Except I was. All I had to do was not show it.

'You know whose murder I'm investigating? The only daughter of the man who can shit on your head and flush you down the toilet. It's in your interests to listen, then give your mouth some serious exercise.'

The muscle beside me didn't like the way I was talking. He took a step towards me, and I could see I was in for a three-spired church smashing my jaw. I gave him the cold stare and beckoned him forward.

'*Arsehole!* You think you can take me? Fuck your mother!'

He didn't like that, but he had just enough discipline not to do anything without an order.

'Let me tell you something. You think I'd come looking for you with just my dick in my hand? Check out the roof; maybe you'll see the night sight of my sniper.'

The muscle's eyes darted upwards, in the direction I'd indicated. Biceps are one thing, but you can't outpunch a bullet. He didn't spot my sniper, which was hardly surprising, since there wasn't one.

The voice from the back of the car was surprisingly patient, but then, this was a guy who'd been smart and ruthless enough to have outlived all his enemies and most of his friends.

'Enough of this shit. I'm not going to put you back in your marriage bed, Inspector. Not yet, anyway. You want to stay out there in the cold, fine. We can talk like this. So tell me.'

I told him about the murders in both countries, about the mutilations.

'We had nothing to do with any of this,' he said. 'We're businessmen. Nobody needs this on our doorstep.'

'There's one more killing you maybe don't know about, and it's going to fall on us all like a mountain.'

I described the murder of the female *Spetsnaz*. I didn't

need to labour the point. Moscow could come back in and smash us into pieces, if doing so would give them an advantage. Don't believe me? Talk to the Chechens, the Georgians, and see what they have to say. The Kremlin was pissed off enough already about the American airbase; if we had anything worth stealing, they'd descend on us like winter wolves hitting the flocks outside Naryn.

Silence hung inside the car like the scent of rotting meat. When he finally spoke, it was with an air of resignation.

'Apart from a bit of piss, the world is full of shit.'

Secretly, I agreed with him, but I also knew who helped make it that way.

'Thanks to your life's work,' I replied, tensing in case the three-spired church decided to show me what disrespect can get you.

'I do what I do, you do what you do. We carry the stink of the grave, both of us.'

I heard him cough, a brutal, rasping hack dragged out of his lungs with meathooks. Maybe cold air didn't agree with him. Maybe a cancer even more malignant than he was had chosen to lodge inside him, on a strictly short-term basis.

'I'll tell you what I think, shall I?'

No answer from the SUV, so I carried on.

'Tynaliev's daughter? Maybe a sex crime, but it didn't

have that smell of testosterone and lust. No frenzy, the way the womb was sliced open. So I figure one of Daddy's political opponents, or a revenge killing. God knows enough people who would like to piss on his grave. You included.'

'*Da*, me included,' and I could hear the scars from the bleach in his words. The *voy* said nothing, but cracked his knuckles with the same glee he'd use on my skull.

'The girl in Karakol, Umida Boronova. We found her body, not her child. The obvious assumption was that she'd been killed for her baby. I got the whisper that there might be Chinese medicine involved, people paying big money for bigger dicks.

'Then the prostitute, Shairkul, the one sliced and diced. Again, not her baby, so maybe the Chinese medicine theory is right. But why kill women who aren't pregnant when you can just harvest the babies of those who are? A warning?'

I shrugged, to hint that I was genuinely puzzled.

'Then an Uzbek Security officer warns me off. That's before someone sets me up, and Tyulev and Lubashov end up on a metal bed. Joy all round; the killer of Yekaterina taken out by brave police officer, end of story. Everyone happy. Except the killings don't stop. Different places, no connection between the victims. It's not sex, it's not revenge, it's not a solo crazy guy, and it's not hawking traditional medicines.'

Silence.

And then, 'Go on.'

'The Uzbek woman tells me her government thinks we're stirring up trouble down in Osh, and my boss thinks it's the other way round. More dead women, including the one who went south to keep safe. And now the Russian military are involved.

'So I ask myself: the Circle of Brothers don't want the Kremlin coming down all mob-handed, looking for revenge and calling it restoring public order. No reason to shit all over what's kept everybody sweet and plump all these years, is there?'

A few flakes were starting to fall, tentative, unwilling to settle on the car and provoke the boss's anger. It would be a long time until dawn, and I wondered if I was going to see it.

Then the voice scrawled some instructions into the air, breath pluming out of the open window into the dark.

'Hurt him.'

Chapter 32

The falling snowflakes, the distant headlights, the wind hustling its way through bare branches had all stopped, frozen into a single moment, slow motion gliding to a complete halt.

Even before the breath of his *pakhan*'s order dissolved into air, I'd swung round to face the muscle, my boot slamming into the side of his knee. His whole leg buckled inward at the joint, bent in a way nature never intended, and I heard the kneecap split, like kindling broken to make a fire. At the same time, the heel of my fist shattered his nose, not so hard as to drive splinters of bone into his brain, but enough to stop him in his tracks. His leg unable to support his weight, he toppled sideways. And as he put his hand out to break his fall, I stamped down on it, bending his fingers back to the wrist.

He gave a surprisingly high-pitched scream, then I was pulling him upright, using him as a shield for whatever might come out of the car, pulling his jaw back to snap his neck if he put up any more fight.

A long gout of blood spasmed out of the remains of his nose, spattering across the snow, and from the smell, he'd pissed himself. With my free hand, I wrestled the gun out of his jacket pocket and pointed it at the open window.

'Enough, Inspector,' the voice said, unmoved by the sudden violence. 'Yuri might be no opposition for you, but you know what I'll have to do if you kill him.'

'Out of the car, fucker,' I said.

I didn't give a shit how old he was, I wouldn't have cared if he died shrieking from cancer in front of me. He knew something, and I'd kick it out of him if I had to, until he bled from every hole.

The door locks clicked open, and the boss slowly dismounted.

'Gun on the floor, now,' I ordered, taking the gun barrel out of the muscle's ear and rapping it against his *pakhan*'s jaw. He held his hands up, showing he was unarmed.

'You think this is a good idea?' he said. 'Just as well you have no living relatives.'

'I've fucked around too long on this,' I said, resisting the urge to hammer his crooked stained teeth out of his face.

The *pakhan* looked around, slightly puzzled, wondering where the rest of his crew were. I let Yuri slump to the floor, and gave him a little steel-toed kiss just to keep him quiet for a while. Then I focused on the *pakhan*.

Maksat Aydaraliev. Seventy years old, deadly as

distilled snake venom. He'd ruled the heroin trade through Chui province since before independence. He'd survived the KGB, the State Police, the Anti-Corruption Police, the Drug Squad, two revolutions and anyone in the underworld stupid enough to take him on. His mobile had the private numbers of anyone who was anyone in the White House. He owned sanatoria for Russian oligarchs on the shores of Lake Issyk-Kul, and a dozen restaurants and clubs around Bishkek. He was decisive and pitiless. I knew for a fact that he'd beheaded two undercover law officers and sent his trophies to their wives. He was a man ready to kick over the table any time, and fuck the consequences.

All this in a man who only hit 160cm on tiptoe, who looked as if a strong wind would hurl him as far as the Pamir Mountains, and who had never been seen in anything other than a hand-tailored suit.

He stared at me, then spat.

'You underestimated me, *pakhan*.'

I gave Yuri another peck, this time somewhere between his navel and his balls, and a little more piss stained the snow.

'Is that why you didn't bring any more brothers along? You thought I'd be easy? Or you know Tynaliev will slice you from arse to armpit if I die before I've found his daughter's killer?'

Aydaraliev reached into his pocket, and I tensed. He

brought out his mobile, and offered it to me, raising his eyebrows.

'Want to call him now and ask?'

It might have been a bluff – anything was possible with Aydaraliev – but right then, I preferred not to tell the Minister that I was no nearer solving his daughter's murder.

Aydaraliev's smile was as brutal as one of our mountain wolves as he put away his phone. Then he looked off to his right, gestured for someone unseen to join us. I was pretty sure Aydaraliev wouldn't shit in his home territory by killing a Murder Squad, but I tensed myself for what looked like an inevitable bruising.

We waited for a moment, and then he beckoned again, impatient this time.

'Can't get the staff?' I asked. If I was in for a beating, I decided to get a few cheap gibes in first.

He looked around, ever so slightly thrown off balance. For the first time in who knows how long, things weren't going according to his very precise and explicit engineering.

'Don't worry, they're out there,' he said. 'And if they're not, well, heads will roll.'

Remembering what he did to the two undercover law officers, I had no reason to disbelieve him. He laughed, the low rustle on the night air like death creeping up on tiptoe.

'So what now, Murder Squad? A tango together in the Sverdlovsky basement? Hope I shit myself with fear? Tell me if I sing like a bird, I'll live in a cage with wider bars.'

Suddenly, he was in my face, flecks of spittle landing on my cheeks.

'Listen, Comrade Cunt, all-important Comrade Prick Inspector, when I was twenty-three, they came to my village, took me away. I was just a yearling, years away from becoming top guy, *bratski krug*. I didn't have clout, no one to look out for me, no one asking for a little sweetener in their pocket in exchange for me strolling down Chui watching the pretty girls in their summer dresses.'

He paused and wiped his hand across his mouth.

'You know what happened, Comrade? When I went waltzing in your basement?'

He waved his hand in my face, and I saw the deformed fingers, missing nails, ancient scars trailing across his palm like albino slugs.

'I didn't just dance, I was taught how to play the xylophone. Not with a mallet, with a ball hammer. One knuckle, one bone, one joint at a time. And the next day, the next finger. Never knowing which one it would be. And as soon as they started to heal, all twisted and splintered, curved like an eagle's claws, well, it hap-pened all over again. Nine months before I danced the polka out of that basement. And you know what? I never sang a single note.'

The same mirthless laugh.

'Those shit-suckers, they broke my right hand in twenty-eight places. Just as well I write with my left hand, eh, Comrade? And once I got out, that wasn't all I did with it.'

He shaped his hand in a parody of a gun, jerked the finger, and then blew imaginary smoke from the tip.

'You won't find any of the uniforms who waltzed with me then walking around today. All in the line of duty, obviously. At least, that's what the grieving widows and children were told. A tough career, but at least it's a short one, right?'

He looked up at me, and grinned, nothing but evil and death in his eyes.

'What can you do to me, bitch, that the real experts couldn't manage?'

I heard the crunch of snow behind me, but I never took my eyes off Aydaraliev. My finger tugged back the trigger, up to the pulling point; if I got hit, then he'd be coming with me.

'The Inspector may not be a real expert, Maksat. But don't worry; I am.'

A voice I recognised. A voice like honey over ice cream.

Chapter 33

Saltanat walked into the SUV's twin circles of light, cradling a Kalashnikov.

Aydaraliev looked puzzled for a few seconds, then nodded in recognition.

'I suppose I've got Otkur to thank for you being here?' I asked. 'No secrets from you, eh?'

'Just as well for you, Inspector,' Saltanat said, her eyes never leaving Aydaraliev. 'Our friend here always travels with precautions.'

Aydaraliev jerked his head towards the darkness from which she'd just stepped, then raised an eyebrow. Saltanat nodded in return.

'One of them will wake up tomorrow feeling like Mount Lenina fell on him. The other?' She shrugged. 'He won't be waking up at all.'

'No loss, if they didn't have the balls to handle a whore like you.'

Saltanat's face didn't register the insult, but she took a quick step forward and rammed the muzzle of the Kalash against his hip. He grunted in pain and put one hand out against the side of the SUV to support himself, staying upright.

'You're the Uzbek bitch?' he said, and contempt dripped from every word. Contempt for her as an enemy, a cop and a woman, all three.

'Think of it as warming up, Maksat, some light snacks before we get down to the main course,' she said, and smiled without warmth.

'It's fucking freezing, let's go and discuss this in the warm, over a bottle, pretend we're friends.'

'Sure,' Saltanat agreed. 'I want you to be my guest.'

She reached down, never taking her eyes or aim off the *pakhan*, and patted Yuri's pockets, finding the car keys, tossing them to me.

'You drive,' she said, 'and I'll snuggle up in the back with my true love.'

And in case I mistook her meaning, she stroked the barrel of her gun.

'Him?' I asked, looking down at Yuri.

'You give a fuck?' she said, and motioned our captive into the car.

Now that she'd mentioned it, I didn't, but I didn't want him to freeze to death either, even if he was gang muscle. I made an anonymous call, and organised a patrol car to pick him up and deposit him in a nice warm cell. Then I slid behind the wheel, fired up the ignition and we lumbered out into the night.

We headed east along Chui Prospekt, past the power station with its veil of smoke hanging in the air. I kept one eye on the mirror, but traffic was light, and I was pretty sure we weren't being followed. Saltanat directed me to the outer edge of Bishkek, towards where a rash of new houses was springing up. The potholed road was replaced by a rutted dirt track, and we bounced and lurched from side to side. Now would have been the time for Aydaraliev to make his move, but Saltanat had her gun pressed firmly into his belly, ready to cut him in half if he tried anything.

We arrived at a large three-storey house, surrounded by a two-metre wall. Someone must have been watching for us, because the blue ornamental gates swung open as we approached, and I steered the car through the gap. The gates immediately closed behind us. I parked beside the front door, and got out of the car.

A guard immediately frisked me, while another pointed his Kalashnikov in my direction. They dragged Aydaraliev out of the car and searched him, much more thoroughly. When they were satisfied, they led the two of us inside. A wooden staircase spiralled up to the first floor and down into the cellar. Other than that, the entrance hall was completely empty. We were pushed forward into one of the rooms at the back, told to sit on the floor. For a safe house, the place seemed pretty basic. There was no heating, and our breath hung in the sour air like steam.

Saltanat walked in and leant against the wall. She'd left her Kalash in the car, but the two guards who flanked her had more than enough firepower. It struck me that the *pakhan* wasn't their only prisoner, and Saltanat had no more reason to feel friendly towards me than she did towards the old man. I remembered she had been sent to kill me, and my stomach gave a lurch.

'No point trying to remember your way here again, Inspector.'

Maybe she meant I wouldn't be leaving here again, or the place was only a temporary bolt-hole. I suspected that the *pakhan* wouldn't be leaving at all. If so, he was showing no signs of it worrying him. He was a murdering bastard, but I had to admire his balls.

He levered himself up from the floor and walked towards Saltanat. The guards tensed, and I braced myself for catching a bullet in the crossfire, but Aydaraliev held his hands apart, stood in front of her.

'I know you're a *torpedo*, you know I'm top boss, a *vor v zakonye*. Let's not pretend. I don't expect you to let me walk out of here with my cock in my hand. It's not in my nature to give out information. You put a bullet in my head, then you get it quick from my followers. Same shot, behind the ear, guaranteed.'

He paused and looked at Saltanat without blinking. His face could have been chiselled out of granite for all the emotion he showed.

'Or, you give me shit. The pliers. The hammer. The usual. I know. I've used them myself. That happens, they find my body, you get worse. Nipples scissored off. Make a movie of you getting gang-fucked front and back by my boys and your tits hacked off, send it to your family.'

He told her this with as much emotion as if he'd been explaining how to distill extra-strength home brew, then gave a gesture of resignation; all this was out of his hands now.

'Or one last option. I should be grateful, you showed me that I've let things slide, maybe got a bit complacent in my old age. Employing useless pricks like Yuri, and those two clowns who let you stroll up and take them. You let me walk, all is peace.'

He looked around the bare room, weighing up whether the beatings and killings, the drugs and the bribes, the *dacha* and the money, had all come down to this, dying against stained and peeling wallpaper in a bitterly cold house.

'You drive me back into town, we draw a line under all this nonsense. But I have to have a little taste of something for my trouble, you know that. Otherwise, someone starts whispering, "Maksat, he's getting soft, lets some pussy take him for a ride, and in his own fucking car." And I can't have that.'

'So what do you want, top boss?'

The *pakhan* gave another of his mirthless smiles, his eyes considering the odds that he might get out of here alive. He looked over in my direction.

'His head.'

Chapter 34

Saltanat looked as if she was considering the option. I wondered what my chances were of getting a Kalash off one of the guards, giving the room and everyone in it a severe chastisement, then getting out and through the gates alive. I didn't rate them. I didn't like the long silence from Saltanat either. I'm not stupid enough to think that a night passed out drunk next to someone constitutes romance, but she and I were at least supposed to be on the side of the men with the white hats.

'Not good enough, Maksat,' she said. 'It doesn't help me get what I want to know. Who's killing these people, and why? You walking out of here with your mouth shut isn't going to happen. You think your shitty little gang can get to me? I had no trouble getting to you, did I?'

She cracked her knuckles and I realised I was involved with a truly dangerous woman.

'Give me your hand.'

He stretched out his right arm, and she took his hand in hers, almost tenderly.

'You know, us Uzbeks, we're pretty straightforward

people, not like you shaman-following Kyrgyz. To us, a storm is just a storm, a mountain just a hill grown too big for its own good. But that doesn't mean we can't look into the future.'

She turned his hand over and ran her forefinger over the scars on his palm, inspecting the twisted and ripped flesh where his fingernails had once been. When she spoke, it was with sadness.

'You suffered a great deal at the hands of the Inspector's predecessors. Your hands are testament to that. But I can read more than your past here, Maksat. I can see your future, see you opening your heart to me. Because you've finally arrived at the place where we bury strangers. You've been brought here by the voices of the dead.'

She nodded at the two guards, who took the *pakhan* by his arms. His face was a mask of resigned defiance, as if he'd always known that this is how it would end. For a moment I was reminded of my mother, the same absolute refusal to submit, the identical unwillingness to accept that anything can exist greater than your own strength of will.

'I had seventy years. A lot more than you will have.'

Saltanat remained unmoved, then one corner of her mouth twitched upwards, and I realised that I'd never seen her smile.

'Perhaps you'd like to look around the house. Not

251

very interesting architecturally, and the decor leaves a little to be desired.'

She reached for a corner of the paper peeling away from the wall and tugged at it. The paper was damp and ripped with no resistance, revealing spots and blisters of mould and damp seeping through the plaster. I thought of the nails torn out of the *pakhan*'s fingers, and felt sick.

'I thought we might start with the cellar.'

We were at the top of the stairs when Aydaraliev made his move. The stairs wound down around a central post, and there was no handrail on the inner edge. So it wasn't difficult for the old man to elbow one guard off-balance, then smash his fist into the guard's shocked and open mouth. The Kalash skittered and tumbled down the stairs, and came to rest on the half-landing. The *pakhan* moved fast, hands reaching out for the barrel.

But the other guard was just as fast, and launched a savage kick at Aydaraliev's ankle. The old man grunted in pain, and lurched back towards the wall. And by then the first guard had recovered, jumping down on to the landing and sweeping his gun back into his arms.

'Surely you don't want to leave already, Maksat? The tour's only just begun.'

And then we were at the bottom of the stairs,

pushing through a doorway, along a narrow unpainted hallway, and towards the furnace room at the back. Smudges and smears of coal streaked the floor, while the walls were black with coal dust. The furnace was made from rough cast iron, with a small glass window where coals would normally glow and burn. But that night, the furnace, like the house, was cold and empty.

A coal hammer, a pair of pincers with which to feed the furnace, and a heavy spade leant against one wall. Aydaraliev's eyes widened as he spotted them. He'd been in cellars like this before, used tools in ways for which they were never meant.

It takes very little to hurt a man to the point where he talks, wants nothing more in the world than to say the words that make the agony go away. Small, innocent things: a sliver of wood, a pair of nail scissors, a needle. That's all you need to make a man weep and scream and piss himself.

Small things, like the rogue cells that feasted on Chinara's breast, devouring it like a child turned cannibal, dragging her down into the earth.

I could taste raw meat in my mouth at the thought of what was to come.

'If I'd known we were having guests, I'd have had the furnace lit, Maksat. Keep you warm; at your age you don't want a chill.'

Her use of his first name belittled him, stripped him

of the prestige and dignity he'd taken as his due for so long. She spoke patiently, as if talking to a retarded child, someone who needs everything explained from start to finish using single-syllable words.

'Saltanat, this isn't going to help.'

She turned to look at me. Out of the corner of my eye, I saw Aydaraliev set his jaw.

'No?' she said.

'Look at him. He's tough, he won't talk easily. But he's old. Probably a bad heart, vodka, a *papirosh* in his mouth for the last sixty years.'

Now there was an amused look on her face.

'Don't tell me Murder Squad's finest is worried about his civil liberties. I'm surprised you're not insisting on the first punch. Or maybe you've forgotten about the headless cops?'

'I'm just saying killing him throws more shit at the fan. How many more enemies do we need while we try to solve this?'

She raised her eyebrow, and the scar that furrowed it gleamed bone-white.

'We, Inspector? I don't recall us partnering up.'

She looked over at Aydaraliev, then back at me.

'What makes you think you're not in for more of the same? Remember, I told you I was sent to deal with you, *da*?'

I hadn't forgotten, but I had hoped she might have.

She took down the pincers from the wall, tested them by snapping the jaws together. The snick of the blades meeting was thin, unremarkable. You wouldn't hear it above a scream or a curse.

She ran her thumb along one edge.

'The trouble with these is they get blunt so easily. So it's much harder to cut through something, takes longer too.'

'Just get on with it,' Aydaraliev snarled. 'If this is meant to terrify me, try harder.'

Saltanat flashed a brilliant smile, and I could have sworn that her eyes sparkled.

'I wouldn't waste my energies, *pakhan*. Everyone in the stans knows how tough you are. So I thought we'd just chat, and I could persuade you to do the right thing.'

Aydaraliev gave a sharp bark of a laugh and spat on the floor, his phlegm quickly absorbed by coal dust.

Saltanat's smile never faltered as she reached into her pocket and took out her phone.

'I'm a long way from home, *pakhan*, you know how it is, you miss your family and friends. But these new phones, you can even get real-time video on them now.'

She held the phone in front of Aydaraliev, angling it so that we could both see the screen.

'Of course, I'm not old enough to have a grand-child. But you are.'

It was hard to see from where I stood, but I could see that an image of a young girl filled the screen. Aydaraliev said nothing, but his lips narrowed.

'Ayana, isn't it? Such a pretty name. A real charmer. Nearly twelve, she'll be a woman soon.'

The girl on the screen waved and was suddenly pulled away off-screen. Her image was replaced by that of a burly man, who grinned, revealing a row of gold teeth. He was unshaven and thuggish, and neither I nor her grandfather were in any doubt about the implied threat, or what would happen if he didn't talk.

Saltanat switched off the phone, and stood in front of the *pakhan*. He stared back at her, his eyes black with hate, but there was a tremor in one corner of his mouth. She pulled the hammer off the wall; one face was flat and blunt, the other tapered to a point.

'It's your own fault really, Maksat. I know that we could give your spine the xylophone treatment, play dentist's visit, even smash your balls into pancakes with this hammer, and you wouldn't sing to us. You'd bite your own tongue out and spit it at me first, right?'

Aydaraliev said nothing, but from the slump in his shoulders I could see Saltanat had won.

'So here's the deal. You tell us what you know – everything you know – and she'll go home tonight. And still be a virgin, to be bride-stolen by some idiot with more balls than sense. Otherwise,' and she pounded one fist on another, the Russian gesture for fucking, 'well, my guys have cameras, and all the other equipment to make a very special film, the sort that's very popular on the internet. Nipples scissored off, tits hacked off, I believe you said. They're small of course, her still being just a girl, but they'll be sensitive enough. What would your gang say about that? Must be hard to owe allegiance to a *pakhan* who can't protect his own family.'

Aydaraliev nodded.

I felt vomit rise in my gut and burn my throat, imagining a *devochka* screaming, begging, her parents being held down and forced to watch as their world was stripped bare of everything decent and innocent. I wondered if Saltanat was human, or merely a psychopath. If she was a *torpedo* who kills to order, you'd have to be on her hit list, money in the bank. If she was a psycho, then no one would be safe until she'd been put down without mercy.

Aydaraliev looked round at us, stopping at me.

'What do you think of this, Inspector? This is how you do your business? This makes you better than me? Maybe even worse?'

'I don't have any more to say than you do,' I answered, knowing that it was a cheap answer; weak, the way that I seemed to be around Saltanat. I stumbled over my words, shut my mouth. I could have made an argument

TOM CALLAGHAN

for this being the quickest way to solve the case. But silence is one, or both, of two things: consent and the desire to survive.

'Let's go back upstairs,' Aydaraliev said, holding his hands wide. 'If I'm going to talk, let's not do it in a fucking coal cellar. If you're going to plant lead in my skull, treat me like a man.'

Chapter 35

Saltanat led us up to the ground floor, into a room at the back of the house, bare as the others, with only three kitchen chairs for furniture. She motioned for the two of us to sit down, while the guards watched from the door.

'It's not a lot to ask for, *pakhan*,' she said, and I noticed that she'd switched back to the honorific. 'We want to sort all this trouble out and end it. It's bad for my business, and it has to be worse for yours. In exchange? You get to foot the bill for your grand-daughter's wedding feast a few years from now.'

She produced her cigarettes, offered the pack around, then lit up. Her smile was encouraging, her eyes trusting.

'So tell me. Who? And, more importantly, why?'

Aydaraliev hesitated. He'd spent his entire life living by *vorovskoe blago*, the thieves' code, and talking about Circle of Brothers business was a major taboo for him. Saltanat remained silent: she knew that this was the point where he would either break and talk or defy her to do her worst.

'I can't tell you why,' he finally said, 'and I can't tell you very much about who. Wait —' and he held his hand up as Saltanat frowned. 'I'll tell you what I can. And after that, I walk.'

He lit one of her cigarettes, inhaled deeply.

'You know I'm one of The Twenty,' he said, 'one of the Circle of Brothers. That's no secret; every cop between here and Moscow knows that. I'm inner circle, but not the Inner Circle. And when they ask me to do something, I tell my boys and it gets done.'

'Like a servant?' Saltanat asked, and there was a mocking tone in her voice.

Aydaraliev frowned, but decided to ignore it.

'I give my advice to the Inner Circle, they appreciate my knowledge, act on my suggestions. And we all make money. But sometimes, they want a particular course of action following, without the need for explanation. And that's how it was in this case.'

Saltanat leant forward, her eyes never leaving the old man. Maybe I was being cynical, but I suspected we were about to get a bigger snow-job than Bishkek gets all winter.

'You were ordered to kill Yekaterina Tynalieva?'

'No one orders me to do anything,' the old man snarled. 'We're a brotherhood, we help each other, one hand washes the other. Say my brother in Tashkent or Almaty needs a favour doing here in Kyrgyzstan. He asks me, respectfully, and if I can, I help him. Then, if I need something – or someone – taken care of in their country, well, that's what brothers are for.'

'So you killed Yekaterina?'

The *pakhan* shrugged.

'I was also asked to supply a dead child, one unborn, a boy. I didn't ask why, and no one volunteered to tell me.'

His matter-of-fact tone sickened me. He knew that I'd seen the carnage under the trees, the humiliation and mutilation, the frozen stare searching for stars between the trees. For a moment I wondered if it was Aydaraliev who had stolen my photo of Chinara, and I pictured myself squeezing that chicken neck until his eyes burst and his head rolled loose upon a snapped spine. I dug my nails into my palms, reminded myself that the most effective interrogations are when you only have to keep quiet to hear the whole story. But sometimes, you have to speak out.

'That would be from the woman murdered over by Karakol? Umida Boronova? Nineteen years old? Pregnant, alone, in the dark, terrified? You didn't even know her name, did you? Just another piece of meat to you, thrown to the wolves you pretend are your friends. But really, you're shit scared of them, aren't you? Just another fucking bully saying that the big boys did it and then ran away.'

Saltanat flashed me a warning glance, but I was sick of pretending that we were in an ordinary interrogation. Right then, I wanted him to move, stand up, say something, anything that would allow me to beat him to death with my naked hands.

Aydaraliev stared at me.

'I've butchered men who've spoken to me with more respect than that. But,' and he gestured towards the two guards, 'it's easy to be brave when someone else can pull the trigger for you.'

'I'd put one between your eyes if I thought I'd hit anything human in there, not just a lump of tissue floating in shit.'

'We'll discuss this another time, Inspector,' he said, his voice calm and emotionless, 'when things are a little more evenly balanced.'

I spat, with all the contempt I could show. I thought of all the dead bodies that Aydaraliev had put into the ground, of the agonies of withdrawal from the drugs he'd smuggled, young women he'd pimped dying of AIDS because he refused to let them use condoms with their customers. I put my face close to his, staring into his eyes.

'Think of your granddaughter when they rip up her insides, screaming for her grandfather to come and rescue her. Begging them to stop, no, please, don't, please. And the knife, moonlight shining off the blade, cold metal stinging against her skin, trimming and slicing away. Because that's what you had done to a nineteen-year-old woman carrying her first child.'

'Inspector,' Saltanat said, 'your outrage isn't getting us anywhere. And I still want to know what's behind all this.'

Aydaraliev shrugged, and dropped his cigarette to the floor, grinding it out with his shoe.

'I told you, I didn't ask, they didn't tell.'

He smiled, and I wanted to take a hammer to his face.

'Is this something to do with Chinese medicine? Smuggling? Supplying raw materials?' Saltanat asked, and I knew she was thinking about the stories of vitamin pills coming over the Tien Shan Mountains, the ones that contained ground-up human foetuses.

Aydaraliev laughed.

'You think the Chinese don't have enough dead babies on their hands? With their one-child policy? They scrape out enough mistakes to fill a thousand pharmacies. No, it was done to create fear. Uzbeks fearing Kyrgyz. Kyrgyz fearing Uighurs. Uighurs fearing Chinese. A circle of mistrust and hatred, you could call it.'

'What could you hope to achieve?' Saltanat asked, and there was genuine disgust in her voice.

'What did I achieve? I got paid, that's what I achieved,'

the old man said. 'Don't ask me what anyone else was hoping for. You want answers to that, talk to them.'

'So you murdered two women on behalf of the Circle of Brothers?'

He nodded.

'The other two, I didn't order their deaths, someone else decided to perform a clean-up.'

I wondered for a moment who he meant, then remembered Shairkul and Gulbara, butchered in their homes, women barely more than girls, who'd not known much else than abuse in their lives, hoping for very little and receiving even less. Shairkul, shivering in the cold outside the Kulturny; I felt a wave of shame at having threatened her. And Gulbara, a nobody who found a body, stole a handbag and ended up with her body hacked in half. I closed my eyes, and wondered if this would ever end.

'They were working for you?' I asked.

'Every pussy you can buy in Bishkek puts a few *som* in my pocket,' he answered, 'it's the way the world turns. Men pay money to fuck, women fuck to get money. But their deaths were not at my hands.'

I pushed the two prostitutes to the back of my mind, a case to solve in the future.

'I understand that you killed Umida to . . . harvest her. But Yekaterina? She wasn't pregnant. And you must have known who she was, the shit storm it would bring down upon your head.'

'She was the one that the contract was taken out on,' Aydaraliev explained. 'The other girl, well, it could have been anyone in the same condition, that didn't matter.'

'How much was the contract worth?' Saltanat asked.

'Two hundred fifty thousand US.'

Even to a *pakhan* like Aydaraliev, it wasn't small change.

'And now, unless there's anything else, you can drive me back to the Kulturny.'

Saltanat considered for a few seconds, then nodded.

'If there's anything you haven't told us, and I find out about it, then we'll be having another little chat. With your granddaughter's head listening in.'

'Listen. I'm not a sadist. I don't take any pleasure in having anyone extinguished. It's business, understand? My men were under strict instructions: a swift kill, painless as possible. The rest, the cutting and so on, well, the dead don't feel what's done to them. I was asked to cause terror and confusion. Which I did. And that's all I can tell you.'

Aydaraliev smiled; he knew he'd played his Get Out of Jail card.

Saltanat nodded at the guards, and they started to

lead the old man out of the room. At the door, he paused and turned.

'Tell me, Inspector, have you ever taken a woman? I mean, really taken her?'

My face must have reflected my disgust, but he carried on.

'I don't mean rape her,' he said, 'that's for low life. But to pound into a woman, give it to her like she's never had it before, over and over, however you want it, until you've broken her spirit, until you just have to snap your fingers and she'll roll over and face the pillow and present herself. The way you tame a dog, or a horse. By breaking the core inside of them to your will. Until they surrender themselves because there's nothing left of them that isn't subservient to you.'

He raised an eyebrow.

'Perhaps that's how it was with . . . what was your wife's name? Chinara?'

'No.'

My answer was flat, deliberately emotionless, but I wanted to kick the brains out of the back of his head. I wanted to see the walls spattered with the filth that lay between his ears, and then I'd stamp on his foul carcass until I'd shattered every bone in that wrinkled old flesh, ripped every sinew apart.

'Well, if you ever took a woman like that, you'd know

what power feels like. Like the best orgasm you could ever have. But better than sex, controlling destiny, the little people, all under your sway.'

I said nothing.

'You've held a gun on a man, Inspector, decided if his life is worth the squeeze of a trigger or not. You've sent men to hell with the twitch of a muscle. Maybe that's how you see power, how you achieve it. Are we so very different?'

I remained silent. The trouble is, I know the feeling of invulnerability that a gun gives, knowing you can make people do what you want simply by being the one with the power to kill. Some detectives never fire their weapon in their entire careers; others, like me, only shoot when they have to. But there are one or two just waiting for the wrong move to unholster and start blasting. They're the ones you don't want minding your back.

'The more power you have, and then you lose it, the more you'll do to restore it, the more you need terror and confusion.'

Another word and I'd slaughter him with my hands, fuck the consequences.

'I hope we don't meet again, *devochka*, for your sake,' he said to Saltanat, and then turned his gaze on me.

It was like staring into the heavy-lidded eyes of a crocodile, unblinking, hungry and totally amoral.

'And you, Inspector? That I look forward to.'

And with that, he adjusted the hang of his jacket, straightened his shoulders, and walked out of the door, his sneer announcing that, once again, he'd won.

Chapter 36

We sat without speaking until the front door closed. Silence hung over us like an axe poised to descend.

'You know he won't rest until he comes after you?' I said. 'And if he doesn't manage to find you, then the Circle in Tashkent will track you down.'

'I don't think so,' Saltanat replied.

'He's going to take you threatening his family and just shrug it off?'

'Of course not. I know he's not a man to leave a threat or an insult unavenged. He'd have cut my head off right now, if he'd had the chance.'

'So why won't he set his team on you?'

Saltanat consulted her watch.

'Because in about twenty minutes, he'll be lying face down in a snowdrift outside the Kulturny. Two taps, one in the back of the head to show he was executed, one in the mouth to say he'd talked.'

She raised an eyebrow, the scar curled like a question mark.

'No one saw me take him, no one knows I had anything to do with his disappearance.' She pointed an elegant finger. 'But his gang will remember he had a meeting this evening. At the specific demand of a Bishkek Murder Squad inspector. Think there'll be any prizes for guessing who they'll come looking for?'

She was right; a bullet or a blade or a simple hit and run would be just a matter of time. But there's one thing she didn't know. I really didn't care. I stared at the bare room, the peeling wallpaper, the stained chairs, and I couldn't imagine a more accurate portrait of my life.

Chinara wasn't the only one who died that day; I just didn't stop walking. The weight of death is too great a burden. It had only taken the deaths of five more women for me to discover that.

Yekaterina, Umida, Shairkul, Gulbara, Marina; they were all watching me, just outside my vision, waiting, wondering if I would avenge them. We have an obligation to the dead, a chance at redemption, the price for continuing to live. Six bullets in the Yarygin, one to avenge each of them, and one to spare. And I knew who it was for.

Saltanat surprised me by placing her hand over mine, her touch shockingly warm in the chill of that desolate room.

'I owe you an apology, Inspector,' she said, and her voice was, for the first time, hesitant. 'You understand that I couldn't know whose side you were on. Everyone can be turned, you know that. For revenge, fear, greed. And for love.'

'It's a corrupt world,' I agreed. 'Why should I be any different?'

'I sent Tyulev to find out what you knew, to send you in the wrong direction if I thought you were getting too close to us. I told Lubashov to keep an eye on things. I shouldn't have relied on a fuckhead like that. He saw Tyulev all secretive and confidential with you, jumped to conclusions, started shooting.'

One mystery solved; I'd thought that I'd been set up by Yekaterina's murderer, that it might even have been Lubashov, acting under Tyulev's orders. That still didn't make me feel any better about killing him.

'That's not all,' Saltanat added. 'The bullet left in your coat; a warning to dump the case and leave it to us. We didn't know where you stood in all this, what you'd been ordered to do.'

I felt a quick wave of anger smash down on me, as if a snow-laden branch had suddenly spilt its burden.

'And my wife's photo?'

Saltanat winced at the venom in my voice.

'Safe. Look on the top of your fridge when you get home. It never even left your apartment. I'm not that much of a bitch. But I had to warn you off, to be sure.'

I reached for my phone, and she took hold of my hand.

'Who are you calling?'

I smiled, but she could see that it didn't reach my eyes.

'I'm Murder Squad, remember? If your boys haven't already killed him, it's my job to stop them. Face down? If he's already dead, I want him facing Usupov on the slab.'

'He killed a lot of people, Inspector, some of them your own. Isn't Bishkek a better place with him gone?'

'I'm not an executioner, Saltanat. It's not for me to say whether he dies or not.'

'I don't think the two dead women he had butchered would think that way,' she replied, pulling her hand away.

Silence flooded the room again.

'Let's get out of here,' she said, getting up and heading for the door.

'How exactly? With Aydaraliev in the car, getting ready for his trip to the morgue?'

She laughed.

'What sort of safe house would this be, if there wasn't more than one escape route? We'll go to your apartment.'

As she reached the door, she turned.

'You can make sure your wife's photograph is still there.'

Chapter 37

From a decrepit shed behind the safe house, Saltanat hauled out an elderly Ural motorcycle that looked like a relic of the Great Patriotic War, and probably hadn't been used since then. Maybe not the quickest getaway vehicle, but I supposed the Uzbek Security Service had as little money as its Kyrgyz equivalent.

She handed me a pair of gauntlets and a pair of goggles, so I pulled my *ushanka* down over my ears and almost broke my foot trying to kick-start the bike. Eventually, the engine grumbled into life, and I ferried the two of us back into Bishkek, the Ural bucking and twisting as we rode over potholed and broken roads.

By the time we reached my apartment, I felt as if I'd been frozen deep into the heart of an iceberg. With no sensation in my fingertips, I fumbled with the key until Saltanat took pity on me and opened the door. A welcome blast of warm air hit me, thanks to the city's central pipes.

'Drink?' I asked, heading for the window sill, wondering if Kursan had finished all my vodka. Saltanat walked into the kitchen, returning a moment later with

Chinara's photograph. I replaced it, looked at Chinara's hair caught in the wind, tried to remember the moment.

When you're the one left behind, memories splinter into fragments, until the most real thing about your dead wife becomes the pictures you keep on the shelf, the scent of her perfume fading in an empty drawer.

I took the Makarov bullet and held it up between thumb and forefinger for Saltanat to see.

'The strong medicine you promised me. Still got my name on it?' I asked.

Saltanat had the grace to look ashamed. She shook her head and, for an instant, her beauty lit up the room. Then she caught the bullet I tossed to her, and she became the ice lady again.

'Bathroom,' Saltanat said, pushing me towards the tub. 'A hot bath, thaw out, and then we work out our next step.'

I was reassured by the 'we'; I hoped it meant that she didn't plan to kill me any time soon. But remembering how calmly she'd ended Illya's career, I waited until she left the room before taking my Yarygin from its hiding place and tucking it underneath a towel by the side of the bath.

Just in case.

Steam swelled and billowed up to the ceiling as I lowered myself into the tub, gritting my teeth against the heat. I could barely see across to the door, so I hoped that Saltanat didn't decide to change her mind.

Lying there, the heat seeping back into my bones, I thought back to what the *pakhan* had said.

'*I was asked to cause terror and confusion. Which I did.*'

I felt tired beyond exhaustion; all I wanted to do was sleep, with no dreams, none of the recent dead opening their eyes and beckoning to me.

Terror and confusion.

The key to all this. But a key I was incapable of turning.

So I started on the long slide into sleep, deep and safe in the embrace of the water.

I was more than half asleep when the bathroom door opened, and I felt a hand on my chest. For a second, I thought it was Chinara, come to tell me it was time to go to work. But then, as the hand pressed down harder and was joined by another, I realised where I was.

Saltanat's weight bore down on me as I struggled to sit up. Unable to move, my arms thrashing by my sides, I started to panic. But I was held fast.

'Relax,' Saltanat murmured, and I felt her hands move down from my chest and over my stomach.

I tried to sit up, water spraying everywhere, and it was only then I discovered she was as naked as I was.

Her hands moved lower down, taking hold of me.

'Don't tell me you didn't think of this when we were back in Osh,' she said. 'That you didn't want me to do this.'

And then she leant forward, and kissed me, and I was lost, as surely as if I was in a dark and lonely forest with no path to follow and no guide to lead me.

Later, after we'd stumbled to the bed, her never letting go of me, dragging me on top of her, we lay with arms and legs as entangled as the sheets, and I started to drift off into fitful sleep. A sense of guilt washed over me; the last time I'd slept with a woman in this bed was with Chinara, the night before her final trip to the hospital. I'd held her close, both of us unwilling to admit this was the end, knowing it all the same. But I'd still gone to bed with Saltanat, willingly, eagerly. Perhaps that's another part of surviving; seeking warmth and comfort, in the arms of a stranger, even an enemy.

I checked my phone. As I'd expected, a whole string of missed calls beckoned me, all but one from the Chief. I anticipated him ripping into me, screaming and wanting to know why the fuck I was still messing around on the Tynalieva case, one sorted out to everyone's complete satisfaction with the corpses of Tyulev and Lubashov.

Pointless to try to explain that they hadn't done it. Even if I told him that the Circle of Brothers had put out a contract on her, he'd only tell me that they hired the dead men to carry it out. And if I was honest, I didn't know how to move the case forward.

Or if I'd see Saltanat again.

Or, more probably, if she'd want to see me.

I unravelled myself from the sheet and her legs, rolled over, facing away from her. The dull ache in my back reminded me that I hadn't done this for a while. And then everything flowed into sleep and the comfort of a woman's body beside me.

When I woke up, I was alone, the radio playing softly in the other room. That was where I found Saltanat, a towel wrapped around herself, inspecting the spines of half a dozen well-thumbed books.

'I didn't think of you as a poetry lover, Inspector.'

'Not me, my wife. You know she's a . . . was a teacher. Physics. She always said that there were laws science couldn't explain, but poetry could.'

'She had good taste, your wife. In poets, I mean. Blok, Pasternak, Akhmatova, Esenin.'

The names brought back memories, of Chinara sitting by the window, in the last of the daylight, reciting the odd line or two, almost chanting, words she believed gave light and meaning to the darkness.

'I'm not much of a reader. I didn't understand most of it, even when she explained it to me.'

What I didn't add was that Chinara believed poems

explained the world, but I sometimes wondered whether only bullets could change it.

Saltanat riffled through one of the books, as if hunting a quotation, something to suit the moment.

'My husband read all these. He taught, as well. But literature; even had a few poems published.'

I felt awkward. A third person had entered the room unobserved, waiting to be introduced.

'Don't look so worried. I'm not married any more. Perhaps I read the wrong poets. The only things his new wife recites are dress sizes and bank statements.'

To move the conversation to safer, shallower waters, I showed her my phone.

'The Chief. I'm summoned. Probably assigned to traffic.'

Her smile made me want her all over again.

'Maybe he wants you to investigate the mysterious death of a leading underworld figure?' she said.

'A Member of Parliament's been murdered?' I asked.

It's common knowledge that half of our elected officials are busy stealing from anyone with two *som* in their pocket, and sometimes the victims take it personally.

'If he asks you to investigate Aydaraliev's death? Conscience or cock?' Unable to reach the former, she stretched out her hand and gave the latter a squeeze.

'Underworld killings are notoriously difficult to

solve,' I said, considering my words carefully. 'And in the absence of any witnesses, or forensic evidence, almost impossible to get a conviction. Someone may have dropped a hint, given an order, but that's not proof. And the public don't like us wasting our time on murders that take bad guys off the streets.'

'I thought you might say that,' she said, and sat back in her chair.

I pulled on my trousers, and fastened my Yarygin to my belt.

'Stay here if you want. Just pull the door shut behind you when you leave,' I said, adding, 'if you want to leave.'

'I look that domesticated? Expecting to come home to an immaculate apartment and stew on the stove? Been there, got the divorce papers, didn't get the apartment.'

I paused, waiting for her to tell me more, then ducked as she hurled a shoe in my direction. I was still grinning as I pulled the front door shut and clattered down the stairs.

It was one of those rare and stunning mornings we often get in the depths of winter, where the sky looks glazed, and the mountains to the north and south of the city gleam with fresh snowfalls. The peaks looked close enough to touch, empty and forbidding, with the farmers' flocks brought down, away from the wolves that descend from the high plain in search of food. That's when I would always remind myself that my country, for all its faults, is one of the most beautiful in the world.

It was early and the roads were still pristine, no tyre tracks scarring the snow. Nothing could look more peaceful. But in Kyrgyzstan, most of the wolves walk on two legs. And further up the street, the remnants of the crime-scene tapes spread around Yekaterina Tynalieva's body still fluttered and twitched in the wind travelling down from the north.

Chapter 38

Sverdlovsky Station hadn't changed in the time I'd been away. A half-asleep uniform still lurked outside the door, Kalash drooping over one arm while he gripped a *papirosh* in the style of soldiers and policemen everywhere, glowing tip concealed by his palm. As I walked past, he glanced away, and I suspected the hot word had gone round the station that I was no longer the Chief's golden boy.

I knocked on the Chief's door and waited for him to bellow. But instead, the door was flung open, and Illya Sergeyevich jerked a thumb over his shoulder. I walked in, and saw he already had a guest, one considerably more important than me.

'Good morning, Minister,' I said, with the humble tone appropriate in front of someone who could ship me off to some shithole at the scrawl of a pen.

Mikhail Tynaliev turned round, stared at me, found my face in his mental card index.

'I hear you've been busy, Inspector,' he said, and gestured at the chair next to him. I was sure the Chief would have preferred me standing ramrod straight while he shoved a two-metre stick up my arse, but what Ministers of State Security want, they usually get. So I sat, got the Chief's 'pay for it later' glare.

In deference to the Minister's visit, there was no sign of the customary bottle, but I'd no doubt there was one quietly hidden away, not that I was likely to be offered anything wet other than blood from a smack in the mouth.

The two men stared at me, both looking as if they intended pissing on me from a great height.

'The Chief tells me you're not convinced that the case of my daughter's murder has been solved.'

I could feel the Chief's eyes boring into me, but I really didn't have any option but to answer the Minister. The Chief could have me shipped out to the border, but I could always resign and become one of the little people again. With Tynaliev, I could simply disappear into a cell somewhere.

'I greatly value the Chief's opinion,' I said, cautious to the point of stupidity, 'but there have been too many crimes with a similar pattern over too great a set of distances, including in Tashkent, for it to be solely the work of Tyulev and Lubashov.'

The Chief scowled, and I did my best to appease him.

'Even if the men I shot were responsible for the murder of your daughter, there is a motive behind it that goes much higher than two small-time *razboiniki* high on something and looking for kicks.'

The Minister dismissed my words with a gesture.

'I told you to bring me Yekaterina's killers. Alive. Instead, you gun down two men who may or may not be responsible. Now you tell me, they possibly didn't do it. And even if they did, they were acting under orders.'

Technically, I hadn't killed Vasily, but it didn't seem a good idea to mention it. Tynaliev stood up, and again I sensed his power, his control over everyone who crossed his path.

'But you still can't tell me who did it?'

I decided it was time to placate the Chief and give up some of what I knew.

'I have an informant, someone high up in the Circle of Brothers here in Bishkek. He says some criminal – and he was very careful not to tell me who – got asked to carry out a few simple requests. Of course, he means ordered to, or face the consequences for disobeying the Inner Circle.'

I turned to Tynaliev.

'I very much regret, Minister, that your daughter was targeted by these people. Why, I don't yet know. But he said the aim of the people who paid him was to spread terror and confusion. His exact words –'

The Chief held his hand up to stop me.

'This mystery informant of yours; does he have a name?'

'Chief, this station has more leaks in it than the Naryn Reservoir. I wouldn't even file his name on a piece of paper, and expect him to be breathing by the end of the day. There's always someone with their palm face up, looking for a few *som* to pay for his beer.'

Reminding the Chief of the force's corruption didn't divert him from the question.

'You know Maksat Aydaraliev?'

'The name, of course,' I answered, all too certain where this was taking me.

'More than just the name?' the Minister asked.

'I interviewed him a couple of times, when we had that little gang war a couple of years ago. Nothing stuck, of course. It's been a long time since he got blood and flesh trapped under his fingernails – if he still had any, that is.'

'You think you should interview him, see what he can cough up, maybe with a little persuasion?'

If anyone could have got answers out of Aydaraliev in his current condition, they'd be the smartest cop in history. But I pretended to think about my reply.

'Chief, he had his hand smashed and his fingernails pliered out two floors below where we're sitting now, and he didn't sing then. I shouldn't think he's mellowed with the years.'

The Chief exchanged glances with Tynaliev, the sort of look that confirmed something they'd discussed earlier.

'You're right, he won't be spilling his guts to you. Maybe his brains, what with having two bullets in his head.'

I did my best to look startled, then shrugged, trying not to let anything show in my face.

'He was the old-school top boss. He made a lot of enemies. Or maybe his own people, impatient for the throne and a bigger slice. If you're satisfied that we're getting nowhere with the other murders, you're giving me his case?'

'I wouldn't waste an hour of a rookie's time on that piece of shit,' the Chief said, then gave me the hard stare. 'Don't you want to know how he was killed?'

'You said, Chief, two in the head. Execution-style, I guess.'

'You don't want to know where?'

I held my hands wide.

'If I'm not handling the case, why should I care where he was dumped?'

The Chief's eyes flashed; I'd blundered.

'Who said he was dumped?'

'The big guys have security wherever they go. His gang must have been taken out, then a *torpedo* takes Aydaraliev somewhere quiet, does him, dumps him.'

285

The Chief considered this, nodded, apparently satisfied.

'He was found outside the Kulturny about five this morning. The funny thing is, someone rang in a call earlier, about one of Aydaraliev's muscle boys, given a kicking outside that shithole. And while the uniforms were loading him into the patrol car, they found one of his pals nearby, with his neck broken.'

I did my best to look unconcerned.

'So Aydaraliev gets done outside the Kulturny, or somewhere else, makes fuck-all difference. His successor will have already called a conference to slice up his inheritance. Maybe a couple of guys will join him on Usupov's slab, then it all calms down. It always does.'

Impatient, Tynaliev turned to the Chief and jabbed a stubby finger at him.

'This officer believes my daughter's death needs further investigation, but you say the case is closed, right?'

The Chief was on the ropes, but he was too skilled a fighter not to defend himself.

'It's the Department's considered belief that the two men killed outside Fatboys were about to murder the Inspector here, to end his investigation. The probability is they were hired to commit her murder, or other murders, with no evidence, no witnesses, nothing to suggest otherwise.'

The Chief placed his hand on the Minister's shoulder, adopted a sorrowful expression.

'You should comfort your wife, mourn your daughter, remember her in all her beauty. Nothing can bring her back, but your memories are always yours.'

He'd said the same anodyne rubbish to me when I returned from the mountains after burying Chinara, and it sounded just as insincere then. Tynaliev was no more taken in by it than I had been.

'Thank you for your advice, Chief,' he said, pulling on his overcoat, turning to me. 'Inspector, walk with me to my car?'

'Naturally,' I said, happy to get out of the Chief's presence.

We walked along the gloomy corridors, down the bare concrete steps, saying nothing. Trudging through the slush in the yard towards his official car, the Minister suddenly stopped.

'Forget what that fat buffoon says. Last time, I told you what you have to do. Nothing's changed.'

He considered his words for a moment, beckoned me closer. I looked up at the Chief's window, but there was no sign we were being watched.

'Do this for me. Off-duty. No one to know you're still on the case except me. Understood?'

I nodded, helpless in the political crossfire.

'You'll find my support very useful in your career,

Inspector,' he said, his narrow-lipped smile never even attempting to reach his eyes. 'And if you fail, well, I'm sure there's a lot more to Aydaraliev's unfortunate demise than you're telling me. And no one is ever above the law. Not as far as I'm concerned, anyway.'

His threat lingered in the air as he clambered into the back of his car. As he pulled away, his driver splashed my boots with muddy half-melted snow and dirt.

Chapter 39

Back at my apartment, there was no sign of Saltanat, no note, nothing to show she'd ever been there, apart from rumpled sheets, a damp towel on the bathroom floor, a scattering of poetry books on the table. As I picked up the towel, I realised I didn't have her number. I wasn't sure if I wanted it. I didn't even know if Saltanat was her real name. I wondered what Chinara would have made of it; the evening before her final trip to the hospital, she'd talked about me finding someone else, but I didn't imagine she had someone like Saltanat in mind.

I opened one of the poetry books, *Collected Poems* by Osip Mandelstam, and read the inscription I'd written there what felt like a million years ago.

> To my beloved Chinara, whose love is all the poetry I'll ever need. Your loving Akyl.

I flipped through the pages, as if they held the solution to the murders, to my confusion, to my life. But the words blurred before my eyes, refusing to give up their understanding of the world. I gathered the books together and replaced them on the shelf, a kind of order whose secrets I couldn't unlock.

'*Terror and confusion, terror and confusion.*'

The *pakhan*'s words kept going through my head, like an awkward knot refusing to come untied. The phrase clung inside my mind, a quotation from somewhere in my past, just out of reach. I decided to think about something else, hoping my subconscious would sneak up on the problem and solve the mystery while my back was turned.

My mobile rang, a number I didn't recognise. Wondering if it might be Saltanat, perhaps even hoping it was, I answered it.

The voice on the other end was male, abrupt, direct. Russian.

'Barabanov here.'

The Colonel from the airbase. What shit was the Kremlin in its wisdom throwing my way?

'Colonel? *Privyet.* What can I do for you?'

'A matter of protocol, Inspector.'

When I didn't answer, he continued, clipped, emotionless. As if discussing missing supplies rather than the murder of the mother of his unborn child.

'The incident involving Nurse Gurchenko has been resolved. The culprit was arrested earlier today, no other further suspects are being sought at this time.'

'Really, Colonel? I have to congratulate you. When will it be possible for me to interview your suspect?'

The Colonel paused, and I knew he was about to lie to me.

'I regret to say that will not be possible. En route to further questioning in Moscow, the suspect managed to disarm one of his guards and was shot dead trying to escape.'

I felt the anger rising, but I kept my voice calm.

'Why was your "suspect" being taken to Moscow? As you know, I am investigating a series of brutal murders across Kyrgyzstan, murders that share several of the same characteristics. It's very doubtful that the Minister for State Security would grant you permission to extradite a Kyrgyz citizen without my having interviewed him first.'

The Colonel's tone was back to being flat and unemotional.

'My apologies, Inspector, I should have made myself clear. The man my military police arrested was a serving Russian officer here on the base. Our *zampolit*, to be precise.'

If there's one thing I know about the Russian Armed Forces, it's that the political commissars they select to spy on their comrades and work up appropriate revolutionary fervour are some of the most unemotional thugs you'd find anywhere. A *zampolit* is about as likely to commit a sex murder as Lenin is to get up from his glass case and run naked around Red Square.

This time, I didn't bother to hide the incredulity in my voice.

'A crime of passion, I suppose, Colonel? A jealous lover driven insane by the thought of his beloved carrying another man's child? Or perhaps enraged by being rejected in favour of a better catch?'

Barabanov didn't rise to the bait.

'I'm sure that with one of those motives you've hit the nail upon the head, Inspector. A pity we will never know the exact reason behind this terrible tragedy.'

I wanted to ask more, but the high-pitched tone told me he'd broken the connection.

'Cheers,' I muttered, wondering if a single word of what I'd just heard bore any passing resemblance to the truth.

I put the kettle on for *chai*, and while the water started to boil I debated just what truth was mixed in with Barabanov's lies. No way of knowing if the 'suspect' had butchered Marina Gurchenko, if he was dead. If he ever even existed. I stirred a spoonful of plum jam into my tea, and thought back to the sight of her, splayed out like a deer gutted during hunting season. It would have taken tremendous strength, and time, to complete such butchery, and all the political officers I'd ever encountered had been weasel-faced weaklings, light flashing off rimless glasses to hide the deceit in their eyes.

The tea was hot and sweet, and I was grateful for the kick it gave. I stared at my phone and wondered if Saltanat would call me, but it remained obstinately silent.

I decided to forget about Marina Gurchenko. Had her death been a personal matter, or part of the bigger picture? I knew that was one murder I would never solve. And if I ever tracked down her killer, it would probably be for something else, and I wouldn't even realise I'd caught him. The Kremlin keeps its secrets locked away in basements that make Sverdlovsky look like a luxury sanatorium on the north shore of Lake Issyk-Kul.

As I sipped my tea, I made connections. Terror and confusion was the instruction given by the Circle of Brothers. But that went against every rule they normally followed.

Vorovskoe blago, the thieves' code, is all about maximising profits without drawing unnecessary attention to yourself, working in the shadows, preying on the weak and paying off the powerful. If you need to make a statement, you make it with a Makarov; you don't slaughter and mutilate pregnant women.

So this wasn't an ordinary criminal enterprise. There had to be big money involved, enough to jeopardise the international heroin trade, the corrupt taxation kickbacks, the bribes, even the regular daily extortion that feeds the Circle.

When one hand is washing the other, it takes an awful lot of cash to make you throw the towel away.

My thoughts were disturbed by a knock on the door.

When I opened it, Saltanat was standing there, frowning, a look on her face I didn't recognise. I stepped out on to the landing and opened my mouth, but before I could speak, a fist the size of a small horse slammed into the side of my head.

The world stopped and twisted with a dazzling firework display that blinded me to everything, and then I was falling into blackness as deep and dark as Chinara's grave.

Chapter 40

I didn't know how long I'd been out when eventually I resurfaced, but I was no longer in my apartment. For the second time in less than twenty-four hours, I was in an unheated empty building, in another dismal basement, but this time I was chained by my ankle to the wall, both my hands cuffed to a table. No sign of Saltanat, but three stocky men standing in front of me made up for her absence.

The thug who seemed to be the leader of this mini gang leant forward and pinched my cheek, with just enough force to show he could do a lot worse if he decided to.

'Well, sweetheart, good to have you back. I was afraid Azad here might have hit you a little too hard. Before we got some answers out of you. And then where would we be, Inspector?'

He grinned, revealing an uneven row of gold teeth. Underneath his leather jacket, I could see the bulge of a shoulder holster, and I didn't think it was for carrying a water bottle.

'On the run, I would think?'

All three men laughed as if I'd told the planet's funniest joke. Leather Jacket patted my cheek, not too gently.

'You think your colleagues give a fuck about a pussy like you? Mister Cleanest Arse on the Planet? Every greased palm who's found his throat dry and his pocket light at the end of the month, thanks to a self-righteous cop like you? Every uniform who enjoys a little taste of the girls behind Panfilov Park but hasn't had a free mouth? There'll be a dozen of them claiming credit when your body turns up; not for solving the crime but for personally giving you the big headache.'

He cocked his fingers, aimed at my head and then spat in my face to emphasise his contempt for police, honest and bent alike. I ignored the thick phlegm trickling down my face, and flexed my shoulders to ease out some of the stiffness. The chain tugged at my leg like a demanding child.

'So that's your big plan? Kill a Murder Squad? That's really going to please whichever boss has the misfortune to lead a troupe of clowns like you. You'll bring down heat on yourselves like you can't imagine.'

'Heat you won't know anything about, once Syrgak has finished with you. You wouldn't think to look at him that he'd had three years' medical training, would you? Very talented with a scalpel. But then you saw some of his handiwork, didn't you? A master craftsman; he'll keep you in agony for hours.'

The trio gave that peculiar mirthless cackle low-grade thugs use to terrify the cell bitches on to their knees when they're behind bars. It wasn't too hard for me to appear unimpressed.

'Heat you won't know anything about,' he repeated, nudging his comrades, who dutifully responded as if they'd never heard anything so witty in their lives.

'Circle of Brothers? Circle of Idiots, more like,' I said, with a confidence I was far from feeling.

'So you know who we are?'

'Well, I know who your boss's bosses are,' I answered, 'and even they aren't big enough to be Circle. As for who you work for, well, you don't any more, do you? Unless the evil old lizard's giving orders from the slab.'

The blow hurled me back against the wall, where my feet got all tangled up in the chain. Leather Jacket rubbed at his knuckles; obviously he was no expert, but I could see he was planning on some serious practice.

He took off his jacket, under which he was wearing a stained and torn T-shirt. His bare arms were pitted with track marks, some already turning black and green. He'd been bitten by the *krokodil*, and the sweet stink of gangrene hung in the air.

'No wonder your *pakhan*'s in the morgue, if he can't even stop his people shooting up that shit.'

The flurry of blows that followed hurt, but the *krokodil* had obviously sapped a lot of his strength.

After a couple of minutes, Leather Jacket stopped for breath and I inspected myself for damage. Nothing that a week in an Issyk-Kul sanatorium with a stockpile of the good stuff couldn't cure.

'Now I know how tough you're not, why have you brought me here? And where's Saltanat?'

'The bitch? She's upstairs, in the master boudoir, waiting for Azad and Syrgak to show her what real men are like. Answer my questions and you can have what's left, if you like. Mind you, after Azad,' and he held his hands a foot apart, 'I don't know if there'll be much left worth having.'

'I don't care what you do to the bitch,' I lied, 'she led you to me. She deserves all she gets.'

'We caught her on the road outside your apartment. We were coming for you already, and we guessed you'd open the door to her. Kicking down doors gets old very fast.'

Leather Jacket jerked his thumb over his shoulder.

'Don't keep the bride waiting, guys.'

Azad and Syrgak headed out of the room, leaving me alone with Leather Jacket.

'You can manage me without backup?'

He smiled.

'Good chain, that. Strong. Shouldn't be a problem. I've got a few questions, and your answers aren't necessarily for everyone's ears.'

'Those two? They wouldn't understand if you drew them pictures.'

Leather Jacket considered that, and nodded. The trio obviously didn't sit around discussing the novels of Chingiz Aitmatov when they weren't terrorising *babushki* out of their pensions. He walked over to a wall cupboard, and paused, his hand on the door.

'The last events, you remember them?'

He meant the riots that burnt down a good part of central Bishkek in anger about the government, with the department stores looted as a sideline. Who says protest doesn't pay?

I nodded.

'I was in Beta Stores, thinking I could pick a few things up. Saw this and thought it could come in handy. For when I met people like you.'

I listened, wondering where this was going, as he opened the cupboard. I was beginning to get a very bad feeling.

'But you know what they say: get mare's milk, make *kymyz*.'

He produced a bottle of cooking oil and a hinged metal contraption. He lifted the lid to show two non-stick enamelled and grooved surfaces. An electrical cable ran from the machine and I watched as he connected it to a portable generator near the door. He pulled the starter cord, and the engine grumbled into a slow pulse.

'It's called a health grill, must be an American thing. These plates here,' and he waggled the jaws of the grill as if it was a small steel crocodile, 'they're slightly tilted so the fat runs out. But both the plates get good and hot; you just put the meat in between, close it, and it cooks in half the time.'

He held his hand above the metal, testing for heat, poured a little oil on to the lower surface. We listened to the oil hiss and spit as it hit the metal.

'Supposed to be good for cooking steaks, that sort of thing, but I haven't tried it out yet. Well, not for cooking anything I want to eat.'

I looked at the metal surfaces. There were fragments of what looked like charred meat, and black stains dribbling down the centre grooves. The knot in my stomach got tighter.

Leather Jacket took hold of my chin and forced me to stare into his eyes. I could smell the *krokodil* sweat on him, the rot of flesh. He looked at me, unblinking, hoping to see fear in my face.

'I'll tell you what it does cook to perfection. Fingers. And the occasional cock, if someone's deciding to be a hero.'

And with that, he forced my left hand between the metal plates and slammed them shut.

Chapter 41

My hand was only trapped between the two hot plates for maybe twenty seconds, but long enough for the pain to flash through my arm and emerge as a scream from my throat. I tugged desperately at the handcuffs. But I was held tight. Then the pain was out of control, and I smelt the flesh on my hand as it cooked.

Leather Jacket opened the grill, uncuffed my hand and plunged it into a bucket of water. The shock was so great, I screamed. My heart felt ready to throw itself out of my chest.

'There, that wasn't so bad, was it? You'd send that back in a restaurant for being underdone.'

I took my hand out of the bucket and looked down. Dark crimson burn lines followed the pattern of the raised grooves of the grill, deeper across my knuckles. My skin had already started to blister and turn an angry red. The soft meat of my palm looked raw, skinned, like a peeled blood tomato. I tried to clench a fist, and the effort flooded my mouth with vomit.

As soon as I could coax breath back into my lungs, I sat very still. The entire centre of the universe had become the closeness of my hand to the grill. Nothing else was in focus; not the killings, not Saltanat, not Chinara.

Leather Jacket poured more oil on to the machine.

'Not hot enough yet, give it a couple more minutes and then we can really get cooking.'

I did my best to muster some courage, some defiance.

'Shouldn't you ask me the questions first? I refuse to answer, then you start to torture me.'

Leather Jacket grinned, and his gold teeth glinted under the bare light bulb.

'You call this torture? Anyway, once they've had a little taste, people get much more cooperative. Why waste time?'

The reek of my hand was making me nauseous, and I wondered if I was going to faint.

'I get the message. You can turn that off and ask away, *droog*,' I said.

Leather Jacket considered this, and pushed the grill to one side. He raised the lid, so I could see the oil bubbling on the metal, and then spat. His phlegm splashed and sizzled, burnt off in seconds. I thought of the *krokodil* bodies I'd seen, with flesh gnawed away down to bare grey bones, and knew that would happen to my hand next time. I wished George Foreman had stuck to making his money hitting other black men in the ring.

'We'll leave the grill just here. If I don't like your answers.'

He cocked his head and looked up at the ceiling.

'Your girlfriend's obviously the well-brought-up type, doesn't talk with her mouth full, eh?'

I didn't reply, but the silence from upstairs hung over us like a shroud.

I remembered the smoothness of her back under my hand. I wondered if my hand would feel it again, ever feel anything again. I wondered who would find my body, and if they'd bury me next to Chinara, in the clean air and solitude of the mountains.

'What do you want to know?' I asked.

'For a start, who killed *vor v zakonye* Aydaraliev?'

I didn't see any point in lying. I'd no loyalty to men who came to my country and acted as executioners.

'Uzbek Security Services. Two men. I don't know them, never seen them before. Probably halfway to Tashkent by now.'

He nodded. My answer made some sort of sense.

'Who gave the order? That *pizda* upstairs?'

I didn't answer; I hadn't yet reached the point where I'd betray anyone or anything to keep the hot metal away from my hand. But I was close. So I shrugged.

'Well, she'll wish she was dead after Azad and Syrgak finish with her.'

He sucked his teeth, considering his next question.

I could tell he'd never done this before: a good inter-rogator says as little as possible. Silence, as much as anything else, makes the accused betray themselves.

'What do you know about the murders?'

'Your *pakhan* boasted about spreading "terror and confusion". It's a quote from a speech by Lenin before the Revolution. About how to overthrow the Tsarist government. And how to keep power once you've gained it. That's what all this is about, isn't it?'

Leather Jacket rubbed at his arm, and I suspected that the *krokodil*'s teeth had just taken a tighter grip.

'Go on.'

'This is too big, too dispersed, for it to be a single team. Killings in Osh, Karakol, here in the city. Across the border. Maybe even on the Russian airbase. There's big money behind this, for sure. But more important, there's also big ambition.'

'Go on. Whose?' Leather Jacket said, but I sensed the uncertainty in his voice.

'That's all I have. You'll know more than me; after all, you were close to the *pakhan*.'

'Not as close as his tongue was to his teeth.'

Now I realised why they were here, why my hand throbbed with a raw pain that pulsed with each beat of my heart. It wasn't revenge for the loss of their beloved leader. It wasn't some obscure part of the criminal's code demanding blood for blood.

It was the hunt for money.

'He didn't tell you where the payment is, did he?' I said. 'All that cash, stashed away, waiting for somebody to stumble on it by accident, and buy the villas and BMWs that should be yours.'

And I laughed, and I kept on laughing even after his punch snapped my head back.

It was all starting to come clear; finally, I spotted a motive behind everything.

'Your *pakhan* was a fool,' I said, wiggling my tongue against a loose tooth, 'so greedy, he couldn't see he was selling his own downfall. And not just his, yours too. All the gangs in Kyrgyzstan, all working for the big guy who will wipe you all out.'

'What are you talking about?' he snarled. 'You're full of shit.'

'Put the grill away and I'll tell you. Explain in simple words that even a *krokodil* like you can understand.'

'Why don't I just cook you one bite at a time? Put your fingers on a plate and make you chew the meat off them? You'll talk then.'

'But maybe I'll collapse, have a heart attack, die without you hearing what you want to know. Where will that have got you? And just how pleased will your bosses be? All those millions missing because you like to smell meat cooking?'

I saw that Leather Jacket wanted to press my face

against the sizzling grill. Thug he may have been, but he wasn't stupid. Reluctantly, he took the grill off the table and went to disconnect it from the generator.

Which is when I grabbed the bucket with my free hand and hurled it at him.

The water hit him, the grill and the generator at the same time, conducting direct current through him and to earth. The plastic casing of the socket exploded, and he fell backwards, his fingers frying and fusing to the grill. The room filled with the sour scent of iodine and boiling blood.

Leather Jacket danced from foot to foot, to an unseen, insane rhythm, jaw wrenched open by the voltage racing through him, a tuneless song spilling from his mouth. His jacket started to char and smoulder, as the lining caught alight. Then his hair was a torch, small flames dancing like a crown around his head. His hips jerked backwards and forwards, in a manic imitation of fucking, the grill still gripped tight in his hands.

A final grunt drove the air from his body, which performed one last convulsive spasm and lay still.

I knew better than to go through his pockets for the handcuff keys; the grill was still plugged into the generator, with the cable's bare wires emitting blue-white sparks and flashes. Instead, I focused on pulling the chain around my leg away from the clasp set into the wall.

With the chain wrapped around my free hand, I used

what leverage I could get with my feet against the wall. I tried to ignore the pain from the chain cutting into my burnt flesh, but there was no give at all. I kicked at the steel of the wall hook, but it was sunk deep into the brickwork.

I was still kicking, hoping to dislodge some of the plaster, when I heard it.

A scream from the bleakest, blackest depths. Coming from upstairs.

Chapter 42

For a couple of seconds, I froze, and I was in the hospital, beside Chinara as she screamed for the morphine to dull the bite of the tumours devouring her.

I was yelling down the corridor, ready to kill whichever uncaring attendant had slipped out for a few drags of a *papirosh*. I was lying beside her, holding her while her nails, made brittle and thin by the drugs, splintered and cracked as they dug into my arm.

She'd howled over and over again, unaware of anything but the fire consuming her, the noise from her throat sounding as if a wolf had made its way down from the mountains and was roaming the hospital in search of food . . .

Syrgak burst through the door, his mouth open, streaming with blood, white stumps of shattered teeth glinting through a crimson mask.

'Boss, the bitch, she just –'

He stopped at the sight of the *vor*, flames flickering from his jacket, blue flashes from the grill sparking against his body.

I tugged on the chain with the last of my strength, felt the plaster finally give way, lost my balance, tumbled back against the table. I swung the chain over my head, building up momentum, took aim, then released my grip. The metal reeled out across the room, the sharp spikes that had held it in place embedding themselves in Syrgak's face.

He gave a high-pitched gasp of surprise, then a howl of anguish as he tried to dislodge the spikes wedged deep in his right eye and cheek. He whimpered over and over, a keening wail that made me sick to my stomach, calling to his mother to help him.

I threw up, uncontrollably, emptying my guts. And I remembered how Chinara would vomit after each treatment, her body shaking with the retching that overwhelmed her, how I would hold the bowl up to her mouth, and wipe the rank sweat away from her face.

Syrgak had both hands covering his eyes and cheek, working out just how ruined his face was.

I still had one hand cuffed to the table, but I used my free hand to pull the leg chain towards me, making sure it didn't touch the water on the floor. I grasped it about a metre from the business end, and got ready to swing it once more if Syrgak came over to finish me off. The adrenaline was hurtling through me; one of these two shitheads must have butchered Shairkul, Yekaterina, Gulbara – and who knew who else?

309

But if I killed Syrgak, the trail died. And this wasn't just about avenging the dead women.

I gripped the chain tighter, picturing how the heavy steel links would coil around Syrgak's face, and I realised I wanted to flog the *sooksin* and flay every inch of skin off his worthless hide.

Once he'd told me what I needed to know.

Syrgak let out a bellow of pain and rage as his fingers told him he'd never be a male model, and he glared at me with his one remaining eye. Unless he was armed, it was a stand-off – at least, until one of us was overwhelmed by pain.

I thought of Saltanat lying dead and butchered upstairs at the hands of these two, and began to wonder if revenge wasn't enough of an ending. Fuck catching the big guys.

That was when the door swung open again.

Chapter 43

'I thought you were dead,' I said, as Saltanat staggered through the door.

'Sorry to disappoint,' she rasped, her voice sounding torn and ripped. She looked like shit, a long streak of blood smearing her cheek and around her mouth. Her shirt was ripped and her bra hung in two halves, dangling where it had been torn apart. There was a purple bruise on her forehead and the knuckles of her left hand were swollen and dislocated. She was also naked from the waist down.

There was no time to swap anecdotes, because Syrgak lumbered towards her, face streaming blood down his cheek. He swung at Saltanat, who ducked, pivoted and lashed out with her foot. She connected with Syrgak's groin and, as he doubled over in pain, grabbed his shoulder, slammed him head first into the wall, once, twice, and then brought her elbow down on to the nape of his neck.

Syrgak's vertebrae splintered and cracked like twigs snapping in a midnight frost. As he collapsed to the floor, his face dragged down the wall and left a vivid red smear, like a child's first attempt at painting. And then the only sound to be heard in the room was the breathing of the two people left alive, and the sizzle of flesh cooking on the grill.

'Handcuff keys are in his jacket pocket. But careful, he's hooked up to the mains.'

Saltanat grabbed a chair and threw it against the generator, dislodging the bare wires and breaking the circuit. She checked one pocket, rolled Leather Jacket's corpse over with no sign of disgust, and found the keys. Half naked, dazed, bleeding, she still seemed more focused and professional than half the uniforms I've worked with.

Once she'd freed me from the cuffs and ankle chain, I made a tentative move to hug her. Not out of desire but to offer some comfort, for myself as much as for her. But she held up a warning hand, palm towards me, and I let my arms drop by my side.

Saltanat seemed to realise for the first time that she was almost naked, and looked around for something to cover herself. Streaks of blood on her face dripped down, and I saw that she was crying.

'Is Azad . . . ?'

'He won't bother us.'

'You killed him?'

Saltanat wiped some blood from the corners of her mouth, then nodded.

'Did they . . . ?'

'Yes.'

Her voice flat, expressionless.

'Let's find you a blanket, or something.'

'I'm not going back upstairs.'

I nodded, understanding. If you'd just been beaten, raped and God knows what else by two psychotic thugs, the last thing you'd want to do is revisit the scene.

'I'll go.'

I edged past the bodies on the floor, held out my hand, but Saltanat stared down, totally absorbed. It doesn't matter how many times you kill a man, whether in the line of duty or not, the dead stay with you, visit you in the long hours before dawn and in the brightest of sunlight. Their eyes stare at you from the reflections of shop windows, car windscreens, ripples on water. They live with you like elderly relatives with nowhere else to go, sneaking up on you unawares with a tap on the shoulder or a half-heard question. All you can do is remind yourself it was them or you, and keep on keeping on.

My hand throbbed as I climbed the stairs up to the ground floor, and then the bedrooms. It was already swollen up to twice its normal size, and the burn marks looked etched in. The muscles and tendons had tensed up, turning my fingers into a set of hooked claws, and

I knew that if I didn't get medical attention soon, the hand would be next to useless. I tried to remember if it said anything in my employment contract about disability pensions. But since I was weaponless, that wouldn't matter if there was someone else up there waiting for me.

I followed a trail of blood spots back to an open door. I could see the edge of a bed and, just beyond that, a foot. It didn't move, and I suspected neither would the body it was attached to. I looked round the doorframe but there didn't seem to be anyone waiting to attack. There was a washbasin in the corner, with towels hanging from a row of hooks. As I took them, something crunched under my feet, and I looked down to see shards and fragments of a water glass, streaked and stippled with blood. That wasn't all that was lying there.

I took a quick look at the thing that had been Azan, and saw that his shirt and hair were drenched in blood. I didn't know who had made the terrible scream I'd heard earlier, but my money was on Azad.

Back downstairs, I handed the towels to Saltanat, looking away as she knotted them around her waist. They looked like a rather stylish multicoloured skirt, at least from a distance.

'Mobile?'

'No. You?'

'Smashed.'

'And a gun?'

Saltanat shook her head. So we were without weapons, wounded and in pain, unable to call for help, we'd just killed three members of the most ruthless gang this side of the Caucasus, and I had no idea where we were.

I knew we'd have to get moving, find shelter somewhere. Leather Jacket's best friend might be on his way over to share a finger or two of the good stuff, and maybe cook one of my fingers into the bargain. I went through Leather Jacket's leather jacket and came up with a set of car keys. I waved them at Saltanat, with a look of triumph I was very far from feeling, and started to head for the front door.

'Wait,' she said, 'we should search the place.'

'You're keen to wait for their friends to arrive?'

She looked at me without blinking, and I discovered again how her eyes had no end to their depths.

'You're Murder Squad. Maybe we might stumble across a clue or two?'

I paused, nodded.

'Five minutes, then we're out of here.'

In fact, it didn't take five minutes to search the entire house. All the rooms were empty, except for the basement, which neither of us wanted to revisit, and the bedroom. Under the bed was a black holdall, containing tightly wrapped packages full of a rust-coloured powder. *Krokodil*, I imagined, maybe twenty thousand dollars' worth, enough to take a lot of addicts in Bishkek to a painful grave. There was also a gallon-sized plastic jar with a handwritten label in Chinese, full of thousands of small red and yellow capsules. I broke one open, and a grey-green powder spilt out. I sniffed at it, but there was no smell, and it wasn't a drug I recognised.

I zipped the holdall closed and checked my watch; time to get out of there before the rest of the gang rolled up for their share of rape and torture.

Our good luck held; on a table in the hallway were a couple of Makarovs. We checked they were loaded, and I slung the holdall over my shoulder. If nothing else, I could use it as a bargaining tool.

I pushed the door open and a shaft of pure sunlight darted through the gap. As we stepped outside, I saw that we were only a few blocks away from my apartment. The sunlight was brutal, and my eyes throbbed in sympathy with my hand. A bus clanged past, startling us as we looked for the car.

Saltanat pointed at a beige four-door Audi. I pressed the lock control, and then we were speeding down Ibraimova. Five minutes later, I parked up the street, a discreet distance away from my building, and we headed for my apartment. A passing *babushka* stared at Saltanat's unusual skirt, spotted the guns in our hands, and decided that none of this was any of her business.

Once inside, I locked the door and edged a chair against the handle for extra protection. Saltanat walked into the bedroom and took the stack of towels from the wardrobe. While she was showering, I laid some of Chinara's clothes on the bed, wondering for the hundredth time when I was going to give them away, thankful that I hadn't.

I called Usupov at the morgue, and explained to him that I was going to need the morning-after pill, some retrovirals and the strongest antibiotics he could lay his hands on. He agreed and didn't ask why; his interest is only in the dead.

I bandaged my hand as best I could, made a couple more calls, put my gun on the kitchen table within easy reach, and waited.

It was almost an hour before Saltanat appeared, and the sight of her in some of Chinara's clothes was an ice pick in my heart. Wearing something other than her customary uniform of black top and jeans, she looked more vulnerable, somehow younger. I had to remind myself that she'd just put down two of Bishkek's most violent criminals.

'How do you feel?'

She shrugged, opened the fridge door and pulled a face. A batchelor's provisions: stale *lepeshka*, a couple of elderly tomatoes and a bottle of vodka. She took the top off the vodka and swilled some around her mouth before spitting it into the sink. She repeated this a couple of times, then recapped the bottle.

The rape hung between us like a curtain. I felt powerless, uncertain what to say or do. I'd seen more than a few sex crimes, but they'd always ended in murder. I didn't know how to deal with a victim who's still breathing.

'I've organised some medicine,' I said. 'We can pick it up later. Or I'll go and get it now, if you want.'

She said nothing, stared out of the window.

'You want to call someone? To take you back to Tashkent?'

Still nothing.

When she did speak, it was in a flat, emotionless tone, as if describing the plot of a boring film peopled by bad actors in which nothing much happens.

'The big one held me down while the other one ripped off my jeans.'

'You don't have to tell –' I began, but she held up her hand to silence me, and continued to stare out of the window.

'While he was inside me, he kept telling me about how they'd killed Yekaterina, how they'd just snatched her off Chui Prospekt when she was getting into her car. Outside a club, people walking past, but nobody did anything to help. They already had the foetus, in a

Beta Stores plastic bag, like a joint of meat they were taking home to make *shashlik*. They'd driven from Karakol that morning, after killing the village girl. Their boss had told them who they were supposed to target. The Minister's daughter, she was picked out to be the victim, she wasn't a random choice.

'He kept pushing and pushing in me, and he got faster and faster as he was whispering to me how he stabbed her, and how when they'd both had as many turns with me as they wanted, they'd cut me the way they'd cut her. And the big one kept sniggering, the way people do when they hear a dirty joke, and telling the other one to hurry up.

'And he was telling me about how they sliced open Yekaterina's belly, how hard it was to cut through the muscle, and then the knife just slid in and her blood spilt out over his wrist, hot and steaming in the night air. And she wanted to scream, as he took her life and spat it away, but his hand was over her mouth, and she could feel the cold snow against the back of her thighs start to melt as her blood warmed it, and her hips were pushing upward against the cold. And then it all started to go dark for her and the stars started to go out, slowly at first and then faster. And finally they peeled her open and dumped the foetus inside, the way you'd throw spoilt meat into the garbage, and that's when he came inside me.

'And I kept telling myself that at least he hadn't tried to kiss me, to force his filthy tongue inside my mouth.'

I said nothing, but couldn't help thinking that they hadn't died hard enough, or slowly enough, or with enough excruciating pain. My hand hurt, and I realised I'd clenched it into a fist.

'He rolled off me, and the big one moved to take his place. But he couldn't get hard, so he pushed it against my mouth. He pulled my jaw open, forced himself in. So I bit down, as hard as I could. And he screamed, he was punching the side of my head, and I had to let go. The other one dived at me, and I grabbed the glass on the bedside table and held it out. He tried to pull back, but the glass broke in his face. I slashed at his throat and missed, and he tumbled off the bed. So I used the glass on the big one, and I cut at his neck and suddenly there was blood spurting through the air, and he took his hands away from me and put them to his neck, but the blood kept spurting through his fingers, and down his shirt and on to the bed. He was grunting and choking, bleeding out, his eyes open with panic, and I kicked him away from me.

'The other one got up off the floor so I lunged at him with the glass, and he turned and ran out of the door. I didn't know where you were; I didn't know if you were dead. So I went over to the big one and I stabbed him in the eyes, and then he stopped whimpering and started screaming like an animal again, and I had to shut him up so I jabbed at his throat and he still wouldn't stop so I cut his throat again with the jagged edge of the glass, and then he stopped.'

And then neither of us spoke for a long time, as she stared out of the window.

We watched the sky darken and turn all the different shades of blue into night.

Chapter 44

It was completely dark when we headed out. The pain from my hand throbbed like ice and fire over my wrist, and I knew that if I didn't get to a hospital soon, infection would race up my arm and finish what Aydaraliev's men hadn't. But I was pretty sure the hospitals would be watched, and there'd be no percentage in me saving my arm if the rest of me ended staring sightlessly up on a slab.

There are no street lights outside my building – precious few in Bishkek – so we had the advantage of cover, even if it also shortened the odds of someone creeping up on us without being spotted. But I figured the *pakhan*'s remaining forces would be in disarray after the call I'd made to the station, saying where to find the bodies and suggesting the three dead gang members were the victims of a takeover bid. An anonymous call: I didn't know who I could trust, and the last thing I needed was to tell some *krisha* hoping to earn a few *som* exactly where we were and what we'd done.

There was enough snow to show us the path but,

even so, I was cautious as we walked down towards the street. Then, as we reached the row of bushes beyond the path, twin headlights snapped into action, turning our shadows into elongated stickmen lying in the snow.

Saltanat had her gun up and ready to shoot in a second, but I pushed her arm down. A gang hit, and we'd already have been sprayed with a dozen rounds.

'Relax, it's fine,' I said, but Saltanat kept her finger on the trigger.

We reached the SUV, where Kursan was grinning at us through the windscreen. He beckoned for us to hurry up, then killed the headlights; anyone watching would be momentarily dazzled. We clambered in and set off at speed for Chui Prospekt, Kursan switching the headlights back on only when we reached the first intersection. He hurtled around a *matrushka* minibus, crashed a red light, left a string of curses in his wake. Saltanat kept watch out of the rear window, until she was reasonably certain we weren't being followed.

At the Metro Bar, Kursan pulled a hard right, heading down towards Frunze, past the University. He finally parked opposite the Grand Hotel, a new building that already looked as if it had seen better days. Even though we were only a few blocks from the White House, the streets were deserted.

'I booked a couple of rooms here, fourth floor. As

long as no one knows where you are, no one can kill you, right?'

Kursan stood watch while we checked in, strictly cash, adjoining rooms. I was certain Saltanat wouldn't want to share a bed, or anything else, with a man for a long time.

We inspected each room in turn, and then headed back to the lobby. Kursan had moved the car further down a side street, so that it wasn't visible from the main road, and he was waiting for us in the Dragon's Den, the small restaurant and bar on the corner. We joined him and I ordered *chai* for myself, vodka for Kursan, coffee for Saltanat.

We sat away from the couples at the bar, so I could watch the street. I'd come here with Chinara, during our last summer. The European owner had gone to some trouble to make the place attractive: art photographs of Kyrgyz scenes on the red-painted walls, a long wood-topped bar and a display of bottles on the shelving against one wall. Chinara always claimed that the vegetarian *pelmeni* soup and *manti* dumplings were better there than anywhere else in Bishkek. And for all I knew, she might have been right. I could picture her, at the bar, drinking Baltika beer and dipping her portion of *manti* into chilli sauce with her fingers, flicking her hair back away from her face.

I shivered, not with the cold. Bishkek is a city of ghosts for me.

'So what's your plan?' Kursan asked. 'You get any further sorting this shit out?'

I told him about the men we'd respectively emasculated, electrocuted, stabbed or executed in the past forty-eight hours. His eyes opened wide when I told him about the death of the *pakhan*. He'd heard the news but, like everyone else, had assumed it was a gang war or an internal job.

'You're a one-man, one-woman death squad,' he said.

I think he meant it as a compliment.

'You've also solved the murder of the Minister's daughter, and that poor girl over in Karakol,' he added, clapping his hands together as if that was the end of the matter.

'Not in a way that's going to please Tynaliev,' I said. 'He was particularly keen to be the one handing out the summary justice.'

'You had no option,' he shrugged. 'He can always go and piss on their graves.'

'We might have sorted out some of the who,' I said, 'but we haven't solved the why.'

'Does why matter, if you've planted the bad guys underground?' Kursan asked.

'Too many unanswered questions that might come back to bite me,' I said.

Saltanat stubbed out the cigarette she was holding,

only half smoked, and reached for my pack. So far she'd said nothing.

'What do you think?' I asked.

'You've dealt with the little guys,' she replied, her voice as expressionless as her face, 'and the top guys will be too big to touch. Even if you know who they are.'

'Maybe,' I said, 'but if Tyulev and Lubashov weren't responsible for the murders, why come looking for me? And who killed the Russian? And Shairkul and Gulbara? And the women in Osh, the ones that got you involved in the first place?'

Saltanat said nothing, sipped her coffee, both hands around the cup, as if for comfort.

'What's in the bag, brother?' Kursan asked.

I looked around to make sure we couldn't be overheard.

'About a million *som* worth of *krokodil*.'

Kursan looked thoughtful.

'No one's cooked that up for their own private weekend recreation,' I added, 'so it's got to be about smuggling. Either into the country, or to go abroad.'

'The connection with the airbase?'

I nodded.

'Make it cheap here, ship it back to Mother Russia on a military plane, who's going to stop and search that?' Saltanat said.

'You think that *Spetsnaz* woman, Marina Gurchenko, was involved?' Kursan asked.

'One way or another. Maybe she was the mule, most likely she found out about the smuggling route and wanted to stop it. And that's what got her butchered. She was a medic, after all, the last person you'd expect to supply people with that stuff.'

Kursan said nothing, but rubbed his fingers and thumb together. Money can buy you almost anything.

'But she was pregnant, like some of the others,' Saltanat argued.

'I'm beginning to think all that was a way to get us off the scent, make us think there was some kind of serial-killer gang roaming the country, a cult. The smugglers hear about the killings; a copycat gets rid of their whistle-blower and points the finger away from the truth. The mutilations, the dead children; who'd link all that to a smuggling ring?'

Saltanat looked unconvinced.

'There are six heroin-smuggling routes out of Osh that we know about,' she said. 'Why not just go about business, nice and quiet, keep your head down, clean the profits and live well?'

I took another mouthful of *chai*, and nodded agreement.

'You're right. There's smuggling involved, but this isn't just about smuggling. There's something else behind all this, something bigger. But I don't know what.'

I drained my glass, set it down, and stared across the empty street. In the last few minutes, it had started to snow, painting the roads a gleaming white, unlike the thoughts in my head.

Chapter 45

We'd been in the Dragon's Den for about forty-five minutes when a battered BMW pulled up outside and Kenesh Usupov got out. He looked around, as if lost outside the confines of the morgue, before coming in, kicking the snow off his shoes, and joining us. He nodded at the waitress and she brought over a hundred grams. Not for the first time, I wondered about what sort of life Usupov led beyond his scalpels and bone saws.

Usupov produced a small paper bag, which he pushed across the table to Saltanat. The look on my face told him this wasn't the time to make one of his jokes. Saltanat looked inside the bag, then took out one of the packets and passed it to me, before taking the rest to the bathroom.

Usupov jerked his thumb at her retreating back.

'I understand the no-baby tablet, but the other stuff?'

I reached forward and took the glasses off his face. He blinked, uncertain, a mole suddenly baffled by sunlight.

'Last night, two bad boys grabbed her. One fucked

329

her while telling her how he'd gutted Yekaterina Tynalieva, the other tried for a *minet*. She killed both of them. Hard. In ways you don't often see, even on your slab. You really want to know some more, Chief Forensic Pathologist Usupov, I'll ask her to explain it all to you?'

The tone of my voice left him in no doubt he'd be on my permanent shit list if he did. And, more worryingly, on Saltanat's. I pressed all the antibiotic tablets out of their blister pack, washing them down with lukewarm *chai*.

'Inspector, we've worked together a long time. You ask for something, I bring it, that's the end of the matter, done and forgotten, *da*?'

With a certain dignity, he fixed his glasses back on to his face. I bowed my head in agreement, wondered how much I could believe him, and then felt bad for doing so. A man who investigates the mysteries of the dead deserves all the trust we can muster.

I poured a handful of the capsules I'd found in the holdall on to the table, making sure no one in the bar saw me.

'I need an analysis of these, Kenesh. Top priority.'

He took one and split it with his thumbnail, examining the contents.

'Any idea what this is supposed to do?'

'None. But they came with a Chinese label.'

'Which you couldn't read.'

'Right.'

'But which you've copied down for me to get translated for you.'

'Mind-reader as well as forensic genius.'

Kenesh nodded. I suspected that was his opinion as well.

'The woman you brought in. Tynalieva. Her father had her buried last week. All the government *nomenklatura* were there, showing their respect. And wondering if their families are next on the hit list, I imagine. Organising bodyguards, security, electric fences, the whole works.'

'Creating terror and confusion,' I said, more to myself than anyone else.

Saltanat had returned and overheard me.

'Sounds like it's working,' she said, waving to the waitress for more coffee.

I looked over at Kursan.

'What do smugglers want more than anything else?'

'Apart from honest customers, you mean?'

Kursan thought for a moment, weighing up all the problems of his trade.

'I stay away from drugs; there's too much money to be made, and so you get people moving into the business who are too greedy, who want the big score first night out. They bring law down on the rest of us, kill each other or get killed.'

He pointed a finger at me.

'Then there are the greedy ones on your side; everybody wants to wet their throat, but some people want to drink the whole fucking bottle. And that's when guns come out.'

Kursan sat back, threw back his drink, watching me sip my tea.

'What do we want? Peace and quiet, that's what, one hand washing the other, everybody watching each other's back, no trouble and happy customers.'

I nodded in agreement; more or less what I'd worked out for myself.

'So terror and confusion doesn't help your business?'

'Trigger-happy border guards? Everybody's mouth open for a bigger slice? Customers who figure it's safer to lie low until the fire burns down? You think that's how to run a business?'

Saltanat looked over at the smuggler with something approaching affection.

'So this isn't about smuggling?'

I shook my head; I was beginning to see some motive behind the game.

'Just as this isn't about serial sex killing, or cannibalistic cults. The murders, the drugs, all pieces in something bigger. We're mistaking pawns for more powerful pieces, thinking there's more than one game and that they're unconnected.'

Usupov finished the last of his vodka and stood up. For a man who spent a good part of his working day slicing up the mangled remains of drunk drivers, he seemed remarkably unconcerned about getting back into his car. Maybe being up to your elbows in death every day breeds a certain fatalism.

'All this speculation is very interesting, Inspector. But hard facts are what give answers. I'll call you if I find out anything about the capsules. And you should get that hand seen to.'

He shook Kursan's hand, nodded to Saltanat.

I watched his BMW disappear into a curtain of snow. There seemed nothing left to say.

Chapter 46

Kursan escorted Saltanat back to the hotel, then drove to wherever he called home. I nursed a black coffee, watched my cigarette smoke sidle upwards towards the ceiling, used the time to gather together what I knew and what I could guess.

Fact: the Circle of Brothers organised butchering the Minister for State Security's daughter, through Maksat Aydaraliev's team.

Fact: the same team also slaughtered a pregnant woman in Karakol, dumped her foetus in Yekaterina Tynalieva's womb.

The same people murdered the two working girls, Shairkul and Gulbara?

The same mutilations were carried out on women across the Uzbek border; by the Uzbek branch of the Circle of Brothers?

Unlikely that the Circle killed the Russian medic; security around any Russian military installation is too tight. Whoever did kill her knew of the earlier murders, but it wasn't identical, even though she was pregnant.

I decided to give up for the rest of the night. Maybe things would look better in the not so clear light of a Bishkek winter morning. If it ever stopped snowing.

Remembering my visits to the Dragon's Den with Chinara, I stared out of the window at the white patterns descending through the cold and the dark. Falling snow caught in the night's street lights always saddens me. It's the infinity of it all, thousands of millions of flakes, all different and all inseparable, trapped by the forces of air, wind and gravity, dragged down from the sky and falling to earth. It means something, I suppose, though I can't say what.

Leaving five hundred *som* on the table, I headed out into the cold, regretting leaving my *ushanka* in the apartment. Halfway across the road, my eyes tearing up against the cold, I heard the first shot. The snow hanging in the air reflected the report, so I couldn't identify the direction it came from. I tugged the Yarygin from its holster and dropped to one knee, all too aware I was a sitting target, dressed in black against an expanse of white. A second shot, but as far as I could tell, nowhere near me. I heard the smash of a window, broken glass tumbling on to cement. Lurching to my feet, I ran towards the hotel. Another shot, and the snow off to my right kicked up in a powder. I ducked, faked a run to my left, then zigzagged towards the entrance. With no target in sight, there was no point in shooting, but I let off a couple of rounds into the air, hoping to distract the shooter long enough to get cover.

I shouldered the hotel door open, raced through the lobby. The desk clerk was tucked away behind the counter, hoping the cheap plywood would deflect stray bullets. The lift doors next to the stairs gaped open, but I knew better than to get trapped inside a moving box with only one exit and plenty of warning of its approach. I took the stairs two at a time, checking the turn between each floor, moving across to the cover of the lift-shaft walls. My heart punched my chest, and adrenaline in my bloodstream was making my hands shake. Not good if you're about to face an armed man.

I waited thirty seconds on the landing below the fourth floor, and listened.

Nothing.

The walls in hotels like these won't stop anything larger than a .22, so the other guests would be in their bathrooms, lying in the tub, if they had any sense.

I flattened myself against the wall to make a smaller target. The door to my room was open, but there was no sign of anyone. I made a quick check, but the room was empty, reeking of cordite and singed bedding. There were two neat bullet holes in the pillow, just where my head would have been if I'd been lying asleep. A glance under the bed, but the holdall with the *krokodil* was gone.

Saltanat's door was shut, but I remembered the third shot and breaking glass, and burst into the room. The bed's thin mattress sprawled on the floor, snow drifting in through the broken window. The frame was one of those that only allows you to open the window so far; I guessed the glass had been punched out to take a shot at me. Apart from that, there was no sign of any disturbance.

Or of Saltanat.

In the lobby, I hauled the terrified desk clerk out from behind his hiding place. He saw the Yarygin in my hand, started crying and telling me about his widowed mother. To get some sensible answers, I put the gun away and showed him my ID.

No, he hadn't seen anyone come into the lobby, no, nobody had checked in after us, all he knew was he heard some shots from upstairs. Yes, he'd called the police, told them, they were sending a police car straight away. Now, please, could he go home?

I told him to wait to tell his story, walked outside, to the flashing red and blue light that had just arrived.

'No need for an ambulance,' I said, holding my ID in one hand and keeping the other well away from my gun. 'No one on the scene, either. The only thing to report is a broken window.'

I didn't say anything about the two bullets meant to excavate my skull; I needed to get on with finding

Saltanat straight away. I half recognised the uniform who got out of the car, then I placed him. The recruit who'd found Yekaterina's body. He didn't look any more sure of himself now than he did then.

'Inspector,' he mumbled, 'the report says shots fired, we have to –'

'Car backfiring,' I interrupted, 'probably a couple fighting over where to eat, and a window got broken. Simple.'

The uniform looked more puzzled than ever, but he took one of the cigarettes I offered him. We both lit up, and I patted him on the shoulder.

'Smart work, though, getting here so fast, you'll be taking my job one of these days.'

As expected, the flattery put him at ease, but he still looked confused.

'Thank you, Inspector, but how is it that you're here as well?'

I did my best to look slightly sheepish but also secretly boastful.

'Officer, I have a lady friend,' I said as I traced an outline in the air with my hands that would make the girls working the strip clubs on Chui look flat-chested. 'And my lady friend has a husband. A husband who maybe doesn't understand that old friends can meet to catch up with each other's news, and to reminisce about the past. I'm sure you appreciate my situation.'

To make sure the message lodged in whatever lurked in his skull, my wink would have looked theatrical from the other side of Bishkek.

He smirked in understanding, and was heading back to the patrol car when a thought struck him.

'Inspector, the Chief sent a message to all active officers. If we see you, you're to report in person back at the station. Day or night.'

'No problem,' I said, though the news had me more than a little worried. 'But no need to mention that you've seen me tonight. You understand, I haven't finished talking with my friend? We've got a lot of catching up to do.'

He grinned, and retraced the imaginary silhouette in the air with his hands.

'Exactly, officer, a man can be forgiven much in the name of friendship, *da*?'

The uniform touched the peak of his cap.

'Funny, really, we almost didn't turn up for the call.'

I was puzzled; trouble at a tourist hotel and officers are always quick to respond, if only to issue on-the-spot fines for 'irregularities in paperwork and visas'.

'Why's that?'

'Well, two minutes before we got here, there was another patrol car racing away down Frunze, and we wondered if they'd picked up the call first. But we thought we'd better check.'

'Good thinking,' I said, 'keep on like this and there'll be a commendation in it for you.'

His broad smile split his face, and I felt almost guilty for leading him on. Once the patrol car had disappeared down Frunze and the coast was clear, I walked round to the back of the hotel, to the side overlooked by our rooms, and checked the snow for footprints, tyre tracks, signs of a struggle. I didn't spot any clues to suggest Saltanat had been abducted by aliens. In fact, I didn't find anything at all.

My hand throbbed in the cold, and I suspected the burns were getting infected. Back at the Dragon's Den, I poured vodka over my hand to disinfect it, rather than into my brain to clear it. For the next two hours, I ran through the same facts in my head over and over again, wondering what it all meant, where Saltanat was, and how we had been found so quickly.

And then everything slotted into place.

Chapter 47

Two in the morning, and the last remaining waitress had been giving me the moody eye for the last hour. I dumped a couple of thousand-*som* notes on the table, waved away the half-hearted offer of change. The bar lights immediately dimmed; she was taking no chances on a thirsty customer strolling by for a nightcap.

The snow had stopped falling, as heartless and final as a whore's kiss. The sky was a delicate tissue of stars, suspended in the stillness and clarity that follows a storm. I checked my mobile; a dozen messages, all from the Chief. I already knew what they contained: a long litany of my various faults, sins and transgressions, ending with an offer of forgiveness, as long as I solved the case.

I remembered the rookie's words: day or night. But at this hour, the Chief would be snoring his way towards a furred tongue and a rough head in the morning. So it was the ideal time to show that I'd obeyed orders by reporting in, without actually having to see him.

A taxi was heading up Tureshbekov with its light on,

a real worthless heap with every panel clearly from a different vehicle, maybe even a different decade. But it was bitterly cold, and I'd no intention of walking. I flagged him down, badged him, made him wait while I told the hotel desk clerk to go home and keep his *rot* firmly shut. When I came out, the taxi was still there, to my amazement, all three of the working windows wound up, the driver creating a cancer cloud that spilt out into the night air.

As we drove down Chui Prospekt, just before we got to the White House – where some of my country's biggest criminals work out new ways of prising money out of the people – I told the driver to stop and wait.

The avenue was empty as I walked towards the monument commemorating the people massacred here during our last revolution, shot down as they demonstrated against the president. At the time, they were described as anti-social forces of lawlessness. Now, they're martyrs in the name of democracy. It's a see-saw; who knows who will get to write the final word?

I stood out of the wind, looked past the marble slabs attached to the White House railings, bearing the names of the dead, and up at the monument. A giant block of a wall, split into two halves, one white, one black, with three men in between them, pushing the black slab away and over on to its side. It's a little old-fashioned – three heroic Stakhanovite sons of toil overthrowing dark repression – but it never fails to move me. Maybe it's the simple division of the world into a good half and a dark half, the belief that people have the power, and can unite to overcome greed and tyranny, terror and confusion. It's a belief I wish I could share, that things can be made better, people whole again, not just slithering around in endless shit and blood and death, the way I do.

The snow was an ermine *ushanka* on the heads of the bronze figures, while the street lights turned the white block a half-glimpsed ghostly grey, floating against the night. And that was a more accurate reflection of the world I inhabit, neither black nor white. I pictured Chinara's grave, under a blanket of ice and snow until the spring thaw, and wondered how soundly I'd sleep when my time came.

I lit a cigarette, smoked that down to the last half-inch, extinguished it in the snow and put the butt in my pocket. It seemed disrespectful to litter this place, where dreams fell and the gutters had carried away the blood.

I sifted through all the evidence again, for patterns, trying to attach motives to actions. Maybe I should have brought a couple of hundred grams away from the Dragon's Den.

Patterns, shapes, epitaphs and reasons.

One by one, they dropped into place, like five-*som* coins into a beggar's grimy hand.

Finally I called Usupov, watching the soft and faithless snow flurry and shimmer in the moonlight, before it buried everything and everyone.

Chapter 48

The driver sounded his horn, impatient for bed, and I got back in the taxi. We headed towards Sverdlovsky, the traffic thin, our bald tyres sliding and slipping on the packed snow. The driver parked outside the station gates, knowing driving out could be a lot harder than driving in. I thrust some notes at him and hauled myself out. The guard on duty at the door nodded as I passed, watched as I signed in, scribbled a short note, then headed to the Chief's office. I'd planned to slide the note under his door, but as I approached, I saw that his light was on.

I swore softly; now I'd signed in, I couldn't just tip-toe away and out of the door. Resigning myself to a whirlwind of abuse, I bruised my knuckles on the door. The Chief looked very pleased with himself; the two brimming glasses on his desk suggested he'd been celebrating.

'Inspector!' he announced, 'at last, an end to this heap of shit.'

He waved at the glass nearest to me, and picked his own up as encouragement.

'The mastermind behind bars, and the Minister off our back, this deserves a drink or two, *da*?'

I waited until the Chief was halfway through his glass before I picked up mine and made a show of raising it to my lips.

'So what's the story? You've lost me,' I said, holding up my cigarettes for permission.

For answer, he pushed an already overflowing ashtray towards me. Stubbed-out *papiroshi*, I noticed, not the Chief's brand.

'It's a triumph of community spirit,' he said, topping up his glass again. 'A public-minded citizen gave us the location of our prime suspect, I personally sent a team down there to facilitate the arrest, and I expect a full confession by morning.'

'Skilled questioning under the gentle hands of Urmat Sariev, I suppose?'

The Chief looked slightly affronted by my tone of voice.

'The officer is one of our most skilled interrogators,' he said.

'Then I'd like to sit in on the gentle interrogation, if I may,' I replied.

The Chief smiled, and waved the half-empty bottle in my direction.

'Inspector, let me be frank. You haven't exactly

covered yourself in glory with this case. I can't write to the Minister and commend your efforts.'

He held a hand up, to forestall a protest from me that wasn't in fact forthcoming.

'I wouldn't want to dilute Officer Sariev's efforts in the pursuit of justice. He's quite capable of explaining the benefits of confession on his own. And besides, when the Umarova trial begins, your involvement might be seen as a conflict of interest, what with you having slept with her.'

Umarova.

So now I didn't just know who was about to be asked the hard questions, I also knew Saltanat's family name.

'It might be best for all concerned, and certainly for your career, if you take a back seat on this one, Inspector. Not that your work hasn't been noted and recognised, but why put unnecessary confusion and doubt before the public?'

'Chief, I know that Saltanat Umarova is Uzbek Security. What does she have to do with the killings? Plenty of Uzbek women have died as well. And you're not suggesting that she killed them?'

'Of course not,' the Chief agreed, 'but something as complex as this, it needs a ringleader, a mastermind, someone who can pull the right strings.'

'But her motive?' I persisted. 'Why would she do all this?'

'Land. Territory.'

I looked at him, saying nothing.

'Let me explain. Umarova is a loyal Uzbek citizen, as well as a senior investigator in Uzbek Security. Diplomatic status, comes and goes as she pleases.'

I nodded.

'The Uzbeks have always considered Osh to be their city; the fact it's in the Kyrgyz Republic is neither here nor there. They want it. Have done ever since Uncle Joe said it was Kyrgyz back in the thirties. So this is how they set out to do it, through terror and confusion. Cause enough trouble, the Kyrgyz in Osh riot against the Uzbeks, the Uzbeks fight back, and the Uzbek army comes in over the border "to protect fellow Uzbeks". And once they're in the city, they won't be leaving any time soon. The Russians advise both sides "to keep calm", and you've got a stalemate, with us Kyrgyz getting fucked in the arse.'

'It's an interesting theory,' I said, and took out another cigarette.

'One you'd have spotted straight away if you hadn't been looking at the world with your little eye,' he said, pointing at my groin, 'and fallen for that whore.'

He saw I wasn't amused, tried another approach.

'Look, it's only been a few months since your wife

died. No one could expect you to be your usual self, not with sorrow blurring your eyes. A pretty girl comes along, life starts to stir again, spring following on from winter. Natural. But not a good idea if you're Murder Squad.'

'So she's Ms Big, the power behind the throne, right?' The Chief winked and shook his head.

'Of course not, there are bigger people behind this. People we couldn't touch even if we found them with a severed head in one hand and a machete in the other. People you read about in the newspapers, watch on TV. But we bite off what we can chew, and we only chew what we can swallow. And in this case, that's your Ms Umarova.'

He opened his mouth and bared his teeth, snapping his jaw shut.

'Case closed,' he smiled and emptied his glass.

Then the smile left his face, and I saw the power that lay behind; it was a face used to having orders obeyed.

'Closed just like your mouth, Inspector. I hope we're clear on that? And while I remember, your case notes, let me have them, all of them.' The smile returned, 'Just for the record.'

'I still have a few questions.'

'I'll let you have a look at the transcript of the confession.'

'Edited highlights, I suppose?'

The smile widened.

'You know us too well.'

I sat back in the chair, tapped the end of my unlit cigarette against the desk to tamp down any loose tobacco.

'The two shitheads at Fatboys, Tyulev and Lubashov, the hit that went wrong. What was that all about?'

'Umarova wanted you dead; she knew you were our best Murder Squad. A high-level killing like the Minister's daughter, no way we couldn't put our top man on it. And you used to be smart enough to be a real risk to her plans. Tyulev was sent to distract you so Lubashov could comb your hair from the inside.'

I nodded.

'And Gasparian? The Armenian high-dive-on-to-concrete champion?'

'A coincidence. He's not the only man to have fucked a whore in this town.'

'So why the jump?'

The Chief poured yet more vodka for himself, raised an eyebrow at my still-full glass.

'You taken a vow of abstinence or something? You should celebrate, not worry about why some low-life loser dies trying to escape.'

I nodded in agreement, raised the glass to my mouth, didn't drink.

'You're right, Chief, it all ties together. Destabilise

Osh, capture it in the name of international law and order, own the most fertile part of our country.'

I smelt the harsh metal scent of the vodka. He was drinking Rasputin, the 70° proof stuff, like gasoline, with lit-match chasers.

'What about the dead Russian woman, Chief? Where does she fit into the Uzbek master plan?'

His face flushed from the vodka, the slightest slurring and hesitation in his words, the Chief frowned with the effort of marshalling his thoughts.

'I think her boyfriend did her, made it look copycat, so we wouldn't look too closely at him. Not that we could, even if we wanted. Russian military, law unto themselves. You know he's got a wife and two kids back in Ufa? A sweet little half-brother or -sister to Boris and Anastasia isn't going to go down well at the *dacha* back home.'

'Sounds like you've got all the pieces in place. All you need now is that confession.'

The Chief raised a hand, in modest objection to my praise.

'Of course, we'll stick to our existing story as far as the public are concerned. No need to inflame public opinion. But we'll let the Uzbeks know we know. And we can always produce your girlfriend as evidence if there's a problem.'

I stood up, and stretched. I was tired, and the

temptation of the vodka was nagging at me like a sore tooth.

'Giving you my notes can wait until morning?'

The Chief was magnanimous in victory.

'Sure, get your head down, take a couple of days off.'

I tapped the desk with the knuckles of my good hand, the sound like distant shots from a silenced weapon.

'That public-minded citizen, the one who gave you the tip-off?'

'Yes?'

I jerked my thumb at the door to the Chief's private bathroom.

'Why don't you ask my old friend Kursan Alymbayev to join us, then I'll explain why everything you've just told me is complete bullshit.'

Chapter 49

The bathroom door opened, and a grim-faced Kursan emerged.

I pointed to the ashtray.

'He doesn't pay you enough to give up the *papiroshi*? Betrayal must come cheap these days,' I said. 'I could smell them from halfway down the corridor. Might as well have painted a sign.'

Kursan shrugged and sat down, no sign now of the carefree bold smuggler. I stared at him without speaking for a moment. My dead wife's uncle, the man who'd danced at our wedding, who'd emptied vodka bottles with us until dawn, who could always be relied on to help out with food and tea when things were scarce.

Knowing I was right didn't make my sense of his complete betrayal any easier. Everything I'd ever considered sacred, family as something honest and intact outside the fogs and mists of deceit in which I lived, all of that had fallen apart when Kursan had walked through the door.

'I always said my niece had married a smart man,

353

Akyl. Maybe too smart,' Kursan said, lighting up the inevitable *papirosh*.

'You found the hotel; no one knew we were staying at the Grand, so it had to be you who organised the snatch. What I didn't know was whose side you were on, who you were betraying us for. Then the *ment* told me about the police car leaving the scene, and I figured it was bringing Saltanat here —'

'As I told you, Inspector, a concerned citizen doing his civic duty,' the Chief interrupted.

'On the side of the angels?' I asked. 'So, of course, you handed the million-*som* holdall of drugs over to the proper authorities?'

Kursan looked hesitant for a second, then the Chief intervened.

'Inspector, everything's under control, accounted for. I suggest you go home.'

'It's just that when I checked in the custody book, there was no mention of Saltanat or the drugs,' I lied. 'As far as the record's concerned, a fender-bender out in Tyngush was the evening's only incident.'

The Chief spread his hands in a conciliatory gesture.

'These things take time. Surely it's more important to interview the prisoner than to spend time scribbling down details?'

'And much more convenient if the interview starts

at the top of some stairs and gets signed off at the bottom.'

The Chief scowled, and topped up his glass.

'I understand you're stressed, but don't push me too far.'

I didn't look too terrified, and that didn't please him either. I finally lit my cigarette, letting the smoke cascade towards the ceiling and join the blue cloud already there. I didn't offer the pack around.

'The problem with this case has always been motive. Lots of connected events, but seemingly too separate to be connected. Unless someone big is pulling the strings.'

The Chief stared at me, unblinking. Kursan was looking at his hands, careful not to catch anyone's eye.

'The *pakhan* told me the motive. "Terror and confusion," he said.'

'Go on,' the Chief growled.

He started to top up my glass, but I shook my head and he put the bottle down.

'To do something this big, all the murders, here and in Uzbekistan, takes real money. The sort of money a government has. Or the people behind a government.'

The Chief sipped from his glass.

'Like I told you, Inspector, it's the Uzbeks.'

I gave him the unblinking eye right back.

'No, it isn't.'

The silence in the room stank of anticipation, of men working up the courage to reach for their guns and turn the quiet into mayhem.

When the Chief spoke, it was in a very calm, measured voice.

'So who is it, then?'

'Which family controlled everything in this country until the last revolution? Which family pillaged the state treasury, the foreign aid reserves, every last *som* they could lay their hands on, then jumped on a private jet with the loot? Leaving their stooges in the army to gun down civilians outside the White House while they celebrated with champagne at forty thousand feet?'

I realised that my voice had risen, and there was anger in it. The Chief shook his head, unable to believe my stupidity.

'And who'd follow their cause now? They're hated from here to Karakol. Believe me, Inspector, that's a crazy theory.'

I nodded agreement, then turned over my cards.

'It's crazy if you think they're expecting the support of the people, the way things stand now. But out of all the millions they took away with them, they found enough to make a deal with the Circle of Brothers. Here's a few million dollars, cause terror and confusion, make the people see they need a tough leader, and we'll cut more deals when I'm back in the White House.'

The Chief looked at me, and there was a sort of grudging admiration there.

'It's a very interesting theory, Inspector. One you could follow that leads all the way to the cemetery next to your wife.'

I nodded.

'Of course, terror isn't enough, not on its own. You need to manipulate it, take each twist and coil and turn them to your advantage. Stir up trouble, quell it, show you're the tough guy the country needs.'

I didn't hear any disagreement, so I pressed on.

'Tyulev and Lubashov, the shoot-out at Fatboys? At first, I did think Saltanat had set me up for it. Then I thought that they'd been involved with the murders, and this was to stop me going any further. But the truth? Tyulev was a *zhopoliz*; he'd kiss anyone's arse if there was money in it. He was too deep into something too big for him, and he wanted to sell me information. So Lubashov was sent to silence him. It wasn't a hit on me, but on Tyulev. He got the long sleep, and I tucked Lubashov away.'

I ticked both names off on my fingers, and moved on.

'Gasparian? Well, that's an easy one. Planning a coup like this isn't cheap. You need someone who can move money around. Word of mouth is all very well for moving money from one country to another, even tens of thousands of dollars. But we're talking millions, and

Gasparian knew how to shift them. The UAE kicked him out for doing just that. I imagine he did a little creative accountancy on his own behalf. The Circle of Brothers found out and ordered you to organise his dive, once he was no longer useful.'

The Chief stared at me, his face unreadable.

'Go on.'

'The two hookers, well, that's straightforward. They were sleeping with Gasparian, and who knows what a man might mumble to impress a woman? Making sure they can't pass on any pillow talk is just an elementary precaution. And if you kill them to make it look like yet two more slayings by some maniac to boost a job, even better.

'The deal with the *pakhan*, the local salesman for the Circle of Brothers? Well, it was a bonus for the big guys if his tongue didn't dance once his usefulness was outlived. And having Uzbek Security take care of it made it even more secure.'

I remembered Saltanat placing a shot into her bodyguard's head next to Gulbara's headless corpse, and blinked to erase the image. For a second, I smelt the cordite and tasted the blood.

'Of course, having a turncoat in Uzbek Security was a great way of keeping track of Saltanat's movements. Until Illya gave himself away. We knew he'd talked, just not who was listening.'

I made a gesture with my hand, like moving an invisible chess piece.

'All the pieces were on the board, but only one player could see them all.'

The Chief considered everything, nodded slowly.

'I don't say I agree, but I can see you've got a case to be made.'

I held my hand up.

'There's more. The dead Russian woman? *Spetsnaz*? Nothing more likely to wind up the Russians than the murder of one of their top force. Pride and revenge kick in. Add the chance to regain more control over the region, and get the US airbase at Manas closed down, and their tanks would be rolling down Chui by the end of the month. And, of course, a Russian air-force plane was the ideal way to get the *krokodil* to all those Russki junkies. But Barabanov found out, and you had his girlfriend slaughtered. Was he paid off by you? A part of it? I don't suppose I'll find out. But it doesn't matter; her death served your purpose.'

I ticked off yet another finger. I needed more fingers. The way the burn was scouring my nerves, like a dog gnawing at the bones, maybe I'd need a new hand.

'It helped to add to the confusion with that fake police ID, to show that maybe I was involved as well. So if I got too close to anything, they could turn suspicion back on me.

'And the death that kicked all this off? The Minister's daughter? No one gives a fuck about some dead peasant girl, but take out a top family member and all the *nomenklatura* start worrying which of their children is going to turn up face down. Government in disarray? Plenty of terror and even more confusion.'

I paused to let this sink in, then continued.

'Easy enough to get the killings done. Plenty of mindless thugs in the prisons, and anyone with access to records could tell you who the rapist-murderers are, who's got some surgical skills for dissecting the victims. Even easier to recruit the *krokodil* crowd and the simply stupid, who don't mind inflicting a bit of pain and shedding someone else's blood.'

I held my hand up to show the little souvenir that Leather Jacket had given me to remember him by. The smell of burnt fat lingered in the air.

The Chief pushed his chair back, but I raised my hand and he stayed slumped.

'Inspector, as conspiracy theories go, there's one major flaw in your argument, but you're probably so blinkered that you've overlooked it.'

He leant forward and waved a finger in the general direction of the vodka bottle.

'Say you're right, just for the moment, for argument's sake. The people you claim are behind this, they're abroad and living very comfortably, thank you. You've got murders, shoot-outs, not just here in Bishkek but all over the country, even over the border. How could they control and coordinate it?'

He settled back with a satisfied smile and poured a short one, tossed it back and poured another.

'You're right, of course, Chief, but I spotted that flaw as well. You'd need to have someone on the ground, directing traffic, making calls, keeping an eye on things, pushing the pawns forward.'

I made the gesture of a chess player toppling his opponent's king.

'And they did have someone. You.'

Chapter 50

The Chief looked over at me. My accusation hadn't thrown him into panic or outrage. Kursan didn't look too concerned either.

The Chief drummed his fingers on his desktop, considering everything I'd just said. When he spoke, his tone was reasonable, explaining to a small child.

'All very clever, Inspector, but hypothetical, circumstantial. You don't have anything to link me to any of this. And without evidence, your career isn't even going to take you to border duties. Or breathing.'

I shifted my weight on to one hip, moved my hand closer to the Yarygin.

'I don't have to prove very much at this stage, Chief, I just have to point the finger.'

I jerked my thumb at Kursan, who watched the two of us play it back and forth.

'There'll be questions asked about your relationship with a notorious smuggler.'

The Chief sat forward, raised an eyebrow.

'A notorious smuggler who's also an uncle of yours by marriage, *da*?'

I continued, wondering what Chinara would have said about giving her uncle up.

'There's the missing drugs, unaccounted for in the files.'

Now it was the Chief's turn to shrug.

'An oversight. Easily rectified.'

'An examination into your finances, bank statements, deposit boxes.'

The Chief smiled, genuinely amused.

'You're saying I dipped my beak? If we lock up everyone who's taken a taste one way or another, Bishkek will be a ghost town.'

The Chief sat back in his chair.

'I'm not like you, Inspector. I'm a pragmatist, not a "justice at all costs" missionary. You're good Murder Squad, maybe the best. But solving something as big as this? That's like picking at Mount Lenina with your fingernails. You end up torn and bloody, and the mountain's still there.'

He stared out of the window, at the city. I watched his reflection dance and flicker on the glass.

'We're a country of nomads; it's in our blood. Even when we have houses, cars, jobs, we refuse to be held down, to go against our nature. In almost a century, the Russkis never managed to smash that out of us. It's more than just pride or stubbornness, it's who we are.'

'So the *dacha*, the Mercedes, the big house; that's your idea of being a nomad?'

'Now you're trying to be cute? You know how easy it would be to leave all that behind? Head up to the high plain and watch the world from a distance?'

Now it was my turn to smile.

'But you haven't. The Merc is still parked in your reserved space outside, the house in the compound doesn't have a For Sale sign on the wall.'

The Chief rubbed his face, a weary man with the world's troubles strapped to his back.

'Inspector, I love my country. But as I say, we're nomads, individuals, tribes, not a people. We need a strong man at the top. Someone to cut through the shit. A modern-day Manas, if you like. Everything for his people, no mercy for his enemies.'

'So you turn the country into chaos, then you and the big man reluctantly climb into the driver's seat?'

The Chief said nothing, continued to gaze out into the dark.

'It's a very clever strategy, to get the Circle of Brothers to do your dirty work for you. Everyone believes it's just the usual business of stealing everything not nailed down. No one thinks there's politics behind it all.'

I reached into my pocket, took out a handful of the capsules from the holdall.

'And how will you pay the Circle, all the bosses and the underbosses and the *torpedos* and the *vory* muscle, when they all come with their beaks open, saying "feed me, feed me"? They're not chicks, they're sharks, and they bite without mercy.'

I scattered the capsules on to the desk.

'Do you know what these are? I got a call from Usupov earlier, he ran some tests on this shit. Stamina-boosters, from China, that's what it says on the packet. Each one supposed to be made up of dried and ground human foetal tissue. You're going to let the Circle make money by turning the Kyrgyz people into cannibals.'

I swept the capsules off the desk and ground them into the wooden floor.

'Except all that's in there is baking powder, brick dust and salt. Nothing but a scam, and a diversionary tactic to keep people off your trail.'

The Chief raised an eyebrow and shrugged.

'And there's the *krokodil*, and the heroin, and any other rubbish that turns a profit. The whores, the casino rake-offs, all of it dirty money.'

I turned to Kursan.

'You always told me you wouldn't touch this shit. I turned a blind eye, because I thought you had some decency about you.'

Kursan stared at me, then finally spoke.

'You don't know what it was before independence.

Back when we danced to Moscow's tune, when we had to pull over to let some Russian boss in a long black Volga speed past us on the way to the lake, when we were supposed to be grateful for any grains of rice that fell from the table.'

I shrugged.

'Ancient history, Kursan.'

'Not to me. Not to people who suffered, who never knew where their next bowl of *plov* was coming from. I learnt that nothing comes before survival, not party, not family, nothing. And if that means selling *krokodil* to the very people that fucked this country for seventy years, that's a sweet bonus.'

Kursan paused, picked a fleck of tobacco off his tongue.

'Akyl, you were married to my niece. I like you. But that doesn't mean you can stand in the way of my business. Sure, I got some small favours from you, an unfair advantage over my competition. But all advantage is unfair, *tovarishch*, that's why it's called advantage. Would you really expect me not to use it? People were happy to work with me, they thought I had protection, whatever we brought in. Despise me, if you like, you know I'm right. Everybody makes money, everybody's smiling.'

'Not everybody,' I said, 'not me. And if she were alive, Chinara wouldn't be smiling either.'

'You ever see a skull that's been picked clean by the worms and maggots? Isn't that smile, at death, the biggest joke of all? And that's the smile on her face now.'

Kursan grinned, his teeth bared, but the smile never reached his eyes. In his face, I saw the mountain wolves that come down in the winter and attack the flocks, ripping and tearing, starving and relentless.

It was time for some creative lying.

'Aydaraliev? The Bishkek *pakhan*? I'm sorry to say, he didn't share the same sense of loyalty and "we're all in this together" attitude. At least, not towards you. He would never have opened his mouth against the Circle, but he was delighted to sing about you.'

The Chief looked wary, then leant forward and spat into the full ashtray.

'One thing to give the old bastard credit for; he was tough,' I said. 'Too tough for us to break. So we told him what we were going to do to his beloved Ayana, his little granddaughter. Not once but over and over again. The scissors, the lighted cigarettes, the video. Payback for the sins of the grandfathers, and all that. He didn't just sing, I thought I was at the Bolshoi in Moscow.'

I reached inside my jacket and pulled out a cassette.

'All the times, the places you met, the instructions you gave, the money you paid. He knew about your side deal with Gasparian, by the way, the foreign bank account, all that. He said, "Let him build it up, we'll take it all back when we're ready. He can choose between gold and lead."'

I let a sneer scar my face.

'Did you honestly think he was going to take orders from you for ever?'

The Chief reached over for the cassette, but I slid it out of reach.

'Don't worry, Chief, it's safe with me. All that high-minded stuff about nomads needing a strong leader? Just another fucking thief, and a stupid one at that.'

The Chief held his hands up in mock-surrender.

'I'm not a stupid man, Inspector, and I don't believe you are either, in spite of your "principles". This isn't a *yelda*-measuring contest. Tell me what you want, we make an accommodation.'

I shook my head.

'I'm not looking for a deal. I want this over.'

The Chief smiled.

'You think I'm going to sit here with a litre and a Makarov, and do the "decent thing"? Killed "while cleaning his gun"? You're not that naive.'

He filled his glass again, sipped this time. This was business.

'This isn't a game of *kok boru*. If all the riders try to grab the headless goat, no one gets a piece worth having. I don't get what I want, neither do you.'

'I've told you what I want.'

The Chief looked at me over the edge of the glass.

'I don't think so, Inspector. I've got something you might well want to swap for that cassette.'

I had a sickening notion I knew what he was going to say, but I kept quiet. The Chief chuckled quietly, tapped on his desk.

'You think she's down in the basement, while Sariev explains to her about how she organised the whole thing, to stir up trouble between the two countries.'

I kept my face impassive, waiting for him to continue.

'Well, Ms Umarova's currently in one of my safe houses. Not so safe for her, of course.'

He paused for effect.

'In fact, I'd be very surprised if she came out of it undamaged. Or even alive.'

He lit a cigarette, contemplated the glowing end, pressed it against a piece of paper on his desk. We both watched as the small brown charring started to smoulder and turn black, before he tipped a little vodka to extinguish it.

'So tell me, Inspector, you still think we've got nothing to exchange? Or would you rather bury your girlfriend next to your wife?'

369

Chapter 51

His threat hung over the room like a grey cloud. But if there's one thing we Kyrgyz are good at, it's not betraying our feelings. My hands didn't tremble as I lit yet another cigarette, threw the empty pack on the floor. Call it contempt, if you like.

'The tape? It's the only one, I hope?' he asked.

I nodded.

'So a straightforward deal, then? Your evidence or your girl. Which will it be?'

'I'll want proof she's alive,' I said. 'Not that I don't trust you, but I don't trust you.'

The Chief did his best to look offended.

'We have to trust each other, *da*? Otherwise we sit here for the next six months.'

'There's a couple of things I'd like to know first,' I said.

'Anything I can do to oblige, Inspector,' the Chief said, taking a small sip from his glass. I noticed that he was no longer slurring his words, a good card player.

'Whose idea was it to kill Yekaterina Tynalieva?' I asked.

'Let me ask you something,' he replied, 'what would have been the consequences of killing the daughter of, say, the head man of a small village up in the mountains? Nothing. Now the daughter of the Minister for State Security, that's a different bowl of *plov*. Show how vulnerable he is, and you send out a message to everyone; we can fuck whoever we want.'

He sat back, narrowing his eyes.

'So, *da*, my choice. The guys picked her up near her apartment. Too independent, that was her problem, we'd have had a much harder job if she'd been living in Daddy's compound.'

'And the mutilations? The other woman's foetus?'

For the first time since my arrival, a genuine look of anger slid over the Chief's face.

'Inspector, whatever you think of me, I'm not a barbarian. But my orders were to create terror. You don't do that with a discreet ice pick. The mutilated babies? I give credit for that particular touch to our friend here.'

I'd almost forgotten about Kursan, but now I turned to him, not hiding the disgust I felt.

'I got offered those stamina-boosters, fuck knows if they work,' he said, his eyes never drifting away from my face, 'but I can make a lot of money from them. Will people believe they're made from human flesh? Not unless we can give them a backup story. We sell what we claim are dead Uzbek children to the Kyrgyz, and Otkur does the same in reverse. "Are they real?" "Didn't you see the reports in the paper?" And the money piles high.'

'And the *krokodil*?' I asked.

Kursan pulled a face.

'It's not a good way to die. But then, what is? Those addicts all have a suicide wish, I just help speed it up.'

I thought of how Chinara died, unconscious, her body ravaged by tumours and the surgeon's scalpel. I pictured the mound of frozen earth above her grave. I remembered the terrified sheep, seconds before its blood geysered from the slash in its throat. And more than I'd ever wanted anything else, I wanted to watch Kursan screaming in agony, begging me to end the pain.

And me refusing.

'My wife would have been sickened to have been born into a family that had you as a member,' I said, as calmly as I could manage. 'If she'd thought she could pass on any of your genes, she'd have had herself sterilised first.'

'She's dead; I'm alive. That's what counts. Everything else is just a scruple that only the rich can afford. If it was her or you under the soil, which would you choose?'

'It's a cheap philosophy, Kursan. And worse than that, it's half right. Sure, Chinara is dead. Nothing can bring her back, and I've got nothing but a collection of memories and out-of-focus photographs. But you say you're alive. Really?'

Realisation slammed into his eyes like a flare exploding on a moonless night. He was already scrabbling in his pocket for his gun when the first two shots from my Yarygin punched into his shoulder and belly. The heavy-calibre bullets hurled him backwards, so that the arterial spray splashed in a long arc across the ceiling, and his gun tumbled to the floor. His grunt of pain mirrored the bleating of the sheep as the knife severed its throat.

Kursan tried to pull himself upright but the damage to his arm was too great to support his weight. He thrashed on the floor, cursing me, trying to reach his gun. I took three steps towards him, waited until his fingers had almost reached the grip, and then stamped down hard on his hand. I wanted to hear the bones grind into powder. I could tell from the smell that I'd punctured his gut, and he'd pissed himself.

I looked over at the Chief, and wagged a finger at him, telling him not to do anything stupid. But he sat in shock, unable to make a move. Too many years behind a desk will do that to you.

Kursan spat at me, the gobbets of spittle falling before they reached me. I took my foot off his hand, and watched him scrabble for the gun. I remembered how firmly his hand had gripped mine in congratulation when Chinara told him of our engagement, had raised a toast at my wedding, had squeezed my shoulder at the graveside.

And as his fingers touched the gun, I pressed the barrel of my Yarygin to his forehead and blew his life out on to the floor.

Chapter 52

The Chief recovered his composure with remarkable speed.

'This won't be a problem for you,' he assured me. 'A notorious criminal attempts to kill two senior police officers, pays the price, thanks to your speed and vigilance.'

I looked down at the corpse, saw the blowback from my final shot covering my hand, the sleeve and chest of my shirt, lukewarm and sticky on my bare skin, and I wanted to scrape and scour until no trace remained.

'No need for an investigation,' the Chief continued, 'not with me as a witness. As long as we have our deal. Self-defence or a brutal killing, it's your call.'

I nodded, as the adrenaline started to ebb, and the nausea kicked in. The room went dizzy for a few seconds, and I wondered if I was going to faint.

'And the drugs?' I asked.

'A two-way split is better than a three-way, wouldn't you say? Yours if you want, no problem. And plenty more in the future. It's a repeat business.'

I started to wipe the worst of Kursan's blood, brains and skull fragments off my hand, then gave it up as a bad job.

'Not like dying, then,' I said.

I put the Yarygin down on the desk. The Chief reached over, very slowly, and with one finger turned the barrel so that it was no longer pointing at his heart. I made a grab at the desk, before my legs decided they no longer belonged to me, and sat down.

'Even if your scheme works, and the old crew come back, the Circle have you by the balls, don't they?'

The Chief looked amused.

'Not with a hard man at the top; we can wipe them out for good.'

I shook my head, my ears still ringing. The smell of Kursan's guts and brains filled the room.

'They've got too much on you, and once the *krokodil* starts biting, you'll have no control. This won't be a country any more, just somewhere to be robbed and raped and screwed for everything it has. And if it gets bad enough, maybe the Russians will come back. Then you and your bosses will be first up against the wall. Or maybe the Chinese will come over the Tien Shan Mountains, and you'll find yourself kneeling in some sports stadium in Urumchi, screwing your face up against cold steel kissing the back of your neck.'

'You're too pessimistic, Inspector,' the Chief said.

'I can put you in touch with a very reliable and discreet company in the Middle East. Everything laundered better than your mother used to do your shirts. Five years from now, sunshine, a penthouse, a yacht, all the girls you can fuck, and no six-month winter. Works for me.'

'Aren't you forgetting one thing?' I asked. 'Saltanat?'

'So there's only one girl you want to fuck, well, I admire true love. Give me the tape, and I'll give you the address.'

I shook my head, and took the tape out of my pocket again.

'Call Sariev and call him off. I'm not giving this up for a dead woman.'

He took his mobile off his desk and dialled a number. He spoke for a couple of minutes, and then broke the connection.

'I've told him to do nothing, to wait for us. She's all right, a little bruised maybe from a couple of taps, but nothing that a few million dollars can't cure.'

He reached out for the tape, and I handed it to him.

'The address?'

'First things first, we're partners and that means we have to trust each other, *da*?'

I watched as he slid the unlabelled cassette from its case, broke the plastic shell open. He spooled the tape into the ashtray, and set fire to it. The shiny brown tape twisted and coiled and melted, the plastic stink over-laying the scent of blood.

'Truth? Lies? A confession? Look where it all ends up, Inspector,' he said, prodding at the charred remains, 'Smoke on the air, uncatchable, untraceable.'

He sat back, reached for the bottle, saw that it was empty, and smiled.

'I would have liked to make a toast to our new friend-ship,' he said. 'Maybe tonight, once that piece of shit on the floor has been scooped up and dealt with.'

I nodded.

'You've made an interesting choice, Inspector,' he continued, 'the country you love or the girl you love. And you know, I don't even think the money played a part in your decision. Maybe you're a romantic, after all.'

'Maybe,' I said, 'but Murder Squad isn't just about solving killings. It's about preventing them in the future. You had Yekaterina Tynalieva turned into something from an abattoir. I didn't want Saltanat to join her on one of Usupov's trays.'

'I did what was necessary. Perhaps one day, you'll come to believe that too. Especially when you look at your bank statement.'

I took my mobile out of my pocket and laid it on the table, next to the Yarygin.

'I don't think I'll ever be rich, Chief,' I said, 'and somehow, I don't think you will be either.'

And that's when three armed men came into the room, followed by the Minister for State Security, Mikhail Tynaliev.

Chapter 53

'It's amazing what you can hear when one of these is left on,' I said, tapping my mobile, 'and you never know who might be listening.'

The Chief's face was as grey as the start of the dawn outside.

'Minister, this is obviously some kind of misunderstanding, a plot, a conspiracy. If you'll allow me to explain?'

Tynaliev said nothing, but watched, impassive, as the three bodyguards hauled the Chief up by his arms.

'Everything you heard, it was just speculation. The Inspector, he lost his wife just a few weeks ago, he isn't well. I told him to take some leave, sort himself out, clear his head of all these delusions, just ask him yourself.'

His voice rose in pitch as he was bustled round towards the door. Saliva dribbled from the corner of his mouth.

'There's no evidence to back up these claims, Minister, maybe I've been foolish in giving the Inspector his head, nothing more than that, nothing any court would convict me for in a trial.'

We all looked down at the tape still smouldering in the ashtray.

'You'd have enjoyed hearing that,' I said, 'if you like traditional Kyrgyz folk music, that is. By the Bishkek Manas Ensemble. Very good, I'm told, by those who know.'

The Chief's eyes closed for a moment. He struggled to break free, but only half-heartedly, as if resigning himself to what was to come.

'This is all circumstantial. No court's going to convict me,' he said.

When Tynaliev spoke, his voice was calm, measured, final.

'You really think there's going to be a trial?'

He reached into his jacket and took out a photograph. A girl in her late teens, taken in summer, sprawled out on the grass outside a *dacha*, her face turned up to revel in sunshine and the joy of being young and alive.

Yekaterina.

Tynaliev nodded at the bodyguards, and they dragged the Chief out of his office. His shoes trailed toes down, leaving faint scuff marks on the wooden floor. I listened to them go along the corridor, and down to a painful, lingering and solitary death, in a snow-white field or some soundproofed basement.

The Minister began to follow them, turned and, after a second, held out his hand.

I stood there, looking into his eyes, my arms by my side.

He frowned, before a kind of understanding crossed his face. Even if this was the only justice the men behind his daughter's murder would ever face, I was still Murder Squad.

Finally, he nodded, left the room, never looking back.

I was in the passenger seat of one of the station's few decent cars, an enthusiastic *ment* at the wheel, ignoring red lights, pedestrians and anyone else foolish enough to be out of bed at this hour.

Tynaliev's team had tracked the Chief's call, and we were heading out past the giant water purifiers to the east of the city. I'd no reason to think that Sariev would disobey his orders, but I still kept my foot pressed hard against the floor of the car, as if I was doing the driving myself.

We pulled up outside a villa on the outskirts, a high wall guarding its privacy, a good place where neighbours wouldn't be disturbed by the occasional scream of agony or a single shot. My burnt hand gnawed at me under makeshift bandages. I checked the load in the Yarygin, and opened the car door. I'd already unscrewed the overhead light. Sariev was expecting the Chief and a big bonus, but I'd seen enough consequences of over-confidence not to put money on his compliance.

The uniform started to speak, but I put my fingers to my lips, walked towards the gates. They were the usual cheap metal affair, spray-painted green with gold detailing, already starting to streak with rust after all the Kyrgyz winter had thrown at them.

I tugged at the left-hand side and, to my surprise, the gate swung open for a couple of feet, before being stopped by a drift of snow. I don't like surprises at any time, particularly when someone might be holding a gun. So I kept still and listened for a couple of moments, hoping anyone inside would think that the wind had blown the gate open.

The yard appeared empty, so I squeezed through the gap, and inched up the steps. Another surprise; the door was ajar. I stepped into the hallway and took stock.

Someone had commissioned an avant-garde mural on one wall, a seemingly random outburst of paint. Except this wasn't paint. And the body that lay at the foot of the stairs wasn't a statue either.

I could only tell it was Sariev by the uniform. His head was a watermelon that had been thrown down several flights of stairs. There was only one eye left that I could see, lolling on his cheek like a drunken afterthought. The other must have been under the mass of bone splinters and split flesh on the other side of his head.

His jaw rested almost under one ear, dislocated and then shattered. Fragments of teeth gleamed upwards, like yellow sweetcorn tipped out from a jar. Both hands had suffered multiple fractures, and his left leg lay at an angle that would defeat geometry. I didn't need a doctor to confirm that Sariev wouldn't be brutalising any more prisoners.

Searching the house confirmed what I already knew; Saltanat wasn't there. Maybe her backup team followed her and waited for the right moment. Or perhaps she killed Sariev all by herself. Impossible to say and, right now, the effort of knowing hardly seemed worth it.

I sensed movement behind me, swung round and came within a tenth of a second of adding to the Department's death toll for the evening. My young driver looked white, whether at the spatter of blood and brains everywhere, or at the realisation that his own might have added a fresh impasto to the scene.

I put the Yarygin away, told him to call it in. Outside, away from the body, I lit a cigarette, watched the smoke trail out of my mouth. I wished I could think of a reason to quit, but none came to mind. What's one more death, after all?

I told the uniform I was taking the car back to the station, and eased myself into the driver's seat. After a couple of complaints and grumbles, the engine turned over and I headed back towards Chui, taking it slowly, breathing deeply, wondering if this was finally the end.

I thought of the Chief, probably naked by now, cut, burnt, gouged, as Tynaliev watched, the expression on his face one of polite interest. No one would find him face down in a snowdrift, or floating down the Naryn in the spring. There wouldn't be any forty-day *toi*, no gathering of friends and relatives to weep and reminisce.

Just a sheep dragged towards the waiting knife, the last sound it heard its own helpless bleat.

Chapter 54

It was an hour or so after dawn when I left the station, my throat raw from too many cigarettes, too many explanations.

The threat of snow still hung over the city, but a thin smudge of blue over the mountains held a promise that winter might be drawing, at long last, to a close.

I walked back to my apartment, leaving fresh prints in the overnight snow. It crunched under my feet, the echo of fingers being broken in a basement room.

As I reached home, the morning was starting to emerge, with new hopes and as many fresh betrayals.

I paused and looked around. Just a few hundred yards up the road was where Yekaterina Tynalieva was butchered, nothing there now to serve as her memorial but tatters of crime-scene tape fluttering in the wind.

I thought of Chinara in the moments before her death, breath rasping in her throat, one thin hand gripping the sheet that would soon become her shroud.

And I remembered how tears stung my eyes as I pressed her grandmother's wedding cushion down upon Chinara's face, to take her away from a hard dying, to a place free from her pain and my sorrow. Her hands rose like startled doves from her sides, settled themselves upon mine, adding what strength she had left. I stared at the thin blue veins beneath the parchment of her fingers, willing them to fade and be still. And after her last breath had fled, I lifted the cushion from her face, wiped a few flecks of saliva from the lace, settled it gently beneath her head.

The end of a marriage, of a life — or rather, two lives.

Perhaps fragments are all that remain of us, fragments and the memories of those we loved and who loved us in their turn.

I wondered if Saltanat would be waiting for me upstairs, if she was already over the border, if I was now only a memory, or not even that.

I can't say if we can create a life for ourselves, if desire can remain and grow into something else.

How long might we have together? Who knows?

I unlocked the door and stepped into darkness.

Acknowledgements

All the characters and events in this book are entirely fictitious, and any errors are mine: what is real is the kindness and generosity of the Kyrgyz people and the beauty of their country.

I owe much to many people.

In China: Zhou Min 周敏.

In the Kyrgyz Republic: Akyl Callaghan, Kairat Jumabaev, Aizat Jumabaeva, Elmira Kalmakova and Mike Atsoparthis MBE.

In Qatar: Charlotte and Richard Forbes-Robertson, Mirna Naccash, Natalie and Tim Styles.

In the UAE: Nick Adams, Valentina and Lyndon Ashmore, Chris Atkins, Scott Feasey, Brad Henderson, Liesl Maughan and Ryan Reed, David Myers, Roger Payling, Craig Yeoman.

In the UK: Stefanie Bierwerth and her team at Quercus, Morag Brennan and Steve Harrison, Helen Brindley and Chris Callaghan, Richard Callaghan, Carol Hannay and Marcus Wilson-Smith, Trevor Hoyle, Shân Morley Jones, Thomas Stofer.

ACKNOWLEDGEMENTS

In the USA: Jay Butterman, Andrew Cannon, Nathaniel Marunas, Peter Spiegelman.

The opening line was given by Mark Billingham.

Special thanks are due to Tanja Howarth, agent extraordinaire, and Simon Peters, for constant support and encouragement.

Finally, and most importantly, love and thanks to my late parents, Vera and John Callaghan.

Anyone visiting Kyrgyzstan will find a warm welcome at the Umai Hotel in Bishkek (www.umai-hotel-kg.com), while Ecotours (www.ecotour.kg) offers unrivalled opportunities to explore the country's natural heritage.